MR MAKE BELIEVE

Beezy Marsh is an award-winning journalist, who has spent more than 20 years making the headlines in newspapers including *The Daily Mail* and *The Sunday Times*. She is married, with two young sons, and lives in Oxfordshire with a never-ending pile of laundry. She is also a karate black belt. This doesn't help much with the laundry though.

This was never going to be enough for a girl from Hartlepool, whose primary school teacher told her to give up her dream of becoming a poet and concentrate on being a nurse instead. Beezy is also a novelist and biographer, with family at the heart of everything she writes – whether it is the life and times of a gangland criminal, or a downtrodden mother's attempt to find the key to lasting romance.

Find out more about Beezy Marsh and read her inspiring, funny and wonderfully honest blog by visiting www.beezy-marsh.com or connecting with her on Twitter, @beezymarsh.

MR MAKE BELIEVE

BEEZY MARSH

ipso books

This edition published in 2017 by Ipso Books

Ipso Books is a division of Peters Fraser + Dunlop Ltd

Drury House, 34–43 Russell Street, London WC2B 5HA

To daydreamers, everywhere.

PROLOGUE

Mrs Make Believe

My blog today features a back-to-basics recipe most of you may already be familiar with. You can pin it on the fridge, to help the man in your life remember what to do, once he gets back from work, football, or the pub.

A NO-FUSS FAMILY

1. *Take one woman – moist, soft but still firm to the touch.*
2. *Strip.*
3. *Blend.*
4. *Roll on a sheet. If you are short of time, any flat surface will do.*
5. *Prick firmly.*
6. *Rest (you won't have time to do this later).*
7. *Leave for nine months. A pinch of humour and a big dollop of understanding will make her easier to handle.*
8. *Tell her to push down. (Note: your woman may crumble. If not, don't worry, she is bound to fall apart at some point.)*
9. *Carefully pat the fruits of her labour and wrap in a warm towel, before sharing with friends and family. Sprinkle liberally with presents if desired.*

10. *To create a whole batch, just follow the recipe again. WARNING! Do not repeat Step 6. You will get your fingers burned. TOP TIP: Get on with your life and leave her to clear up the mess in the kitchen, for the rest of hers.*

I love being a source of inspiration. Do let me know if this recipe helps to establish a good domestic routine in your home.

CHAPTER ONE

Marnie couldn't remember exactly when she lost her fashion sense. Though it was painful to admit, she knew why it had gone. Somewhere along the way, her style had zipped itself into her teeniest cocktail dress, grabbed her Gucci heels, snatched her Prada purse and fled, screaming, into the night, in search of a worthier woman.

And it was all her fault.

why would a size 10 want to hang around with someone who saw relaxed-fit as a godsend, who revelled in wearing baggy sweatshirts and had been known to do the school run in her jim-jams on more than one occasion?

As Marnie turned around to face herself in the mirror, the horrible truth dawned: motherhood had robbed her of the magic thing that made people look twice. Now, if she merited a second glance, it was only because there was yoghurt in her hair or ketchup on her tracksuit bottoms.

She should never have let herself be seduced by snuggly loungewear. The sheepskin-shod path to the plus-size department was wide and smooth; the road to the designer denim store steep, winding and full of women with pinched faces, rumbling stomachs and sprained ankles.

Oh, she should have fought, sweated and starved her way back into her party-wear, like any other self-respecting mother.

But she hadn't. The endless scoffing of snacks to combat tiredness, the hoovering up of children's leftovers, the milky lattes, had all taken their toll.

And, right now, her furry slipper socks and fuzzy legs weren't helping to set off the only little black dress in the wardrobe that she could manage to squish into.

She sighed to herself, as Charlie, her youngest, thundered down the stairs and his older brother, Rufus, started yelling for the telly to be switched on.

There was no time to go shopping today. Besides, she couldn't really afford anything new.

Marnie squidged the roll of fat around her middle. She couldn't bear to waste money on a new outfit in a size…a size larger than she wanted to admit to. She still had to lose her baby-weight.

Well, when she said baby-weight, she meant toddler-weight. Charlie was nearly three, so he was still a toddler, wasn't he? Yes, she still had to lose her toddler-weight and regain her figure.

Matt, her husband, strode in to the bedroom fresh from the shower, a towel tucked around his waist – which was looking a lot leaner since he'd started going back to the gym – and stopped dead in his tracks.

"That's rather dressy for the school run, isn't it?"

She tugged the clingy fabric down over her hips a bit as he spoke. Her frock seemed to have developed an annoying habit of rucking up every time she inhaled, turning it into a minidress – not a good look for someone whose thighs were kissing.

"It's for our big night out," she said, flushing a little. "I wanted to ask your opinion. Do you fancy me in this?"

She gave him a self-conscious little twirl.

There was a horrible silence.

She could almost feel his embarrassment at having to be seen with her at the Legal Eagle Awards, looking like she should be carrying a "wide load" sign. As she breathed out, a button detached itself from her front and ricocheted off the wardrobe.

"Oh, Marnie," he said, clapping a hand to his forehead, "I thought I'd told you! It's a work do, strictly business and no wives or partners."

"But I've got a babysitter!" They hadn't been out together in ages! She felt a large stab of disappointment, as she pictured another evening, alone, with only the television and her movie box sets for company. Plus, a family-sized bag of crisps.

A muscle twitched in his cheek.

"I'm so, so sorry darling. I've got so much work on, I don't know whether I'm coming or going at the moment. And to top it all, I've got lumbered with George, my new pupil, tonight," he mumbled, bending down, so that all she could see were the dark curls on the top of his head, as he rummaged in the sock drawer.

"Socks?" he said, casting a questioning glance that would not be out of place in a courtroom.

"They must be in the clean laundry pile," she said, through gritted teeth, pointing to the clothing mountain, which languished in a wicker basket in the corner. She hated herself for being so disorganised. "I haven't had time to do socks reunited yet this week."

Their little Victorian terraced house could have been quite light and airy, like the ones gracing estate agents' windows along Chiswick High Road, but she'd have to get rid of the detritus of family life first – and a skip-load of kids' toys.

Matt walked around the bed, pulled her to him and gave her a quick peck on the cheek. "I'm sorry about tonight.

You'll give the rest of the mothers a bit of a shock at the school gates this morning if you turn up looking so…" His eyes made the arduous journey across her curves, as he struggled to find the right word. After a pause that lasted just a second too long for Marnie's deflated ego, he said: "Lovely."

❧ ❧ ❧

Sitting down on the bed, she gazed at her reflection.

A ridiculous little space hopper of a woman, squashed into a too-tight party frock, gazed back.

What had happened to her? Where was the svelte little thing, who used to slide into something form-fitting, zip into the office and take on the world? And where, oh where, was her bloody waist?

She hauled the dress over her head and it got stuck on her massive mono-boob, formed, quite unhelpfully, by her sports bra. The nearest thing she got to exercise was lifting coffee cups to her lips and lugging Charlie about, but all the other bras were a bit tight at the moment.

The yelps of warring children bounced off the sitting room walls and carried up the stairs. She still had to do breakfast and get them dressed for nursery and school.

Marnie tugged harder and heaved off the dress from hell, before throwing it on to Mount Clean Laundry. She would have to conquer that later.

Then, she pulled on her mummy togs for the day: Ugg boots, baggy jogging bottoms and a hooded sweatshirt, featuring stains (by accident, not design).

Marnie stood at top of the stairs, her thick, dark brown hair, greying at the roots, pulled up into a scruffy ponytail.

"When are we getting rid of this damn thing, Marnie?" Matt shouted, as his tried and failed to untangle his raincoat from the folded up buggy stashed underneath the coat rack in the hallway.

"Charlie doesn't need it any more, does he?"

"I haven't got around to taking it to the charity shop, sorry," she said, doing her best to ignore the pang of emptiness at the thought of letting her pram go for good. They might still find a use for it...

He stopped wrestling with the buggy and looked up at her.

"You look more like yourself now," he said, with a smile that lit up his face and showed his dimples. He was so handsome in his business suit and crisply ironed shirt; tall and imposing, just like a barrister should be.

She felt like a complete bag lady.

"Thanks," she mumbled. "Have fun. And don't be back too late."

But the pinstripe of his jacket had already departed through the front door, in a blur.

❧   ❧   ❧

Marnie Martin had committed career suicide by having kids.

That was how it felt at least.

Once upon a time, she had an awe-inspiring job, writing news stories for the front page of Britain's favourite quality tabloid, *The Sentinel*.

She'd door-stepped politicians, covered gritty court cases, listened intently as people poured out their hearts to her, turning their words into tomorrow's headlines. Now she was clinging on by her fingernails, working from home part-time, filing a cookery column, which seemed to be shrinking in size each week. That was not a good sign.

Why had she even let herself be talked into writing a bloody cookery column in the first place? She found oven chips quite a challenge, for a start.

The words of her scary News Editor, Barker, rang in her ears: "What's your problem? You're a mother, you've got kids, you want to work part-time. You can cook, can't you? It's a bleeding busman's holiday. Seriously, Marnie, you should be paying me for this."

So, unlike her cakes, she'd risen to the challenge, raided her mother's old recipe books, updated a few ingredients, altered quantities here and there and hoped no-one would notice.

It had worked. Well, to be fair, there had been a few readers' complaints about things not setting or cooking quite right, but she'd managed to sweep those under the carpet – was it a gas oven? Aha! She'd used an electric. Electric? She'd used a microwave! And so on...

Her phone rang: "Wakey-wakey, slummy mummy, where's your bloody copy, then?"

It was Barker. He barely spoke to her these days, unless it was to shout at her for her shortcomings. Or her shortbread.

"I'm just finishing it," she lied. She hadn't even started.

"Give me your top lines. You know the Editor's wife reads *Home Life* before anything else. She wants a preview of your recipe for her dinner party tonight."

Glancing around, she spotted a half-eaten double choco-muffin on the table.

"It's about muffins."

"Muffins?"

She'd been meaning to work on her recipe all day, really she had, but she got distracted chatting to her mate Belle from *Sentinel Showbiz* who was off on maternity leave and was in the grip of precious first-born mania.

Then, she'd heroically tackled a huge pile of ironing and the washing up, before rewarding herself with some me-time. Actually, she might have spent a bit too long watching that Maddox Wolfe movie.

Two hours precisely.

Maddox Wolfe. It was almost impossible to say his name without going "Mmmm".

Maddox Wolfe was handsome, but not in a pretty way, with blue eyes crinkling at the edges. His hair, once black, was now flecked with grey but still flopped over his resolute forehead when the role required. Sometimes he swept it back to emphasise a very fine set of cheekbones, giving his face a charmingly chiselled look. Maddox, like Marnie, had definitely seen a few late nights but he was all the better for it. His were spent partying, of course, and hers were spent burping her babies, but she didn't begrudge him that.

Marnie found his lived-in look reassuring and he – or, rather, his films – were such great company too.

His name had been in lights for as long as she could remember, which made it OK to have a bit of a, well, a lot of a crush on him, didn't it? He was tall – well over 6ft – lean but broad-shouldered, giving him the ability to either lope or tower, depending on his mood. Clothes hung in a very pleasing way on him, particularly his trousers.

And, Marnie had noticed, in his last outing as sexy superspy Seb Winter, even his forearms were good-looking. With the sleeves of his linen shirt rolled up, as he trekked through the desert in search of his foe's lair, those arms looked capable of anything. His muscles were honed to perfection. Had he done particular exercises to achieve that, or was he born that way?

Was it normal to fancy someone's arms?

"What is so special about your bloody muffins recipe then?" said Barker, icily.

Marnie pulled herself, reluctantly, from Maddox's powerful embrace.

She stood up, to make herself sound more authoritative: "It's more than just a recipe, David, it's actually an exclusive about muffins."

Tumbleweed blew across Marnie's open-plan kitchen-diner. She sat back down.

"Mummee," came a little voice from the downstairs loo. "Will you wipe my bottom?"

"What was that?" said Barker.

"I might be able to do something for the news pages about muffins and the obesity crisis," she gabbled into the handset, before the loo voice could speak again. "Why women are seduced by sugary snacks, you know the kind of thing. It wasn't like that in the good old days, when women were thin and happy and knew their place."

The Sentinel loved the good old days; that was bound to work and get her back on the news beat, where she belonged.

"Have you lost your marbles? You know the Editor's wife is the size of a bouncy castle. We can't print that, Marnie," he said.

"She's got a very important dinner party coming up, find a decent recipe for that, or you can consider your goose well and truly cooked."

"Mummeee!" The voice grew more insistent.

"Remind me again, why I am paying you, for fuck's sake?" said Barker. "You've got ten minutes to file it to me. You do want to keep your job, don't you?"

"Yes, David."

"And wash your hands before you start typing up your copy," he added. "I'm sure there are food hygiene rules about that. Turns my stomach."

He hung up.

Ten minutes!

Marnie still had to pick up Rufus, who was in Year One at the eye-wateringly expensive Astral Prep School in Chiswick. Other mothers were already competing over who had the highest reading age, the best swimming grades and the neatest cursive script. Some were secretly tutoring them to speak Mandarin.

She was just grateful that her son had stopped demanding to wear his Spiderman suit over his school uniform.

She glanced at the clock and flicked open *Perfect Dinner Parties*, which featured lots of pictures of women with beehive hair-dos and pointy shoes handing around trays of vol-au-vents.

Chicken Liver Parfait.

A perfect, moussey pâté to serve as a starter at the most sophisticated parties.

Has your husband invited the boss to dinner? Don't panic, this easy but impressive little recipe will prove you are the perfect hostess. Serve with French toast for a certain je ne sais quoi!

Sod the toast. Half of London was wheat-free these days and the Editor's wife needed to shed a few pounds, so Marnie just stuck to the pâté. Brilliant. She was saved!

She had measured out the afternoon in episodes of *Peppa Pig.*

The boys were tucked up in bed, at last.

And she finally got to sit down on the sofa. Well, she had sat down on the sofa earlier, to be fair, but not for *that* long. It was just a snatched hour or two. Now, she could luxuriate a bit, ignore the washing up and really enjoy the movie. Maddox Wolfe's films were a public service to bored housewives everywhere.

After a glass or two of wine, Maddox had this amazing habit of leaning out of the television, taking Marnie's face in his manly hands and kissing her passionately.

Then, he would carry her upstairs and lay her gently on the bed, run his fingers through her hair and down across her collarbone before starting to slowly unbutton her, murmuring sweet nothings in her ear, nibbling a bit, making her tingle all over with anticipation, and...

Marnie heard the patter of tiny footsteps overhead.

Charlie was out of bed again.

He always settled better when Matt had read to him. That was yet another reason to feel cross about the Legal Eagle Awards.

"Charlie?" she called softly, as she trudged upstairs.

He was waiting by the bedroom door.

Picking him up, she kissed his cheek and he put his arms around her neck.

"When's Daddy coming home?"

"Soon, darling," she said. "Just go to sleep and he will be here for you in the morning."

Here for all of us.

❧ ❧ ❧

Marnie was awoken by a thudding noise coming from downstairs. They were being burgled!

She leapt out of bed, heart thumping in her chest, and crept to the top of the stairs.

He was swaying in the hallway, clutching what looked like a trophy of an eagle with a scroll in its claws.

"I'm Legal Eagle of the Year! The best barrister in town!" boomed Matt, loud enough to wake the dead, never mind the children. Or the neighbour's children, for that matter.

"Matt," she whispered. "For God's sake! It's 3am. You gave me the fright of my life! Where on earth have you been?"

"Celebrating!" he slurred. "Marnie, I won. I actually sodding won. I've never won an award before. But I won this!" And he thrust the eagle skywards in triumph.

She came downstairs.

"It's so late. I was worried."

"I thought you'd be happy for me," he said, his lip curling, as he plonked the award down on the hallway table, and collapsed on the bottom step. "Of course, you just want to tell me off for being a bad man and staying out late."

"I am happy, ecstatic," she lied. "But I will be miles happier to celebrate in the morning, not the middle of the night."

He pulled off his shoes and stomped upstairs, before falling, fully clothed on to their bed.

"I spend all my life working, Marnie," he muttered, as he rolled over and turned his back on her. "Just to be appreciated, for once, is all I want. The Legal Eagle Awards appreciate me, my colleagues seem to appreciate me."

Stung, she slipped back under the duvet. She was too tired to even cry.

And anyway, Legal Eagle of the Year was already snoring like a bear in the woods.

⚜ ⚜ ⚜

She became dimly aware of a buzzing noise by her ear. Her phone was threatening to vibrate its way off the bedside cabinet and onto the floor.

It was barely light outside.

"Hello?" she whispered.

"Turn on your television," said the voice, which she recognised immediately as Barker, her News Editor.

Marnie sat up.

"David, it is 6am and I have a family, I really don't think you should be calling me at this hour," she said.

"Just go and put the news on."

He was not going to let it drop.

The Legal Eagle of the Year was still snoring like a train next to her and the stench of stale beer was seeping through his clothes and onto the bedsheets.

Phone in hand, she crept downstairs and flicked on the TV.

A massive front page from rival newspaper *The Globe* flashed up on the Future News screen in front of her.

"PRIME MINISTER FORCED TO CANCEL SUMMIT MEETING – MYSTERY FOOD BUG TO BLAME!" screamed the headline.

The presenter said: "Downing Street sources have confirmed the Prime Minister was taken violently ill late last night with a mystery bug, which has also struck down several other members of the Government, who were rushed to hospital for emergency treatment.

"It is not known if the illness is contagious but investigations are continuing. Unconfirmed reports are that the Premier and several colleagues were taken ill at a dinner party in Hampstead. Inquiries are centring on a suspicious pâté."

She froze. Time stood still.

Marnie didn't hear the rest of the news report because it was drowned out by the monstering she got from the boss. The suspicious pâté was her pâté. The moussey pâté made from chicken livers; pink, undercooked chicken livers. Salmonella simply hadn't crossed her mind. Those women with bee-hive hair-dos in the 1950's recipe book probably had stomachs lined with asbestos to withstand food poisoning.

"I'm so sorry," she said. "It's … it's an old family recipe. Tried and tested. I thought it was safe."

"You have poisoned half the fucking cabinet," said Barker, with machine-gun-like precision. "The Editor would have bollocked you himself, Marnie, but he is still on the porcelain telephone, talking to God."

She was a pathetic excuse for a journalist, Barker was right.

She was a waste of space, more bothered about wiping her bloody kids' backsides than coming up with a recipe which could pass a basic health and safety test.

She'd dropped her game when she dropped her sprogs.

She thought muffins were hot news.

She was a useless fuckwit.

She was fired.

CHAPTER TWO

Mrs Make Believe

Dear Reader(s),

Thank you so much for looking at this little blog!

I have a confession to make. I am worried I may be a bit hooked on fantasy.

I don't want to sound like some weirdo, it is just an innocent thing about a movie star, which appears to be taking up most of my free time – which isn't much. I am a busy mum, probably like you!

Lately, I made a terrible mistake at work, which cost me my part-time job, actually. It was mainly because I had spent two hours watching one of his films instead of doing what I was paid to do. It wasn't a case of just skiving. It was his company I craved.

When I'm not watching his films, I am thinking about his body or day-dreaming about him. Specifically, I am fascinated by his forearms at the moment. They are just perfect: manly and strong.

Don't get me wrong, my husband has a perfectly serviceable pair of forearms, it's just the movie star's are something special.

Does anyone else out there do this? How can I make it stop?

On a positive note, the fact that I lost my job means I have found myself with a lot more time on my hands and I am excited to be embarking on life as a "stay at home mum". A SAHM, yes, that's me! No more work to get in the way of the most important job in the world: being a mother. Right? Before this, I was a working-part-time-and-sort-of-stay-at-home-mum. That's a WPTASOSAHM, so I am grateful for the abbreviation, to be honest.

I am slightly worried that I will now have even more opportunity to pore over the box sets featuring my movie star crush. Is this harmful in any way to my marriage, do you think?

Crushes aside, I'm hoping to share with you my views on life, which can be a bit crazy at times. I'd also love to hear yours. There are so many hilarious moments, I bet you can think of a few!?!

Does anyone have any ideas for rainy day activities in West London? Got any tips about making bed times easier for a three-year-old and a five-year-old? I have tried telly on and I have tried telly off but they still seem to go a bit mad around 6pm, just as I am trying to cook something for my husband's dinner. Help!

M arnie sighed. Well, at least she'd started her blog, which was something positive. It was just a silly little thing, really, to take her mind of the fact that she had no career left, whatsoever, and was never likely to work in journalism again.

Other than that, everything was fine, really great. Besides, she had loads more free time to do all the things she'd always wanted to do with the kids; all that licking and sticking and making and baking and clearing up. Lots of clearing up.

And cooking.

Maybe she should actually learn to cook properly, in case she ever got her job back? She twiddled her thumbs. That was never likely to happen.

The PM had to cancel his appointments for an entire week and the Ministers for Education, Health and Defence lost so much weight due to salmonella they were now nicknamed the Shadow of Their Former Selves Cabinet.

On a positive note, the Editor's wife was also apparently looking trimmer.

But that wasn't enough to make Barker take Marnie's calls.

So, the blog was just to keep her brain active.

Besides, she'd had ten Maddox-related thoughts before breakfast this morning. She needed to stop that.

She couldn't tell Matt about that and, frankly, he seemed to be leaving for work earlier than ever in any case. She hadn't even had the chance to bother him with the fact that she had lost her job. She'd get around to telling him eventually.

Anyway, he was going to be working late again, tied up with some difficult legal arguments at the office. Luckily, George, his new pupil, was helping him out, so he might be back before midnight. Good old George. He was turning out to be a real tower of strength and Matt said George's legal opinions were quite brilliant for someone who was only just 23.

Her email pinged.

Her friend, Belle, had posted a comment on her blog. Her first reader!

Dear Mrs Make Believe,

As a new mother, I am very much looking forward to your wise words.

Re work, what on earth happened? They are idiots to lose you!

I wouldn't worry about your movie crush, unless it is still that ageing spy bloke, in which case, we need to get out to have a drink together, and soon.

How long are babies supposed to stay in their bouncy chairs for? I worry that it is making Gabriel's neck go all scrunchy.

Belle x

P.S. The thing about fancying his forearms is a bit strange. We need to talk.

Marnie rang her: "How's Gabriel?"

"He's fine," said Belle. "It's just, I can't work out what to put him in. Should he have a hat on indoors? And this bouncy chair thing ... are you sure he can still breathe in it?"

"Yes, he can breathe I'm sure," said Marnie. "Is his chest moving?"

"Hang on ... yes," said Belle. "What about his clothes?"

"Well, I would say today is very much a vest and Babygro day, socks optional, but no need for a hat indoors. Check the back of his neck for his temperature, rather than his hands, which might feel cold."

"Oh, thanks so much," said Belle. "It's just, when they can't tell you, it's so hard, you know?"

"Are you getting any sleep?"

"Not much. He doesn't do what the book says he should be doing."

Marnie looked down at Charlie, who had wellies on the wrong feet and, having pulled her lipstick out of her handbag, was in the process of smearing it all over his face.

"Yes, the thing is Belle, none of them actually do what they say they should in the book ... "

"But I did everything that the book said I should do in pregnancy!" cried Belle. "Where have I gone wrong?"

"You haven't gone wrong," said Marnie, gently. "You have got a beautiful, healthy baby who doesn't sleep much. That is entirely normal in my experience. What about Jonah?" Marnie couldn't help but say his name in hushed tones.

Jonah Bevan, Belle's delicious rock-star boyfriend, who had graced Marnie's bedroom wall with his band Destroy during her student years of big hair and black eyeliner, was now an occasional, thrilling fixture at her dinner table. Plus, he was very hands-on with his baby, which just made her insides go all squishy.

"Yes, he's helping but he doesn't do it right," said Belle, huffily. Marnie held the phone away from her ear as Belle shouted: "No, Jonah! He likes bunny in the chair with him, not teddy."

Marnie heard Jonah shout back: "Amazing. He's only two months old and he can tell the difference."

"We're really looking forward to getting out for a quiet dinner together tomorrow. Are you still OK to babysit?" said Belle, ignoring his remark.

"Of course," said Marnie. Damn. She'd totally forgotten. "All organised. I'll be there."

"And we need to talk about your obsession with Maddox Wolfe," said Belle.

"It's nothing serious," said Marnie. "I just think about him quite a lot, that's all."

"How are things with you and Matt?" said Belle softly.

"They are, well, they are just fine, I suppose, but we never have the time to…"

"Look, I'm sorry, I've got to go, Marnie," said Belle, "Gabriel has some dribble running down his chin and it is going to ruin his outfit."

Rufus wandered through from the lounge and shoved the iPad under her nose.

"It's a funny lady. Look!"

A woman flashed up on the screen of the iPad, naked except for an arrow over her crotch.

"I'm Muffy, click me!"

What the hell?

"It's OK, Ruf," she said, struggling to maintain her composure. "You go and watch CBeebies and Mummy will sort it out."

Rufus reached up and grabbed a marker pen from the kitchen island while her back was turned, before wandering back through to the lounge.

Avoiding a splodge of half-eaten cereal on the chair, Marnie sat down at her dining table and checked the search history.

Someone had been looking at porn! It wasn't her.

So, it had to be Matt.

Something twisted in her stomach at the thought of him looking at X-rated stuff in secret.

All the years they'd been married, he'd never been into that sort of thing. She certainly wasn't.

When did they last have sex? Marnie couldn't quite remember. It must have been sometime around Christmas? Or, was it a few months before that? On his birthday?

Of course, it was not an issue for them! He was exhausted by the daily grind of representing his clients in court.

She was just worn out by running around after the kids.

She looked more closely at Muffy, who had nice breasts, a trim waist and amazingly long legs, which she appeared to be able to hold at 180 degrees to each other with ease.

It wasn't jealousy. No, it was more a feeling of total and utter inadequacy. She was a mother. She had given up her skinny jeans and the desire to wear sexy underwear in order to bear children.

What did Muffy have that she didn't? How dare she just pop up, uninvited, in her kitchen!

Marnie clicked on her.

Muffy had everything, neatly packaged and quite bare. Marnie zoomed in on the image to get a closer look.

A message popped up on the screen: "Hello Matt, want to chat?"

He had betrayed her with Muffy. The bastard.

Marnie stifled a sob.

So, all his understanding little cuddles when she'd been too tired for sex had been a cover for his hot-blooded internet passion for some loose woman with a perfect figure!

She squidged a handful of fat that was bulging over the top of her jeans.

Who could blame him, when he was married to a manatee?

She wasn't a prude! Far from it. But this woman represented something so unreal, so unattainable and it just wasn't fair that her husband was going to look at the likes of Muffy and get turned on because, well, it made her feel so bloody frumpy and unattractive.

It was a bit like enjoying a nice long ride in the family car and then secretly salivating all over the sports car section in Auto Trader, because the tyres had got a bit worn and the suspension was clapped out from carrying all the kids.

There was a horrid, empty feeling in her stomach and not just because it was nearly tea-time.

She didn't have time to work out what she was going to do about Muffy, because at that point Charlie wandered through to the kitchen, sucking on a yoghurt tube, sporting a thick, black pair of scribbled spectacles on his face.

And a little moustache to match.

Marnie ran into the lounge.

Rufus was still at the scene of the crime, clutching the most unfortunate of weapons – a permanent marker pen.

※ ※ ※

Why was she even bothering to look? Propped up in bed, as the clock ticked closer to midnight, Marnie found herself poring over *The Sentinel* website. It was like being at a sweetshop, with her nose pressed to the glass and not enough money in her pockets to buy anything.

She took a quick look at the sidebar of shame – the celebrity and gossip panel.

COURTROOM CUTIES!

A hitlist of the hottest barristers in town is sweeping the internet and causing near-riot in the robing room at the High Court.

That sounded funny! She'd be able to have a laugh with Matt about that later.

She read on.

Clerks and barristers have secretly nominated the top totty in their chambers, in a move denounced by the Bar Association as "completely sexist".

We say, stop being so prudish! It's just a legal laugh!

Topping the list, from Zenith Chambers, is raven-haired temptress Georgina Flaherty. Dublin-born Georgina, 23, known as "George", is making her mark as a pupil, with a keen eye for detail... and great legs.

Zenith Chambers was where Matt worked.

Marnie tried to ignore the sinking feeling in her chest, as she studied the picture of the beautiful young woman, with a great sweep of raven hair, skin like porcelain and startling blue eyes. There must be an explanation, another George, that's all; one with a deep voice, as well as one called Georgina, who was a total fox, with great legs.

A key turned in the lock.

She heard him take off his coat, try to hang it on the overcrowded coatrack, swear and chuck it over the bannisters, before stomping upstairs.

She had been planning to tackle him about this silly Muffy porn business, but now Marnie's throat had gone quite dry. She tugged at her top, remembering – fleetingly – the times she used to like to wear little babydoll nighties to bed, instead of pyjama bottoms and a T-shirt big enough to make a ship's sail.

As he came in to the bedroom, she rasped: "How's George?"

"Fine," said Matt, pulling off his court shirt, revealing a very toned set of biceps. "We had a long day."

"George is a woman, isn't she?" She traced a pattern with her fingers on the duvet.

He gave her a puzzled look.

"Sorry?"

He was stripped to his boxer shorts now, looking fitter than ever, with his long legs and firm, high bum, which she found irresistible.

"George, your pupil, the one you took to the Legal Eagle Awards instead of me. She is a woman," she said, more loudly.

"Yes," he said, glaring at her and hurling his socks into the laundry basket. "She is. Now, I'm very tired."

He climbed into bed, yanked the duvet up so it touched his chin and turned over on his side.

"She's very pretty," said Marnie, quietly.

But he was already asleep.

CHAPTER THREE

A thena Maldon was flicking through the latest edition of *The Sentinel*, as she nibbled a crumb from the tiny sliver of coffee and walnut cake in front of her.

Spring had well and truly sprung in the countryside, which meant the bloody birds had been twittering in the garden of her Cotswold cottage at some unearthly hour again, robbing her of precious beauty sleep and making her crave sugar.

To make matters worse, her former West End co-star Cecily Hayward was grabbing headlines in *The Sentinel*. Cecily was such a Miss Goody Two Shoes, all swept back hair, perfect skin and wreathed in smiles, talking about her latest movie. All of life's troubles, should she encounter any, would simply slide off Cecily, who was so smooth, she practically had a non-stick coating.

Athena swallowed hard and felt her pride sticking in her throat. If it hadn't been for that horrid little tabloid reporter Marnie Martin ruining her chances of stardom, those headlines could have been hers. She'd been papped falling out of Kabaret with a half-full bottle of Jack Daniels clamped to her lips, flicking the Vs at a photographer. True, she'd got a bit carried away celebrating an offer of her first movie role in LA and the bird's eye view of her knickerless undercarriage was rather unladylike – but that was not the point. Marnie Martin had used her as an example of ladette drinking culture in an article head-lined "Boozy Britain". The very next day, the movie bosses rang her agent to tell him that the role had gone to some other starlet, who was a decade younger than Athena and whose image "fitted with what the studio wanted" – and that was that.

Now that bloody unflattering photo was the first thing that popped up every time she did an internet search for herself. She'd been on the brink of the big time, she was sure of that, but that picture made her famous for all the wrong reasons. To make matters worse, her agent had stopped taking her calls.

Athena turned the page – there was another photo-graph of Cecily, this time with movie god Maddox Wolfe hugging his wife, his dark blue eyes twinkling. Was his nose really that cute? It was almost indecent for a man in his fif-ties to be so handsome. He and Cecily looked like Barbie and Ken. Thanks to a liberal use of the airbrush and copy approval, no doubt.

It was enough to make her want to vomit. But this cake was rather tasty, so perhaps not just yet.

All Athena's hard work, hoofing it in the chorus line of grim pantomimes in coastal towns, accidentally-on-purpose getting pregnant by a theatre impresario who gave her a leg up in the business in return for getting his leg over, had been for nothing. Her carefully-crafted chirpy blonde image, cemented by her starring role in the TV sitcom *Au Pair*, was tarnished forever.

She now only got invites to functions graced by Z-listers – soap stars and assorted flotsam from the provinces, who never quite got it right, no matter how much they spent on designer labels.

Athena's eyes hardened to little pebbles of hatred as she marched over to the newspaper cutting she kept on the fridge, and came face to face with her nemesis.

Today, she added another set of horns and a moustache to the picture of the cheerful-looking woman with long wavy hair, her hand resting on her heart-shaped face. Then, to calm herself, she methodically scratched Marnie Martin's eyes out with her Montblanc pen. That was much better.

Athena was working hard to atone for her loutish behaviour. She appeared to be living the dream as a single cake-baking, gardening, do-it-all mother in her sleepy Cotswolds village. She was building quite a following on Twitter, enduring mindless banter with women who lived to bake cakes all day and liking – yes, liking – their cupcakes.

She'd recently managed to strong-arm the married theatre impresario into paying for their son Tristan to go to boarding school – which was a relief. However, she was still stuck in the sticks.

But her time would come. She could feel it.

Her moment needed to hurry up, though. She'd been in her late twenties for over a decade now.

She flicked over another page and felt her heart miss a beat as she clapped eyes on Vladimir Shustrov, the Russian oligarch, whose wealth was almost matched by the size of his gut.

Ignoring the Slutlana in a dental floss bikini at his side – a mere detail who would be no match for Athena at her most persuasive – she read on. Vladimir was coming to the UK. That was interesting.

He had just purchased the luxurious, five-star Shilling Hall Spa and Hotel, nestling in acres of parkland in leafy Surrey, and rumour had it he wanted to buy up a large stake in the UK media.

With lightning speed, she swept the rest of the coffee and walnut cake into the bin. And the home made loaf from the last meeting of Little Gidding Women's Institute, plus six scones that her housekeeper Mrs Rolfe had left for her earlier.

They had all been uploaded on to her *Living the Dream* blog anyway. The Twitterati loved her perfectly-presented sponges, advice on bottling jam, growing vegetables and generally living an organic lifestyle, purloined from the good women of Little Gidding WI.

They were only too happy to share their knowledge gleaned from years of Cotswolds life. Athena was only too happy to pass it off as her own.

She ran a finger along the wooden worktop – just to check that Mrs Rolfe hadn't been slacking – before picking up the telephone and dialling the number for *The Sentinel.*

"Hello, this is Athena Maldon. I'd like to do an interview on stars ageing gracefully," she said, sweetly.

"Hmmm," said Barker. Athena Maldon was a nobody these days. He had been quite amused by the sitcom star's drunken antics, flashing her pants falling out of some West End nightclub, but she hadn't done anything newsworthy since. And he didn't really have time to chat.

But Athena was not going to be deterred by the lack of enthusiasm at the end of the line.

"It's just so nice to see Cecily Hayward hasn't a shred of vanity," she said into the silence.

"She is an inspiration to us all – these days she mostly goes out looking like an unmade bed. I looked at *The Sentinel's* article today and marvelled at the wonders of photoshop. I hope I can be as relaxed as her when I'm that old. It's a really difficult choice for women of Cecily's age. I thought about that a lot when we were on stage together in the West End and I got to see her crow's feet on a daily basis. How long will she be able to take her clothes off and look gorgeous in front of the unforgiving movie camera lens? Will she look back on her life and wish she had spent more time with her children, rather than pursuing a career based on vanity?"

Barker sat bolt upright. This would make great copy: "What strong views you have!"

"Yes," said Athena, smirking to herself, "I have turned my back on all that artifice. And I am much younger than her. Much."

"Where are you exactly these days?" said Barker, in his chummiest tone.

"Oh, I'd love to welcome you into my home in the Cotswolds, away from all the noise and hassle of the big city," said Athena. "In fact, I'll bake some scones." She'd better get Mrs Rolfe to put that on her to do list.

"If this is going to make a little story for you, would you mind terribly giving my blog a teensy mention? It's called *Living the Dream*. It's for all those mothers out there, like me, who are toiling away in the background, raising their young and finding real pleasure in baking, cooking, sewing – what I like to think of as the real beaux arts of the fairer sex."

"It could be a real talking point," said Barker, envisioning a double page spread and a squillion internet hits worldwide. Tweets, retweets and maybe a TV segment. Those menopausal moaners on *ChitChat* would jump all over this. Actress friend of movie star slags off the vacuous existence of her former co-star, whilst bravely baking cakes and making jam.

Barker ran his fingers through his greased-back hair as he surveyed the paper in front of him. Some of his triple-shot latte had splatted onto the front page of today's *Sentinel*. The inky lifeblood was leaking out of the paper.

Why couldn't his female reporters stop breeding? The only ones left in the newsroom were those old enough to be a news story themselves if they got pregnant and girls who barely looked old enough to go on the pill.

He needed to find a replacement for Marnie Martin.

It didn't matter whether she could actually write or not. Athena could be his Next Big Thing and she could cook.

Good. Problem solved.

❧ ❧ ❧

Athena finished the call and stood up.

Her size 8 jeans didn't hang off her hips any more, in the way she liked. Athena grabbed a teensy bit of flesh from around her middle. She had let herself get fat.

It was no carbs from now on. She had serious work to do.

She stepped out of the jeans, pulled off her t-shirt and wandered outside across the flagstones to the pool house. She cut quite a figure as she strode semi-naked, her long mane of golden hair swishing about, but there was little chance of anyone seeing her: Athena did not have any friends. Nor did she want any, here in Nowhereland.

London was different. It was important to have frenemies there – girl friends to go out to lunch and dinner with, to surpass in every way and to bitch about behind their backs. She'd ring a few of them later to let them know she was coming to town soon.

Athena's behind was encased in a tiny pair of red silk knickers. She whipped them off and undid the matching bra, tossing it by the pool side, before appraising herself in the floor to ceiling mirror, ignoring her forehead – too high, too broad, hence the fringe. Her cheekbones were still razor sharp, thank God, her jaw line well-defined and her big, grey eyes framed by the darkest lashes (those permanent infill ones were a miracle, as long as you got them replaced every six weeks). Her breasts jutted upwards, even without support, her limbs were lithe and bronzed (thanks to careful applications of fake-tan). She was still gorgeous in the eyes of most civilians, but Athena needed to look superhumanly good for what she had in mind.

Then, she dived naked into the water and started ploughing up and down, doing length after length of perfect front crawl.

Athena was on her way back.

CHAPTER FOUR

Mrs Make Believe

Well, I'm joining a book club!

It's going to be brilliant. I've always wanted to be able to sit and discuss the latest good reads with like-minded people and I'm also really looking forward to having an evening off with a large glass of wine or three. Only joking!! I don't really like to drink too much, because the school run is a bit tricky if your breath still reeks of alcohol in the morning, isn't it? Whoops, sorry, headmistress! Don't call social services. Please.

I'm really hoping that the book club might take my mind off my favourite outfits of all-time (as worn by my movie star crush).

These are, in case you are interested:

1. Tight swimming trunks.

2. Bath-towel, tucked around waist, top-half naked.

3. Bed sheet, not covering much.

While I am on the subject of my hunky actor, I thought I may have seen him driving a sports car down the high street in my West London suburb yesterday. Is this even remotely possible? (Note to my one reader, don't answer that, you will spoil the fantasy.)

I resisted the urge to throw myself on the bonnet.

Marnie sighed. The blog currently had a readership of one – two if she counted herself, as well as her friend, Belle. Was she allowed to count herself?

Crisp packets had more readers than she did.

On the bright side, Marnie was thrilled and quite honoured, actually, to have been asked to select a text for the book club, especially as she'd only just joined.

It put quite a spring in her step as she pushed her trolley around the supermarket.

She'd managed to grab a couple of pasta meals for the boys, while they ripped the heads off their gingerbread men. Now, they were corralled at the magazines for a moment's peace.

She picked up a copy of *PerfectBaby*, which happened to be right in her line of vision, and flicked through. Just for a millisecond.

Prams had changed since she bought hers. They were cool and zippy and came in such great colours now.

And, oh, that little baby looked so adorable in his cashmere cardi and hat.

"Having another one?" said the shop assistant, blonde hair scraped back to reveal her blackened roots.

Charlie threw his dummy at the woman's feet.

"What have you been up to, drawing on your face?" she teased.

No amount of scrubbing could shift the Groucho Marx graffiti.

The shop assistant picked the dummy up, wiped it on her overall and popped it back in his mouth as he grinned at her.

"No, gosh, not planning any more at all!" said Marnie, hurriedly replacing the magazine on the display stand. "My friend has just had one, I'm looking for some tips for her, really. You know how hard it can be first time around." She felt a little tug inside as she said those words, remembering the haze of love for her first-born.

The shop assistant smiled to herself as she tidied the display.

"I was just looking for this, actually," said Marnie, with a little shrug.

She reached over and grabbed a book to her left, which had a picture of a woman wearing a fur coat on the front, with snow-capped mountains in the background. A man's hand was around her waist, clasping her tightly. In his other hand, he brandished a revolver.

She glanced at the title: *Harsh Winter.*

Flipping it over, she read the blurb on the back.

In a chase from the ski slopes of Switzerland to Russia's remote Altai Mountains, can superspy Seb Winter find a way to thaw the heart of lethal double agent, former model and Nobel-prize winning pharmacologist Katya? Only she holds the antidote to a deadly new plague released by terrorists, hell-bent on bringing the West to its knees. The fate of the world once again rests in Seb's capable hands – but time is running out.

Seb Winter was Maddox Wolfe's most famous role! This was meant to be! The book had found her.

She loved his capable hands, not to mention his forearms. In fact, she just adored all of him as sexy superspy Sebastian, breaking codes and hearts all over the world. Dare she bring it to the book club?

Perhaps they could do a post-feminist examination of female roles in Seb Winter novels? She was something of an expert in the genre.

"Want a poo," said Rufus, picking his nose.

"Can you hang on till we get home?" said Marnie, shoving the book in her shopping trolley.

Rufus nodded, thank the Lord. The last time they'd had to go in the supermarket, Charlie locked himself in a cubicle while she was washing Ruf's hands and the manageress had nearly split her skirt clambering over the top to rescue him.

Picking up a magazine each for the kids – that would cost a small fortune – she wheeled and wheedled them over to the checkout, avoiding old ladies with bunions, old men with walking sticks and the child-free, who looked on her with a mixture of pity and horror.

"You've got your hands full!" said the check-out girl, as Rufus threatened to climb into the trolley and Charlie tried to climb out.

She picked up the book before she rang it through the till and gave Marnie a little smile.

"I loved this one," she whispered. "He gets his kit off a lot, I don't think you'll be disappointed. And it is 20 per cent off. What a bargain!"

"Mummy," said Rufus, rather loudly, "What does get his kit off mean?"

"It's just another way of saying someone is taking their clothes off," said Marnie, feeling the beginnings of a blush.

"Why is the man in your book taking his clothes off a lot?" said Rufus, causing the military-looking gent at the next till to drop his apples.

"Because he keeps getting dirty and needs a bath," said Marnie, pushing the trolley at breakneck speed to the exit and through the car park. "Oh, look, an aeroplane!"

Charlie sucked happily on his dummy, which was bright pink, covered in flowers and, Marnie recalled to her horror as they drove away, had not been in his mouth when they arrived at the shop.

❧   ❧   ❧

After unpacking the shopping, she barricaded herself in the downstairs loo for a minute, just to have a quick read without some child with grubby paws snatching her new book away from her.

"Mr Winter, I've been expecting you. Drop your gun."

My cover blown, I pull off my balaclava and throw it on the floor in disgust. It was such a basic error: sneaking through the back door instead of bursting through a window. Am I losing my touch?

Logs crackle in the fireplace as my target steps out of the shadows, towards me.

Outside, the lights of St Moritz stud the hillside.

I catch my breath. She is more beautiful in the flesh, blonder, every curve revealed in a figure-hugging, strapless gown, the colour of amethyst; the same colour as the gem on a pendant at her slender throat.

She smiles, her face lighting up in triumph.

Her eyebrows arch, almost daring me to move towards her and the barrel of her 9mm Beretta.

I step forward.

My heart thumps in my chest, I feel my pectorals rippling in an involuntary dance beneath my skin-tight ski-suit. She almost devours me with her eyes.

"Not so fast, Mr Winter." Her finger lightly strokes the trigger and I can't help but notice her scarlet nails, gripping the gun. What would they feel like, running down my back?

"Now," she orders, "drop your trousers."

"Mummy! I want my Lego!"

Marnie landed back in Chiswick, and reassumed her role as Toy Management Executive (Lego).

One day, she would open her front door and be swept away by a great tidal wave of the stuff.

Damn. *Harsh Winter* was just getting good. Would Seb manage to overpower Katya? Would Katya make him take all his clothes off? Would Marnie ever manage to get to the end of the chapter and find out what was under his ski-suit? It was quite a gripping read.

After heaving a massive box of Lego into the lounge for Rufus to play with, she took the time to check and re-check her blog, just in case there were any mums out there who wanted to know more about her book club. Or, indeed, if anyone had given her any tips on getting the kids to bed. There was nothing. Never mind, it was early days and she was new to blogging, so she couldn't just expect people to want to read her stuff, could she? It wasn't like writing for a newspaper. That thought made a tear spring to her eye, so she pushed it away.

Later on, as she cooked dinner, Marnie meandered into a surprisingly pleasant daydream. She was not here, in Chiswick, but licensed to thrill, in a mountain hide-out somewhere in Switzerland, brandishing a Beretta, making Seb Winter peel his trousers down his muscular thighs.

She was interrupted by a knock on the door. Karen, her lank-haired, pallid teenage babysitter, was standing behind it, with her earphones in, as usual. Marnie gasped. She had totally forgotten her promise to babysit for Belle and Jonah! There was no way Belle would leave the baby with just any old babysitter, only Marnie would do, she'd made that clear. Oh, God, she was such a rubbish friend! Marnie ran her hands through her hair in exasperation and her fingers got stuck in a big tangle at the back. Karen's signature look of thorough boredom had turned quizzical. "Come in!" Marnie mouthed. There was little point in actually speaking to the babysitter, as she couldn't hear a damned thing with those ear phones in, in any case.

Marnie grabbed her handbag, silently thanking God that she had at least remembered to book Karen because there was no chance of Matt making it home in time to put the boys to bed. Yes, funny how he was never around during the witching hour.

After kissing the boys and giving strict instructions to Karen to read to them, rather than let them play games on her phone, Marnie clambered into a cab and set off for Notting Hill.

She'd managed to download *Harsh Winter* onto her iPhone. Brilliant! She could snatch a few minutes here and there and find out whether Seb managed to get the better of evil Katya. And whether his pants came off altogether. As the taxi inched its way around Shepherd's Bush round-about, there was still time to read a bit more.

I comply, unzipping myself and shucking my shoulders free, slowly rolling the suit down my thighs before stepping out of it.

I stand before her in my jockey shorts, aware of her eyes making their way south of my navel and lingering there.

"Take those off too."

I yank the shorts down and toss them aside. I know I won't disappoint, but I wasn't planning on revealing my credentials just yet.

Eventually, she meets my gaze, my blue eyes boring into her grey, limpid pools of malice. How I'd love to punish her for this.

"You are so much more impressive in the flesh, Mr Winter." Her finger squeezes the trigger a little harder, damn her.

"You don't really want to do that," I smile. "We haven't had the pleasure of each other's company yet."

She throws her head back and laughs, strands of silken hair falling on her bare shoulders, eyes closing, almost consumed by her own delight.

In an instant, I am beside her, on top of her, inhaling her scent and grappling for the gun, my fingers tearing at the delicate fabric of her dress.

⚜ ⚜ ⚜

With Jonah and Belle out for dinner and the baby settled for the night, Marnie kept her promise to check on him regularly. Perhaps not as regularly as Belle wanted – every five minutes did seem rather excessive. The baby monitor was a really hi-tech affair which beamed pictures to her phone but if she looked at that, she couldn't get *Harsh Winter* on it at the same time, so she huffed up three flights of stairs for the fourth time that evening.

When she got to his room, Gabriel was smiling at her. Just at her. Waving his arms and legs happily in his cot.

Marnie gazed into his gorgeous eyes which were still denim blue but would probably soon turn a lovely green, given that Belle and Jonah were green-eyed good-looking types.

"Hello, baby."

Marnie felt such a longing inside her. He was supposed to be asleep now but she couldn't help it. She'd just have another quick cuddle. He was bound to be spark out by the time the two love birds got back from dinner. She picked him up and sniffed his head; his little baby head covered in fluffy, downy fair hair. He smelled divine, so sweet and fresh and babyish. His stocky little legs were wriggling about, just like her babies when they were tiny.

Marnie was so careful to support his head but his neck was strong and he looked right into her eyes. He dribbled a bit and then smiled again. At her. Just at her. Her hormones were screaming it loud and clear. That was it. Marnie knew right there and then. She wanted, no, needed, another baby. But what would Matt say?

❧ ❧ ❧

Marnie was just flicking through Netflix to see if there were any good Maddox Wolfe films for her to watch when she heard the sound of a key turning in the lock and Belle, followed by Jonah, appeared in the lounge.

Marnie glanced at the clock. It was only 8pm.

"You're early, was dinner OK?"

Jonah grimaced: "Well, the starter was delicious but we didn't quite make it to the main course…"

"Did you check if he is still breathing?" said Belle.

"Well, I was up there half an hour ago and he is sleeping fine, I promise," said Marnie.

"You mean, you haven't checked him for a full 30 minutes?" said Belle, panic rising in her voice.

Jonah mouthed "I'm sorry" to Marnie over Belle's shoulder.

"I was watching him on the baby monitor the whole time." She lied. But Belle had already scarpered up the stairs.

"Is it normal for first time mothers to be so anxious?" said Jonah, slumping next to her on the squishy sofa. She still hadn't quite got used to the fact that one of her teenage idols was now a friend and had to stop herself staring too closely at his perfectly-chiselled jaw.

"Well, I suppose it is," said Marnie, "but I think lack of sleep doesn't help. Can you get someone in to give her a break?"

"That's a great idea!" he said, brightening. "I'm a bit worried about how she's going to manage when I go to LA to finish the album. I've asked to her to come with me but she won't in case it upsets Gabriel's routine ... "

Marnie rolled her eyes.

Jonah smiled at her: "I know you'll keep an eye on her for me. She really does appreciate you coming over. We'll repay the favour, I promise. Let me call you a cab."

When she got in, Matt was sitting at the table, going over some court papers.

He glanced up. "Oh, you're back early. What's for dinner?"

As Matt kissed her briefly on the cheek, the tell-tale whiff of beer on his breath gave away the fact that he'd been to the pub with the clerks again.

A risotto congealed horribly in a pan on the stove. Three hours ago, it had looked quite appetising, sod him.

"I cooked this earlier for you," she said, apologetically.

"Great," he said, his lack of enthusiasm all too evident.

During dinner, she found herself washing down her risotto with a large glass of white, while Matt polished off the rest of the bottle. He really was drinking too much these days. She wanted to raise that with him but didn't want another row – he was so stressed about work.

She still hadn't quite found a way to broach the issue of him looking at Muffy-porn online.

It was just so hurtful. It pushed her into a position of having to confront him, which she hated.

She'd got over the thing about George being Georgina, quite brilliantly. Of course, it was fine. He had to take her to the awards because it was a work do, there was no point sulking about it or even mentioning it ever again; even if Georgina did have legs as long as the A1 and the prettiest face in Chancery Lane.

There was no easy way to start the conversation about the internet porn star, though.

"Muffy," she said, loudly, before she could stop herself.

"What?" He glanced up, perplexed.

"Stuffy, it's stuffy in here, that's all."

"Mmm." He went back to the financial pages.

Perhaps there was no point talking about it? It was much nicer – and more interesting, actually – to think about *Harsh Winter*, which was very challenging on so many levels.

For a fleeting moment, Marnie absent-mindedly transposed herself and Matt into a sexy spy thriller. Maybe she could order him to undress and they could tussle with each other on the bed, just for fun? It just wasn't quite as delicious as Seb Winter and Katya, though.

She studied Matt's face for a second, as he carried on reading the papers.

His eyelashes were so long. All the years they'd been together, she'd never really noticed that before. His jaw had the first signs of stubble on it and his lips were pursed and almost moving as he read, his brow furrowed intently. Even when concentrating like that, without really caring if she was there, he was still handsome.

She traced the line of his collar with her eyes, travelling downwards. The top two buttons of his shirt were undone.

That drew her to the broadness of his chest, just visible.

And he had the faintest smell of sweat. It wasn't exactly pleasant – he'd had a hard day – but it pulled her to him.

Before she knew what she was doing, she leant over and touched him, lightly, on the shoulder.

"Do you fancy coming to bed soon?"

He gave her a quizzical look and then muttered, "I'm tired, Marnie, I can't. I've got lots of work to do tonight."

"Of course," she said, as a small flame of desire snuffed itself out. "Silly me."

CHAPTER FIVE

"Running away from me is pointless."

Marnie gasped as he pulled her into his arms, catching the fraying edge of her bathrobe and yanking it open.

"What are you hiding in here?"

His hands brushed across her chest and she felt her nipples harden under his touch.

"Nothing much," she mumbled. "I've still got my sports bra on."

"I may have to strip search you," he said, his blue eyes unblinking, staring into hers, turning her insides liquid with desire.

His breath was warm and sweet on her face, moving down to her neck, his hands wandering, pulling at an invisible thread of longing deep in her groin.

"I'm not sure I have time, the kids will be late for school," moaned Marnie, turning over and waking up, with a jolt.

Matt was a lump in bed beside her.

She rolled on her side and clamped her hands between her knees.

There was an unmistakable warm, stickiness between her legs. And it had nothing to do with the body snoring softly beside her.

Oh, dear God. She had betrayed Matt with the actor!

Mr Make Believe had actually got inside her head and into her dreams and they had *done things* together.

Marnie lay quietly for a moment, staring at the ceiling.

What was wrong with her? She was married and she loved her husband, not some silly imaginary bloke in a dream.

She turned and studied the back of Matt's neck. It was perfect, broad and manly, and his hair was cropped close from a recent visit to the barber's.

She fell in love with the back of that neck when she saw him at the bar in the Student Union at university. Twenty years on, she still adored it.

Ignoring the plus-sized stab of guilt over her sexy fantasy with her imaginary lover, Marnie leaned across and kissed his neck. No wonder she'd had his babies...

He turned over and opened his eyes, slightly startled.

"There's something I need to ask you," she said, earnestly.

"OK," he replied, rubbing sleep out of his eyes and looking dubious.

"You know I looked after Gabriel for Belle last night," she said, propping herself up on her elbow.

"Yes," said Matt, looking into her heart-shaped face.

"He was really easy."

"Mmm."

"Such a lovely baby. It made me feel..." She couldn't finish the sentence. What if she got washed away by the emotion of what she was trying to say?

He sighed and there was a hard look to his eyes that she hadn't seen before.

"Marnie, you know we already have two healthy boys and we are neither of us getting any younger."

"Oh," she said.

"School fees for two of them are going to kill me financially. With three, you can forget it."

Case closed.

"But we've got most of the baby stuff still," she said, meekly. "I've even kept the pram ... "

"We both need to start earning more just to keep pace with our outgoings," he barked.

Oh God, it was like a board meeting. She wanted to stop up her ears. She hadn't quite got around to mentioning that she had lost her job at *The Sentinel*. Perhaps now wasn't a wise moment to talk about that.

Matt was getting into his stride now. The thought of going back to the endless round of sleepless nights and Babygros and nappies when Charlie wasn't even properly potty-trained was too much.

He moved in for the kill.

"And besides," he added, "you can barely cope with two."

But she hadn't seen that coming.

"What did you just say to me?" she sat up straight.

"Marnie, you know you struggle with them. You should hear yourself. Your voice rises an octave when you talk to them. You are stressed around them half the time. You can't control them. I feel like recording it sometimes and playing it back to you. You don't like keeping house. That wasn't what your mother raised you to do. Your work is important to you as well and with a third child ... "

There were so many assaults she didn't know which one to tackle first. How dare he mention her deceased mother! She had died shortly after they graduated and he barely even knew her.

She wanted to cry but he had wounded her so much that there was just shock.

All the things she did with the boys, all the fun they had. All the wiping of noses, drying of tears, the reading, the play dough, the painting, the trips to the park, the Lego, the making cakes – well, OK, not very successfully, but still. The doctor's, the dentist's, the playdates, the swimming, the haircuts, school runs, assemblies, the cooking, the cleaning up, the washing up and the laundry. The relentless fucking laundry.

The love.

So much of it. She could never give them enough. And that included Matt.

She didn't tell him half the things she did with them during the day. She wasn't expecting a medal, but she didn't deserve this.

"That is the meanest thing you have ever said to me, Matt," she said, brushing away tears which were spilling down her cheeks.

She felt like howling and burying herself under the duvet for a week but she could hear the boys chattering to each other in their bedroom and, any minute, their cheeky little faces would appear around the door.

"I'm sorry, that came out wrong," said Matt, putting his arms around her and pulling her to his chest.

"You are a great mother, Marnie, it is the hardest job in the world and you really do your best." He sounded far from convinced or convincing.

She stared straight ahead.

"It's just with three, I think things would spiral out of control and we cannot afford it either. You need to cut back on the weekly shopping bill anyway. I've been meaning to ask you to cut down on expensive stuff that we really don't need. The clerks have had to slash my fees, clients are not paying on time and I still have to pay taxes on what I've billed for. And the way things are going with the economy, it's going to get worse before it gets better … "

She heard his voice but it was growing more distant.

Marnie let him hug her as the boys clambered onto the bed and started squealing and laughing, their faces alive with the sheer joy of being with Mummy and Daddy. While they laughed with the kids and made pillow mountains for them to explore, a sadness crept over her. She glanced away from Matt. It was as if part of her – the part which longed for another baby – had just slipped quietly from the room.

Matt hadn't noticed a thing.

CHAPTER SIX

Two figures moved slowly together in the semi-darkness, legs and arms entwining.

Maddox Wolfe froze in the doorway. His big, blue eyes filled with tears as he took in the half-lit scene. There was a stabbing pain in his chest. The lovers embraced, the silk sheet slipping down to reveal the curve of the man's firm, muscled backside.

She wrapped her legs around him, pulling him in deeper, gasping with pleasure. It was a sound Maddox knew so well. For this woman was Cecily. His Cecily. Somewhere deep inside, a knife twisted in his heart. She had betrayed him. And this man was everything he was not – young, fit and able to perform.

He wanted to cry out in anguish but no sound came.

Before he could stop himself, Maddox very quietly picked up the priceless vase from the antique console table by the door.

Stealthily and silently, he crept across the thick carpet towards the couple, who were lost in each other's embrace. Drawing himself up to his full height, Maddox loomed like a Colossus over the bed. He raised his arm high, brandishing the vase, hesitating for a second as he appraised his target, before bringing it down with all his might on the head of the man who was making love to his beautiful wife.

There was a sickening thud and the air was filled with the sound of Cecily's shrieking, as blood oozed from the motionless body on top of her.

"And cut!" yelled the director.

Byron Hunt brushed some chunks of plaster out of his hair and sat up, grinning at Maddox: "That was harder than it needed to be, mate, but it is always such a pleasure doing your wife."

Maddox gave him a playful shove before leaning over and kissing Cecily, who was naked from the waist up and being openly admired by Byron. Maddox gritted his teeth. Actors were meant to be relaxed about nudity, but he couldn't help being possessive about his wife's body. He was rather relieved when a wardrobe assistant ran in to give her a silk robe.

"Darling, you were wonderful!" she breathed at Maddox, batting her eyelashes at Byron Hunt, who had the taut six-pack and bulging biceps of a 20-something all-action hero and blue eyes, which glittered with appreciation as she fastened her robe loosely, leaving a great deal of cleavage on display. Her blonde hair fell to her shoulders, giving her an effortless beauty that women worldwide wanted to emulate.

Maddox felt like an intruder all over again. If he could just lean over and tie that belt so tight that not an inch of flesh was left showing, that might improve his mood. Or, better still, pull it tight around Byron's windpipe.

Instead, he quietly chewed a spot just inside his left cheek that he used to calm himself when particularly stressed, staring impassively.

Feigning happiness at starring alongside blonde demi-god Byron Hunt was his most challenging role to date. For a start, he had to overcome his mounting chagrin at missing out on the starring role of this action thriller *Whitehouse*.

Maddox had to attempt to relish the role of the impotent President, while his ambitious wife, Marie – played by Cecily – cheated on him with political correspondent Damian Kirsch – played by Byron, of course.

Four, maybe five, years ago he would have been dry humping Cecily in this bed on the set. Or maybe, they would have done it for real – just to turn each other on and keep the crew guessing.

But he was too old for the lead role now, at the wrong side of 50 and sliding towards 55. Sure, some stars managed it alright, with a strict personal training regime and anabolic steroids, but not when the hot poster-boy for horny housewives everywhere was reading for the same part. Maddox felt like strangling his agent for making him go through with it. Then again, he had numerous homes on two continents, a small army of staff, private school fees for two teenage boys and a pre-teen princess, plus the spending habits of Cecily to contend with. Nope, he needed this job. Plus, sharing the movie billing with his wife guaranteed acres of news and magazine coverage, which was good for both their careers.

The director, a picture of permanent, low-grade exasperation, stalked over and forced a smile.

"That was great guys, just great. But Maddox, I just need a bit more emotion from you. In that split second before you bring the vase down on his head, I need you to reach into the depths of your soul to give me that special something. You know what I mean, don't you?"

"Yes, Jack, of course," said Maddox. What was this little prick talking about? "Let's get cleaned up, then I'm ready to give it my all."

The director chomped on his biro.

"Great, great, Maddox. Now, although I need you to look like you want to kill him, don't actually hit Byron as hard as

that again, will you?" he laughed. "We can cover it with special effects you know! I'm not looking for a fractured skull!"

"Sorry, Byron, hope I didn't hurt you?" said Maddox, as
he ruffled the young actor's hair.

"No, I'm fine," said Byron, looking even more perfect
when he smiled.

"Good, good," said Maddox, beaming back at him, his
eyes creasing at the corners in a way that film reviewers
always said made women go weak at the knees.

Next time he would do his damnedest to hit the little
fucker even harder.

Maddox didn't hear the director whisper to the make-
up girl: "Do something about granddad's bald patch will
you? The light's bouncing off it like a laser off a glitterball,
for Chrissakes."

⚜   ⚜   ⚜

The last of the film crew had sloped off to the pub to discuss
the day's action. Cecily Haywood slunk back to the bed on
set where she had spent the best part of the day, still naked
but for her silk robe. She was not alone for long.

As she lay back on the pillows, she reached out and pulled
Maddox to her, running her fingers through his hair, which
used to be jet black but was now greying at the temples. She
did her best to ignore the thinning bit on the top.

Soon she would raise the issue of a hair transplant. Her
beauty specialist Dr Tolko would be sure to help. He could
probably iron out a few of the creases around Maddox's eyes
at the same time, or maybe give him laser facial rejuvena-
tion at the very least. The possibilities were endless. And
Maddox would benefit from it – he was known for being
boyishly, if a bit devilishly, handsome. Being blessed with

cutesy features was no good if things started to look too creased. It was beginning to show in the roles he was pulling in. If he wanted to stay at the top, all those little lived-in laughter lines would need to be sorted, and soon. She'd been thoughtful enough to take care of her looks. Why should it be any different for him?

Maddox still believed that Cecily's face and body were the result of sheer hard work and will power, rather than liposuction and fillers. Those long stays away when he was filming on location came in very handy for maintenance. The time had come for her to have "the talk" with him about the need to get a little surgical enhancement.

But, for now, being in bed with Byron Hunt all day had made her needy, so needy, for sex. And if she couldn't have Byron, Maddox was going to have to give it to her. Hard and fast – right here. If she closed her eyes, she could imagine it was Byron, sliding in to her, putting every one of those muscles to good use.

"Come on honey, there's no-one here, just us. Don't you feel like playing?" she teased, as she slowly undid the silk ties of her robe to reveal her beautiful breasts and tiny waist.

"Of course I do," he said, his voice a whisper, as he traced his fingers across her milky white skin.

He started to kiss her, feeling her mouth, soft and warm. His hands were on her breasts as her nipples started to harden beneath his touch and Cecily murmured her appreciation.

"We can pretend you caught me with someone else and now you have to make me yours, just yours," she said.

She put her hand down the front of his jeans and felt something disappointingly soft.

Maddox flinched and pulled away.

"I don't know what's happening with me at the moment."

Cecily sat up and folded her arms. "I think you are taking the method acting too far Maddox. Get out of character for a minute, will you? You haven't managed to get it up in over a week. What's going on?"

"I'm sorry honey. I really want you ... "

"Well, maybe you need to see a doctor."

"No, no. I'm sure it's just stress. Working with Byron is getting me down. He's such an arse. He couldn't act his way out of a paper bag."

"He's a good looking arse, though," teased Cecily.

Maddox pulled her closer. "That is really not helping me at all. I want you so much it hurts. It's killing me seeing you in bed with him, day after day."

"Oh come on, you're not jealous are you?" said Cecily, pouting a little. "You know you are my leading man. I just want you to take care of me. And only you know how. You know I need you, Maddox. I need a real man, not a boy like Byron."

He was stroking her hair as she laid her head on his chest. This had never happened to him until he got this damned supporting role in this bloody film. It was demeaning and the little man in his trousers knew it and was refusing to play ball.

The fact that Byron Hunt was being touted as a replacement for him in his most famous role, superspy Seb Winter, wasn't helping matters either, but Maddox didn't want to discuss that with Cecily now. It was ego-shattering stuff.

"I know, honey. I'll sort it. I promise."

In the editing booth, the sound man, who had been listening to every word via the ambient overhead microphone, pressed save on the recording he had just made. It would have been better to catch them screwing on set. That would have been hot. Really hot.

But A-list movie star Maddox Wolfe talking about his erectile dysfunction problems with his Oscar-winning wife and slagging off his co-star had to be worth a couple of thousand at least from one of the national newspapers.

CHAPTER SEVEN

"Hello, sis!"

He was standing on the doorstep, looking as if he hadn't washed for at least a decade. And he was carrying the same rucksack he had used to trek around Thailand during his gap year.

"Dylan!" said Marnie. "What are you doing here?"

"That's no way to welcome your little brother, is it?" he said, pushing past her and into the hallway.

"Had you forgotten I was coming to stay?"

"Stay?"

He put a hand over his mouth in mock-horror: "Don't tell me you didn't get my emails?"

She put her hands on her hips: "No, Dylan. I did not, mainly because you didn't send any."

"You can't prove that," he said, slipping off the back-pack. "And, anyway, I'm family. I just need somewhere to stay for a few..."

"Days?" Marnie cut in.

"Weeks," he corrected her.

"Oh, Dylan," she said. "I don't want to be uncharitable, it's just I've got so much on with the boys and Matt..."

"Yes, how is little Rupert?"

"It's Rufus," said Marnie, "And he has a three-year-old brother called Charlie."

"Of course he has!" said Dylan. "I am dying to be a good uncle to them. We need time to bond and I think you could use my help, Marnie. I will be your manny on my days off."

"My what?"

"Your male nanny. Free babysitting. You and Matt can go out and enjoy yourselves, in return for letting me stay for a bit."

Marnie bit her lip. That was a very attractive prospect. Maybe she and Matt could go out for an evening and really enjoy themselves? It had been such a long time, although, the idea of leaving Dylan in charge of a pet rabbit – let alone her precious boys – was rather daunting, to say the least.

He had already wandered off down the hallway and was peering into the lounge, where an old Seb Winter spy film, *Nuclear Winter*, starring Maddox Wolfe, was on pause.

Her new book, *Harsh Winter*, was open at chapter three – the bit where Katya forced Seb to undress at gunpoint. Marnie had been re-reading that, just to be sure she fully understood the sub-text, for her book club.

She rushed in and shoved it under a cushion, before Dylan spotted it.

"Yes, you seem very busy, Marnie," he smirked, sauntering into the room. "What if I tell you I'm working on his new film?" He pointed to the television and the frozen image of Maddox Wolfe, stark naked in a decontamination facility shower, save for a few strategically placed soapsuds.

"Are you?" she clapped her hands together, before she could stop herself.

"I am," he said. "And that means I might be able to sneak you some gossip from the set. Or at least get you an autograph. I had no idea you were such a big fan."

"I'm not," she said, flicking the telly off. "It was just research for a story."

Oh, what a lie. She didn't even have a job any more, but there was no need to tell Dylan that.

"I'll make myself at home," he said, throwing his backpack over his shoulder and making his way up the stairs to the loft. "Then, why don't I do the school run for you?"

✤ ✤ ✤

With Dylan out on the school run, she had time to check her blog for any new comments. There were none, so she went on Facebook and had a look at her friends' amazing lives. Everyone seemed to be going to better places or having more fun than she was. Other families seemed to find time to explore, to go for long walks, to have weekends away. She just did laundry, shopping and cleaned up after the kids and Matt was so exhausted he barely had the energy to go to the park. Matt didn't even bother liking any of her posts either.

There was a time when they'd send each other little love texts or emails during the day. That never happened any more, most of their exchanges involved childcare or their internet food order for the week. It was as if the desire to flirt with each other had deserted them, or perhaps she was being paranoid and he was just busy?

She looked up his Facebook page. That was strange. He seemed to find time to like a lot of other people's stuff and even comment on what they were up to. One name in particular was all over his page like a bad rash, with chirpy little comments and emojis. Belinda, his old flame from university, who had got her claws into Matt during Freshers' Week, was now engaged in a game of verbal ping-pong with her husband, sharing little jokey asides and digs at each other.

Marnie swallowed hard. She didn't even know that he was still in touch with Belinda! He'd never mentioned it, that's for sure. Belinda lived in Australia, for God's sake, and was last heard of saving the whale or whatever it was that eco-warriors do these days. Marnie clicked on Belinda's profile. Swampy-Belinda had certainly cleaned up her act. Gone were the grungy dreadlocks and in their place was a perfectly respectable blow dry, which emphasised her almond-shaped eyes. Marnie zoomed in on that picture, checking for wrinkles and sun damage. There wasn't any, which made her feel even worse.

There was a knock at the door. She really must tell Matt to mend that bloody doorbell instead of mucking around on Facebook so much.

The courier was holding a package that was expensive-looking and very pink. It had her name on it, but who could it be from?

Heart fluttering with excitement, Marnie carried it inside and laid it on the kitchen island. She carefully opened the envelope accompanying the parcel and found a little card: "Sorry for upsetting you, love, Matt x"

He had bought her a present to make up for being so beastly to her the other day! Oh thank God she hadn't lost the plot over that silly Belinda thing. Of course, lots of people were in touch with their friends from uni on Facebook.

She placed the card next to the weighty recipe book, which Matt left open, hopefully, every morning at the page with the meal he would most like to eat that evening. Every day, she ignored that page and shoved the book back on the kitchen shelf.

To be honest, sometimes, she quite fancied slamming his stupid head shut in it; it was quite a heavy book.

But today, perhaps, she might actually go ahead and cook – what was it? – lamb tagine.

Her fingers traced the ribbon tied around the parcel and gently tugged it open.

Layer upon layer of cerise tissue paper rustled in her hands. She inhaled deeply. Wafts of delicious scent emanated from the most luxurious gift she had ever received. He really was trying to say sorry.

A small silk bag, fastened by a single mother-of-pearl button, lay at the heart of the box.

She was trembling as she undid it and gently reached inside.

First, she pulled out two very small thongs – one in leopard print and the other bright red, in a material that bore no resemblance to the silk purse they had been presented in. Too much friction and these knickers would create a fire hazard.

They practically screamed pole dancer.

She put her hand back inside the silk pouch and slowly drew out a pair of sheer black pants, which, on closer inspection, appeared to have the crotch missing.

Oh, and they were in a size 10.

There was more.

He had even bought her a pair of furry handcuffs. Those would come in handy for chaining him to the oven while she went out on a three-day spa and shopping spree to get over this.

Winded, Marnie sat down at the kitchen table. When had she *ever* wanted anything in leopard print, let alone worn it?

He saw a sexy come-hither glance à la Muffy in those thongs and she saw cheesewire, a bad case of thrush and half a tube of Canesten.

And the crotchless knickers! Well, they were just unspeakable.

How dare he impose his sexual fantasies on her in this way!

It just was not on. She picked up the phone and rang him. "Hello, Matt Martin."

Why did he always do that when he knew her mobile phone number off by heart? Was it to make a point about being at work and oh-so-flipping important?

"I got your present," she said, flatly.

"Did you like them?"

She could hear the grin in his voice.

"No, but I think Muffy would."

"Who?"

"The online porn-star you have been chatting to."

"I ... I don't know what you mean."

"Yes, you do, you bloody liar."

"I only did it once."

"You only got caught once, Matt. Does that make it OK? Is it not enough that I have wrecked my body having your babies? Don't you find me attractive anymore? And you never mentioned that Swampy Bloody Belinda had been poking you on Facebook ... "

"Of course I find you attractive! That's why I bought you those nice knickers and you know Belinda is just an old friend from college ... "

"Nice knickers?" she spat. "What's wrong with my normal knickers? Not sexy enough for you?"

"Of course they are sexy," he whispered. "Look, my clerk has just come into the room, can we talk about it later?"

"Perhaps," said Marnie. "Then again, perhaps not. You might be too busy chatting to Muffy or Facebook flirting with Bloody Belinda!"

There was silence.

"And Matt?"

"Yes?"

"I haven't been a size 10 since you ruined my life by marrying me."

"Marnie," he began.

"Don't 'Marnie' me!" she said. "There's something else you need to know."

"What?" His voice was a whisper.

"I lost my job and I was too scared to tell you because you already think I am a huge, unattractive failure."

"I don't think that!"

"Yes, you do. I am so busy trying to be everything to everybody in this house that I can't be a good journalist, a good mother, let alone a good anything else, if Muffy is anything to go by," she sobbed. "We need counselling!"

And she threw the phone down so hard that it bounced off the kitchen island.

CHAPTER EIGHT

Jonah was getting ready to take the baby out for a walk in the park – some boys' time together before Destroy's warm-up gig tonight for the music industry's head honchos and hangers-on.

Having wrestled successfully with the straps on Gabriel's pram, he was about to place teddy in his allotted spot, when he became aware of an agitated presence at his shoulder, waving a muslin and a different stuffed toy.

"No, no, you have got the wrong one!" said Belle, barely disguising her exasperation.

Then she plonked a massive changing bag on Jonah's shoulder.

"For God's sake! I'm only taking him to the park for a walk!" said Jonah.

"You always need to be prepared," Belle tutted. "You never know when he is going to do a poonami."

"A poonami?"

"It's like a tsunami – of shit. You don't want to be stuck in Hyde Park with one of his dirty nappies and no change."

He held his hands up in defeat – slightly lopsidedly due to the sheer weight of the changing bag. What the hell had she packed into this thing? The entire contents of Mothercare?

He pleaded with her back as it departed down the hall-way: "Will you at least have a lie down?"

As the door banged shut, Belle ran up three flights of stairs to check and re-check the room thermometer in Gabriel's nursery.

Was it warm, very warm or too hot in here? Or too cold? She darted across to Gabriel's cot, which was carved in the shape of a guitar, sticking her hand underneath the mattress, pulling out the movement sensor to check that the batteries hadn't run out.

Black and white images of Jonah, Belle and Gabriel – taken by *The Sentinel* – adorned the walls. They all looked so happy and relaxed. They were only taken a few weeks ago but it felt like a lifetime.

Belle ran back downstairs to the open-plan kitchen, which she kept spotlessly clean. A sterilizer was ready to empty on the stainless steel work surface and the sink was full of the next lot of bottles. She had to wash them by hand and then give them a good rinse in cold water. There were all kinds of chemicals in the dishwasher that she didn't want Gabriel ingesting. Yes, she had a cleaner, but this was her baby, her job.

Belle was so tired, her breastmilk had virtually dried up. She was bottle feeding, secretly. She couldn't tell the other mothers at her Natural Mums' Group, who were all bright-eyed, glossy haired, committed breastfeeding types, who produced home-made scones from their Birkin bags with one hand and a sleepy, downy-haired little babe from the folds of a baby sling with the other, as if by magic. It could make meetings at her house quite awkward. Maybe she could pretend it was her milk, expressed into a bottle?

Why was she so rubbish at this?

A weighty tome by baby guru Alexa Joy, *The Joy of Parenting in Ten Easy Steps: How to Be a Better Mother*, glared at her from the kitchen table, open at chapter three, "A

Good Night's Sleep". She had done chapter one, "Simply the Breast", without much success but chapter two, "Raising Einstein", wasn't too bad if you bought enough toys from her online store, Bundle-of-Joy.com. Chapter three had proved an insurmountable hurdle.

It advised minimal cuddles and controlled crying at all times, even in the small hours. Belle had watched Alexa Joy dispensing advice to fraught callers on housewives' favourite lunchtime slot, *ChitChat*, smiling beatifically as she poured her own soothing brand of baby oil on troubled bedtime waters. Women were cajoled into admitting that they hadn't quite followed her advice to the letter as their babies screamed their heads off in the background.

"And that, you see, my loves, is where you are going wrong," chided Alexa Joy, firmly, her bony little hands rapping her thighs. "You have let your baby down, you've let yourself down. Of course your baby is angry with you! To Be a Better Mother requires discipline. Lots of it, in such a loving way. Your baby will thank you for it. That is the true Joy of Parenting!"

Each of Gabriel's wails was a like a knife in Belle's heart and he seemed to settle much more quickly if she cuddled him. All the Notting Hill mummies thought Alexa Joy was so clever at getting babies to sleep through the night. Most of them made sure their maternity nurses and nannies employed her methods while they got a full eight hours.

Alexa Joy had never had children.

Sighing, Belle picked up a mirrored baby toy from the kitchen floor. She would have to sterilise that as well. The mirror distorted her face and made it look even more hideous. She had dark circles under her eyes and a deathly pallor from broken nights with Gabriel. Jonah was often out late rehearsing with the band and he needed his rest, so she didn't want to disturb him. With her hair pulled back, she did a passable impression of Golum.

Jonah had offered to pay for a full-time nanny or a night maternity nurse but this made Belle see red. She was a top-flight showbiz reporter who was used to lots of pressure and little sleep. She worked for one of the toughest Newsdesks in Fleet Street. Having hired help would be like admitting defeat, really.

Besides, motherhood simply couldn't be that hard. Her mother had done it twice over but was now too busy to come up from Plymouth to help out, even though she would run barefoot to London if there was the offer of a celebrity-filled event to attend.

Of course, she would need a nanny when she returned full-time to the showbiz beat at *The Sentinel* when Gabriel was nine months old or so. She wanted to keep earning her own money. She couldn't just be the kept girlfriend of a rock star. That was not what she had spent her whole life building a career for, was it?

Belle felt her eyelids closing as the water gushed over her hands in the sink and the bottles clunked together in the suds. Tears started streaming down her face. Gabriel was so little, so vulnerable, and the most perfect thing ever. So why was being a mother making her so miserable?

❧ ❧ ❧

Belle was curled up and dozing on the sofa in her tracksuit bottoms and one of Jonah's old tour T-shirts when he came in. Her hair was still wet from the shower and hung in damp waves. She looked more like a teenager than a mother in her late twenties.

"Hey," he said, gently stroking her face.

Belle sat bolt upright, panic rising in her voice: "Sorry, I must have fallen asleep. What time is it? Where's the baby?"

Her cheeks were flushed slightly from her doze. She looked adorable.

"He's fast asleep in the pram, honey. He's fine. And that means we may have at least," Jonah looked at his watch, "five minutes before the little bugger wakes up. Come on!"

She laughed and her whole face lit up for him. The nap had done her good.

He dived on top of her and started wriggling her out of her jogging bottoms. She was still so lithe. And those little white cotton shorts underneath made her look sweet and sexy.

He was already in possession of a raging hard-on. How did she do that to him, even in her sweats?

Belle was desperately tired but also desperate for Jonah. She missed her pre-baby days of lazing about in bed together. They used to be insatiable.

She was already stripped to her bra and boy-shorts now. She got to work on his jeans and his erection sprang free.

She pushed him back on to the sofa, leant forward and took him in her mouth, making him groan as she moved up and down his considerable length. The taste of him, the feel of him. He was delicious. And he was hers.

A little cry came over the baby monitor in the hall.

She paused looked up at Jonah and his eyes met hers imploring her to continue. She swirled her tongue, making him judder a little, watching him all the time. She knew that would drive him wild.

"I want to be inside you, honey," his voice was hoarse with longing.

It had been ages since they had found the time or the energy to do this.

Quick as a flash, she peeled off her shorts and straddled him, plunging him deep inside her. It took her breath away. She started to move, slowly up and down as he put his hands up and squeezed her nipples through her bra, turning her on even more.

Her breasts were even more full and womanly since the baby. He loved that.

A warmth was building in her lower belly. She was lost in sensation as he started to thrust back at her a little, his hands steadying either side of her hips and then stroking down, over her bottom. He knew just what to do to take her over the edge.

More noises came from the baby monitor. They looked at each other again. He was too far gone to stop now and so was she. She started to grind against him. Harder. Faster.

"Come with me, Belle." He looked deep into her eyes. That smouldering look did for her every time. Her stomach did a funny little flip which connected with the warm feeling and a jolt of electricity shot through her groin and down to her feet as she arched her back for him, feeling the clench and release as he came inside her at the same time.

"Oh, thank Christ for that," he said, encircling her in his arms as she rested her head on his shoulders, feeling complete and peaceful and...

The baby was howling now. They looked at each other, their moment of post-coital bliss shattered by parental guilt.

Belle dashed into the hallway and popped the wailing infant on to her shoulder, patting his back to calm him.

Jonah stood in the doorway, appraising her form, her hair tumbling down over her shoulders.

"You really are the most beautiful creature," he said, putting a protective arm around her back and patting her on the bottom. "And you, little boy, are the luckiest young man in the world because you get to spend all day with her!"

"I think he's hungry," said Belle, shifting her weight from one foot to the other, trying to shake off the guilt of ignoring Gabriel's cries as well as Jonah's hand, which, for some reason, was irritating her now. "Could you get him a bottle and I will go and get sorted for this evening?"

"Dress sexy for me," he said, adding quickly, "If you want to. It makes me play better when I am admiring you."

Belle gave him a withering look which passed him by completely: "Thanks, I'll try."

Dress sexy? With breasts like watermelons and an extra stone to shift. Great.

The doorbell rang.

Jonah ran to pull on his jeans, carefully laying Gabriel on the thick-pile Union Jack rug in the lounge. Then, picking up his son and still naked from the waist up, he sauntered to the front door.

Marta, his PA, stood glowering at him. She hated to be kept waiting and it was perfectly obvious what her boss had been up to in his state of undress, with wildly ruffled hair.

He was jaw-droppingly handsome, every inch of his honed torso on show, chiselled cheekbones and green eyes peeking out from long, dark lashes. But even that didn't improve her mood.

He gave her a lopsided grin.

"Sorry for the wait."

He handed Gabriel over to her

"The bottle's in the kitchen," he said, as Gabriel dribbled on her immaculately pressed T-shirt and she shot her boss an even filthier glance. "Would you mind feeding the baby?"

CHAPTER NINE

Hugo Hansen hated having to get up early to pap celebs on their doorsteps.

The Picture Desk had issued last minute orders for him to be waiting with his long lens by Primrose Hill at 6am. It was just not on for a photographer of his calibre. Yes, he had no problem roughing it in the field if there was a war on, but trying to catch a movie actress going for a run? Really?

By the time he'd showered, dressed, had a fag and a coffee, cleaned his camera lenses, plucked his nose hair and defluffed his belly-button, the clock had reached the slightly less anti-social hour of 7am.

Hugo sat patiently in his Porsche a few doors down from the imposing Haywood-Wolfe family home, cameras slung around his neck, with one eye on Primrose Hill and the other on the morning paper.

Hugo's grey-blue eyes glinted as Cecily Haywood trotted into view at the top of the hill. He determined to make his quarry look absolutely awful. If he had to be inconvenienced in this way, then his pix were bloody well going to make the paper.

He waited until she was half way down the hill before slowly climbing out of his car, pushing his Ray-Bans on to the top of his head, and firing off the first set of shots. Nice and easy.

She was huffing and puffing in spray-on black running tights and a form-fitting sweat top, hair flying about, and she hadn't seen him.

Just as she reached the park gates, he shouted her name and she squinted at him, trying to make out who was calling her. The sunlight was in her eyes but he did seem kind of familiar. He was quite good-looking, with a boyish crop, sandy blonde hair and regular features. Where had she seen him?

He fired off another shot. What a beauty!

Then, realising what was happening, a look of horror crossed her very pink face and her mouth twisted, as if to say something. She thought better of it and her hands flew up to her cheeks. By then, it was too late. He had caught the whole lot. Smirking, he waited for her to jog past to get to her front door, taking more snaps than were strictly necessary of her lycra-clad bum. She was in great shape for someone over 40, from the back at least.

Cecily didn't dare scowl at him in case he caught that as well.

And she couldn't slow down because then it would get reported that she wasn't fit enough. So, she stuck her nose in the air and just jogged by as if she hadn't a care, before opening the front door and shutting herself off from the horrid world outside.

⚜ ⚜ ⚜

Cecily didn't have to wait long for Hugo's handiwork to appear.

It made a double page spread the next day in *Sentinel Woman*, as part of a very upsetting article headlined "The Ugly Truth About Ageing Stars", quoting her former co-star and slut Athena Maldon at length and deriding not only Cecily's looks but her very existence! Bloody Athena was even getting her own column out of it too – talk about scraping the barrel. Why did no-one come to ask her about her witty opinions on life as an international movie star?

Most upsettingly, it was the most viewed article in the online showbiz section, with people worldwide logging on to discuss the state of her face. The topic "Should Cecily Buy a New Look?" was trending on Twitter.

Awful.

Maddox thought she was just being overly sensitive and didn't bother with all that Twitter nonsense anyway. A look of concern flashed across his face as he scanned the paper, clasped in Cecily's perfectly manicured hands.

"Athena isn't worth a second thought honey," he said, stroking her hair. "I know you are gorgeous and so does the rest of the world. Athena's just got an axe to grind. She's jealous of our love, our success. In fact, she's just jealous." He thrust his hands deeper into the pockets of his faded blue jeans, which hung off his lean waist. He chewed his lip as Cecily watched him a bit too closely, searching for something in his face.

They'd both had their conquests but none of it had threatened their marriage.

Something about the sheer determination, beauty and youth of Athena unsettled her. Was she losing her grip on Maddox along with her looks? And he was losing his, she really did need to have a chat with him.

"I'm not sure we can really do anything because the photographer didn't snap you on private property," he said. "That's why I work out in the gym downstairs, sweetheart. I don't want some grubby little snapper getting a picture of me working up a sweat, unless I am being paid thousands for it."

Tears started to well up in Cecily's eyes.

"Hey," he said. "Don't cry. Do you want me to get on to the lawyers?"

They would relish the chance to get heavy with the Managing Editor of *The Sentinel*.

But Cecily refused.

"It will make more of it than we need to," she said, "I just want it to blow over." She was actually desperate for Maddox to leave her alone so that she could make an urgent appointment with her skin specialist, Dr Tolko. Without the doctor's input, she would have to remain under self-imposed house arrest, in case any more nasty photographers wanted to take shots at her. "I was caught from an unfortunate angle, that's all."

Papped looking rough in the harsh light of a Primrose Hill morning. Frankly, the dogs-on-string hippy brigade in nearby Camden looked better than she did in those shots. How many creases were there around her eyes, exactly? It was like facial origami. And why was her mouth drooping in that manner? Her hair, instead of its usual silky loveliness, looked like straw. She needed help.

Plus there was the issue of Maddox's little problem, which was still bothering her. Byron Hunt was looking more attractive by the minute and his tumescence during their love-making scenes seemed to be getting not only harder by the day but harder to ignore. She was sure – very sure in fact – that he fancied her. Now this nasty set of photographs would put him off.

There was no way he would want to grab a granny.

❧ ❧ ❧

Later that day, Cecily swept into the offices of leading beauty specialist Dr Tolko in Harley Street, wearing vast shades, her face covered by a large scarf.

As she was A-list, he had managed to squeeze her in. Mere mortals couldn't even get a foot over the threshold.

She was welcomed by a lithe, white-clad assistant with, Cecily noted, very peachy, flawless skin.

The soothing white walls of the clinic were adorned with pictures of impossibly beautiful naked women. Piped music – a hypnotic mixture of sighing and violins – floated through air that was scented by the most delicious-smelling candles.

Cecily was ushered past the white leather banquettes in the waiting area and upstairs into Dr Tolko's office.

Daylight streamed in through the huge windows and as if that wasn't bad enough, he had very, very bright lighting. There was nowhere to hide here.

The doctor got up from behind a glass desk – with nothing on it other than a flatscreen computer and a large bottle of mineral water.

"Miss Haywood, how nice to see you," he extended a long, thin hand towards her, his grey hair scraped back into a little ponytail, thin lips barely moving as he spoke, eyes growing wider as they studied her every pore.

Never mind his creepy looks, those fingers worked magic and right now, she needed a miracle.

"You have come about your recent pictures in the newspaper?"

So he had seen them too! How awful.

She nodded, mutely.

"Today we will start with some Botox to help the immediate situation, but I'm afraid it is no longer a solution for you."

So was this it then? Haggard ever after! She couldn't live with herself if that was to be the case.

"Relax, Miss Haywood, I have a facial. Very new, very

exclusive." He was already at her side running his bony fingers over her face, squeezing here and there, testing the plumpness of her cheeks.

Something about the way was squinting now told Cecily he was not happy with what he had found.

"This facial, I want it. I need it," she said, like a little girl begging for a new dolly, as he propelled her towards his leather examination chair and gently pushed her back into it.

"First, you must get pregnant."

"What?" She sat up.

"Relax," he soothed. "You are still young and anyway, there is IVF! I have the best doctors at my disposal. I like to call this, The Baby Facial."

"But Maddox really doesn't want any more kids." She managed to leave most of Persephone's care to the nanny – although she was showing signs of turning into a pre-teen little madam – and the twins Hector and Ajax were off at boarding school.

Never mind what another baby would do to her body! Was the doctor insane? Why not just smash a wrecking ball through what was left of her looks – and her pelvic floor.

Dr Tolko let out a shrill laugh, which echoed around the room: "Since when has pregnancy had *anything* to do with what the man wants? Think of your face. You will get pregnant. You have the baby, which of course is loved and wanted, but you also get some very special stem cells from the cord blood."

"The what?"

"Think of them as the most wonderful, miraculous little cells your body can produce."

He started pacing the room, waving his arms around, as if he were conducting an orchestra: "I am there at the moment of the birth – I collect the umbilical cord blood, I harvest the cells, we grow a stem cell line in the laboratory, we create a lifetime's supply of your very own rejuvenating facial cells! No more depleted collagen."

He turned and poked her very hard in her cheek to ram the point home.

"Ouch. No more depleted collagen," she said.

"The face of a 20-year-old!"

She was flushed with excitement: "The face of a 20-year-old? I'll do it."

She could always spend every waking moment working off her baby-weight down the gym. Especially if she had the face of a 20-year-old! Beauty is hard work, after all.

Mollified, Cecily lay back in the chair, but a look of concern made her furrow her brow – as much as she could with a Botox needle sticking into it.

"There's one problem. Even if Maddox did want to have more kids – and I'm really not sure that he does – he is having trouble, in the trouser department."

Dr Tolko shrugged his shoulders. "It happens, especially to men his age. Don't worry. I have something that might help. But it is very exclusive, very secret. You must not even tell your doctor he has got this. It is still in development."

"Is it safe?"

"Of course! It has been tested on thousands of volunteers worldwide. Just not here. Our laws are so tight. They strangle breakthroughs. They are so much more creative in Russia, China, Korea, parts of South America. Maddox will find he has more stamina. You will have more fun together. I guarantee it. And your face will love you for it!"

She wrote out a large cheque and took a month's supply of pills in a box marked "Obduro".

The doctor went on: "But once he has started it, don't let him stop. He must take the whole course."

"Wonderful," said Cecily. "And I'll keep you posted on other developments."

"Make sure you do." He added: "Before it is too late!"

CHAPTER TEN

The light shimmered off the myriad of tiny iridescent tiles lining the walls, as Athena Maldon completed her thirtieth lap of the infinity pool at Shilling Hall Spa.

Day membership had cost her a bloody fortune – and one that she could ill afford – so she was going to make the most of it.

Rumour had it that film demi-god Byron Hunt liked to come here to have massages, which meant the management had to keep prices high to prevent fortysomething mummy-civilians from over-running the facilities and ruining the air of calm with their fervent star-spotting and damp gussets.

Athena was attracting a few stares and glances, but she wasn't a civilian of course. She wasn't a movie star either. Yet.

Exiting the pool and drying herself on the thickly-tufted towel, she spotted a pair of pneumatic breasts, barely contained in a gold bikini top, bobbing about in the outdoor hydrotherapy pool.

They were attached to Slutlana, girlfriend of Vladimir Shustrov. There was almost as much silicone pumped into her lips by the look of it. Her dyed blonde hair streamed out behind her as she let the jets of water pummel her scrawny body.

Athena pulled her hair back into a neat chignon, kicked off her Havaianas and slipped into the pool beside her.

She had planned to lock her in one of the herbal saunas, or better still, the ice cave – but no matter.

Slutlana didn't open her eyes but lay back, hair still billowing.

It only took a minute for Athena to achieve her goal, fingers working deftly. Then, she stepped back out of the pool and made her way, swiftly, to the sleek changing rooms.

She was shrugging off her fluffy white robe when a therapist bustled in, whispering in panic to her colleague on the towel desk: "She's got her hair tangled in the bloody filter. Get me some scissors, quick, before she screams the place down. I'm going to have to cut her extensions off to get her out."

Athena stifled a giggle.

She really wanted to luxuriate in the cavernous marble showers but no time for that now. She needed to move quickly.

After drenching herself in Chanel Coco Mademoiselle, she wriggled into her dress and pulled on her heels.

Then, she crossed the flagstone path from the spa to the grand old ivy-covered hotel, breathing in lungfuls of fresh Surrey air and smiling coyly at the doormen.

Surveying the bar, she spied her target engrossed in the financial pages, sitting in a big armchair overlooking the manicured grounds, guarded by two burly men with thick necks.

With any luck he may have spotted her strutting over from the spa in her red bodycon minidress and Manolos. Normally, she would go for something more gamine to seduce a man of Shustrov's age but he was Russian, so it was less complex. She'd selected her highest heels and a microdress in red, to remind him of his formative years in his home country, of course.

Settling herself in the plush striped velvet chair opposite, she took out her mobile phone and started crossing and uncrossing her legs. She wasn't wearing any knickers. He ignored her for a whole minute – she was timing it on the phone's stopwatch. Most men would have crumbled at 30 seconds. She hoped this wasn't a bad sign.

"Have we met?" He glanced up from his newspaper, his eyes the most startling, mesmeric shade of aquamarine. She inhaled sharply and recovered herself.

His face was broad, framed by salt and pepper grey hair and his features were round and slightly piggy-looking, but that mouth, curling slightly at the corners, had a very full pair of lips, which she couldn't stop staring at.

"No, but I'm a columnist for one of our national newspapers," she purred. "And I was hoping not only to welcome you to the UK but also to get your views on English women."

One of Shustrov's heavies moved closer to his side, but was waved away.

"No need, Petya." He leaned forward and smiled at Athena, revealing two gold teeth: "You were saying?"

Instead of being revolted by his dentistry, she felt butterflies rising in her stomach and hitched her dress a bit further up her thigh.

"I was wondering about your views on English women. How do we compare to our Russian counterparts, that sort of thing?"

"Why don't we continue this little chat upstairs?" he said, extending his hand to her, "I didn't catch your name?"

⚜ ⚜ ⚜

As he pushed open the door to the master suite, Athena was almost knocked sideways by its opulence. A sumptuous bed, piled with the most decadent, deep red silk cushions and covered with a wine-coloured velvet quilt, formed the centrepiece of the room, which was painted in burgundy, with the same accents of colour picked out in the sofas, armchairs, vases and the heavy, brocaded curtains.

Her spindly stiletto heels sank into the thick, cream carpet as she entered, inhaling the luxury, admiring the massive crystal chandelier twinkling overhead.

An ivy-clad balcony was visible through the French windows, with a bottle of champagne chilling in an ice bucket on a little table – for afterwards, how nice.

A frosted roll-top bath peeked through the open door to the marble bathroom. She couldn't wait to splash about in there.

Athena spied his paperwork strewn across a big desk in the corner and felt her heart beat faster as she imagined him signing cheques for million dollar deals.

As Shustrov turned his back to fix them a drink from the silver tray on the side, she whipped off her dress and stood there naked, looking like a goddess, albeit one wearing high heels.

His eyes lit up as they travelled across her body, the perfect breasts, slender – almost boyish – hips and her pubic hair waxed into the shape of a downward-pointing arrow.

"I don't think I am going to need directions, dorogaya," he chuckled, enveloping her in his bear-like grasp. Athena felt herself getting wet at the sound of his mother tongue. That was unexpected. What was happening to her? He smelled musky and exotic and...

Someone hammered on the door.

A woman was shouting what sounded like obscenities, in Russian.

"Svetlana," he said, with an apologetic shrug. He pushed a button on his mobile phone. There was a scuffle outside the door for a few seconds, then silence.

"Would you like her to join us?" said Athena, smiling sweetly as she peeked up at him through her blonde fringe, resting her head on his (very expensive) shirt. She quite wanted to see what Slutlana's new haircut was like.

"Point one for your article: it's good to know that English women are so open-minded, more open-minded than Russians it would seem," said Shustrov, as he ran his fingers down her back, fondling her toned bottom with his massive hands, sending tingles up and down the length of her spine. She was like a cat being stroked by its owner. "But right now, Athena, I want you all to myself."

He picked her up and whispered in her ear as he carried her over to the bed: "And next time, you don't have to dress like Eurotrash. You could even put some panties on. Less is more, Athena."

For the first time in her 28 years – say it often enough and the world will believe it – Athena was admonished by a man and blushed accordingly, turning as red as her dress, which lay discarded on the floor.

CHAPTER ELEVEN

Barbara, the counsellor, had the most magnificent hair that Marnie had ever seen. It was a bright ginger and sprang from her head in wonderful, mesmerising curls. They were the kind of curls that you could twirl around your fingers, for hours on end, without ever getting bored.

"So," said Barbara brightly. "I know from your initial phone call that you have some issues to talk about. Who wants to start the ball rolling?"

Matt shrugged his big shoulders: "Search me. I'm afraid I've no idea why we are here. In fact, I think we should be resolving whatever 'issue' there is ourselves. We don't need counselling."

Marnie surveyed the sparse room at the Family Matters Centre. Woodchip on the walls, a low table in front of them and the world's most uncomfortable wooden chairs, except for Barbara's. Hers looked quite nice and squishy.

"OK," said Barbara, "reluctance is quite normal. It can be a shock to find out your partner is feeling in need of help from a third party. There really is nothing to worry about, Matt," she leaned forward and gave his knee a little pat. "I don't bite and I'm just here as a neutral facilitator."

"A what?" he said.

"A neutral facilitator."

Matt looked upwards and sighed. Barbara ignored him and smiled again.

"Marnie. What about you? You initiated the session. Can you tell Matt why you are here today?"

The box of tissues on the table was just out of arm's reach. If she could only grab it and have it on her lap, she might feel strong enough to speak. Marnie opened her mouth, as tears pricked her eyes and started to roll down her cheeks. She sobbed and sobbed. And sobbed. Then she wailed a bit and hid her face in her hands.

Matt went to get out of his chair and hug her but Barbara got out of her chair first and stopped him.

"No, Matt. Let her cry," she said firmly.

"But…"

"She needs to do this. Once she stops, she'll be able to talk. If you hug her, you will stop the flow."

"I was rather hoping to stop the flow," he said, exasperated. "She's upset. She's my wife."

Barbara offered Marnie the box of tissues and she clung to them like a liferaft, taking first one, then another, then another, blowing her nose intermittently.

Twenty-five minutes and one box of tissues later, she finally stopped crying.

She was gathering herself to explain what was wrong when Barbara looked at the clock on the wall and stood up.

"Well, I hope that was as helpful for you as it was for me. I think I'm beginning to see what the problem is and I will be very happy to work with you as a couple. There's a lot of work to do. I need to see you at least twice a week."

Marnie and Matt exchanged glances. They couldn't really afford to come to counselling that often.

Matt opened his mouth to say something but she ushered them both out of the door, with a breezy: "Same time on Thursday?"

Outside in the cold night air, Marnie linked her arm through Matt's.

"I'm sorry," she said. "I wanted to talk and I don't know what came over me. It's strange but I do feel lighter."

Matt scowled: "So does my wallet. By about 50 quid, to be precise."

⚜ ⚜ ⚜

LIVING THE DREAM!

Welcome, Mummies everywhere!

I know you are all dying to know how I manage to be such a wonderful mother, as well as an actress of great repute.

Well, guess what? I now have this thrilling column to give you the inside track on my fabulous life, week in, week out.

Please feel free to write or email me your views but don't bother to ring – I'm far too busy to answer the phone!

Firstly, I want to share my thoughts on a serious problem that can cause havoc around the home: dust.

There is, quite simply, far too much of it around these days. Is it increasing?

How do you manage to keep it bay? When I talk to my cleaner, I find she usually manages with a good, old-fashioned duster. It helps to keep an eye on things, by running a finger over the mantelpiece, once in a while.

I don't know about you, but I bake every single day. I find it such a total pleasure, especially the fun of sharing it with my little one. How we laugh as he throws flour all over the place! We have advanced from simple cupcakes to choux pastry and millefeuille. Haven't you? His petits fours are quite dainty and delicious.

*Never mind, there is still time for you to catch up, but you
will have quite a long way to go before you are as brilliant as me!
Until next week, Mummies, keep on Living the Dream!*

It wasn't fair. That used to be her slot.

Athena Maldon's massive picture byline loomed out of
the page like a ship's figurehead, blonde hair billowing,
teeth gleaming in a smile of triumph.

Marnie picked the icing off another cupcake as she read
through the celebrity column, which had replaced her cookery reports. It was her own fault, of course, but at least she
wrote recipes that were relevant to the readership. Unlike
Athena's mummy-twaddle.

The phone rang.

"Hello, Marnie, how's the playgroup going?"

It was Barker, trying to rub salt into the wound.

"Actually, I'm really busy, David," she said, clattering
plates into the dishwasher.

"Oh, I bet you are, with all those trips to the park, or
perhaps you've been baking some killer cupcakes?"

"Yes, I am busy!" she said, a bit too curtly. "I have got a
new project."

"What's that?" She could hear him smirking.

"It's a writing thing."

"Writing? Who for?"

"Myself," she said, quietly.

"Well, I suppose we should all be grateful you aren't
launching a career in catering."

She'd managed to get three readers now, including herself. One of the girls from the book club had signed up for
the blog, which was very supportive of her.

"I am getting quite a lot of followers for my project, actually." She wanted to put her fist right down her

throat to stop herself rising to his jibes but it was too late, as usual.

"Well, in that case, you might not be interested in the little job offer I was going to put your way," said Barker, with a laugh.

"No!" she cried. "I mean, yes! I am interested." Oh, she sounded pathetically grateful. She just couldn't help it.

"I need you to ghost write something for me and sub it too."

"So, I'm not actually going to get a byline?" she murmured, her pride shattering into a thousands pieces.

"After your colossal fuck-up, I don't think you are ever going to get another byline in this newspaper again, Marnie," he said. "But I am offering you work. Unless you are too busy, of course."

She sucked in a breath.

"OK," she said. "What do I have to do?"

"Athena Maldon thinks she is writing a weekly column called *Living the Dream*."

Marnie shrieked: "But she hates me! And her stuff is ... "

"Popular, Marnie," said Barker. "Incredibly popular. She writes fun opinions. The readers want fun opinions."

"I can write fun opinions," said Marnie, unable to keep the irritation out of her voice. "Why don't I just do it under my own name?"

"I know, but you are not a name, a celeb, are you? The focus groups say we need a name and I have found a name. Plus, you have ruined the Editor's special relationship with Number Ten with your pâté a la puke. I really don't think now is the time for you to ask for favours, you fuckwit."

"I'm sorry," she whispered. She could never apologise enough for what she had done. "What if Athena finds out it is me rewriting her column?"

"Athena will never know. She will file 250 words of pointless guff and you will provide another 500 a week of scintillating, fascinating copy. Your copy is always clean, you can write your own headlines and sub it too. That will save time and money. And I will see my way clear to giving you a grand a month out of my very tight budget."

"A thousand a month! Is that all?"

"Marnie, these are tough times. Money does not grow on trees."

"That is hardly anything compared to what I used to earn!"

"Marnie, you may not have noticed, but you are in no position to bargain with me. If you don't want this job, I have a whole list of increasingly desperate freelancers to work my way through. In fact, maybe I should just leave you to your little writing project."

"Please!" she cried. "I'm sorry. I'll take the job."

"That's better," he said, satisfied that he had made her grovel. "Just remember, you are now *Living the Dream!*"

And he hung up.

CHAPTER TWELVE

It was just like giving medicine to a child.

Cecily crushed the Obduro pill and whizzed it up into the spirulina powerdrink that Maddox was now obsessing about – ever since he'd overheard Byron Hunt revealing what he ate for breakfast.

She wouldn't tell Maddox about his little helper just yet. If it worked – and she sincerely hoped it would – she might discuss it with him. For now, she just needed him to be able to get hard. She wanted this baby. More to the point, her face needed this baby. Maddox would get lots of sex from her and if that wasn't enough, they could always try IVF.

They could both use this new addition to their family to give their careers a bit of a boost, Maddox would come round to that idea, with a bit of feminine persuasion, Cecily was sure. The infant would be their little miracle. She would net a few more headlines and a nice spread in *Vision* magazine, with them both hugging the baby.

Perhaps she could then launch her own range of designer baby clothes? The possibilities were endless.

⚜ ⚜ ⚜

Maddox strode on to the set with a spring in his step and something stirring in his trousers. It was his big scene – as

President, he had the power to ensure reporter Damian Kirsch never saw his name in print again, especially as he was schtupping his wife, played by Cecily. But Kirsch, played by Byron Hunt, had an exclusive about terrorists planning to bomb Capitol Hill and needed to warn the President. Could both men find a way to put aside their differences to save Washington from the bomb?

Something was definitely moving in his groin as he rehearsed his lines. He felt blood rushing to it.

Oh, Lord. Why was this happening?

Could he even stand up?

Maddox sat down behind the Presidential desk, with his head in his hands.

Jack, the director, came over to see him, splintering bits of biro all over the place, as he chomped in agitation. They needed to get on. It was already getting late.

"Problem?"

"Yes," said Maddox, pointing to the bulge in his trousers.

"I see," said Jack, flushing. "Take five, everybody!"

An hour later, Maddox's rather big problem – which gave the wardrobe girl a bit of a shock – had still not subsided.

Filming was suspended for the rest of the day.

He drove home. Cecily looked extremely pleased to see him back early, particularly when he got out of the car.

"Why don't we put that to good use?" she said, unbuttoning her blouse. "I'll just go and get us both something nice to drink."

He lay on their sumptuous bed and surveyed the flagpole in his silk boxer shorts.

What the hell was going on? He'd never heard of men his age being affected by anything like this. One minute, the little man was refusing to play ball and next minute he was raging around in his pants like a teenager on heat.

Cecily shimmied over to him with two large glasses of white wine.

He took a large slug and lay back as she stripped off her underwear, giggling, and straddled him.

"Drink up!" she said, picking up the glass and pouring the rest of the wine down his throat.

She opened her mouth and started to run her tongue from the base of him to the very tip. She circled. She sucked. She flicked. She took all of him in her mouth – which was no mean feat, he was enormous.

Maddox smiled at her. He was extremely grateful and outwardly very turned on but something was missing. He couldn't say anything to her, she was so enthusiastic and gorgeous, everyone's fantasy of the perfect woman, servicing him in their luxurious bedroom in the middle of the afternoon.

She stopped, her fingers still gripping his shaft, and sighed, as if she were doing a close-up, before giving him the most smouldering look: "I know what you want."

Cecily clambered on top of him and started to bounce around, moaning and making sure that she jiggled her breasts. He usually liked that.

She closed her eyes and thought of Byron Hunt's body, taut, toned and delicious, as she squeezed her pelvic floor muscles for all she was worth to finish him off and get this over with.

He felt his orgasm building, envisaged his favourite porn star straddling him, instead of his wife. And maybe she was snogging her girlfriend at the same time, just to make things a bit more interesting.

"Oh, God, yes!" he groaned, as he felt himself going over the edge.

"Yes! Don't stop!" shrieked Cecily, faking it for Queen and country.

Afterwards, they lay together in each other's arms, a picture perfect scene.

"You're the best, Maddox," she cooed. "You're every woman's fantasy."

"And you are just a dream lover," he replied. "How did it ever get so good?"

Chapter Thirteen

LIVING THE DREAM!

Welcome, Mummies everywhere!

And what a hard job we all do, don't we?

I do so love knitting. I expect your mothers all knitted. Mine did – everything from complicated cardis to my undergarments. She was thrifty and stylish, a real role model – in fact, both of my parents were perfect in every way. Wasn't I lucky?

These days I have taken up my own needles, but only using the finest cashmere gleaned by hand from the two dwarf alpacas I keep in my ten acres in the rolling Cotswolds' hills. I expect some of you could find a little space in your back gardens to keep some alpacas of your very own and have an easy, homemade supply of the softest yarn. Don't forget, you need to leave room for your raised beds, in order to grow your own veggies!

If you are unfortunate enough to live in a flat, just ask Fortnum and Mason for a delivery of organic produce, like I do when I am in London. They are frightfully good value. Try to eat only seasonal fruit, grown from your own orchard so you know that there are no nasties like pesticides on your apples. And stick with homegrown, heritage brands, with unpronounceable names, like Crumhorn Firkin. I do, and I feel SO much better for it.

Until next time, Mummies, keep Living the Dream!

A flame mail, in shouty capital letters, from Barker, landed on Marnie's iPhone with a little ping: "GET INTO MY OFFICE IMMEDIATELY. SANS KIDS. I NEED TO SWEAR AT YOU."

Marnie sighed.

This really was most inconvenient.

Barker didn't own her anymore and she would make that quite clear. He only paid for a certain amount of her time now and she would only give him exactly what he was due.

She dug a smartish print dress and some medium heels out of the wardrobe. She was only going to look fairly professional at such short notice. Charlie was in nursery today and Rufus was at school but she had a whole spaghetti Bolognese to cook up and an entire set of uniforms to label because she forgot to do that at the beginning of term and the headmistress had made a point of mentioning her by name during their last parents' briefing.

"There is an embarrassing amount of lost property and one child in particular has taken jumpers from *six* different classmates in the last two weeks because his is still not correctly labelled. And I prefer sewn in, to iron on, Mrs Martin."

If she left it much longer, she might end up on the naughty step.

❧   ❧   ❧

Marnie made it to *The Sentinel*'s Kensington HQ just before morning conference.

Harry Hedgeson, the newspaper's louche journalistic journeyman, was lying quietly under his desk, trying to recover from yet another massive hangover. Marnie almost tripped over his feet.

"Morning, Harry!" she said, loud enough to make him sit up, sharply, and bang his head.

Newsdesk secretary Bryher Greerson scowled and flicked her lank hair over her shoulders as she saw Marnie approaching. Bryher was a glass half-full kind of girl – half full of wine mostly.

Her mother was a columnist on a rival paper and she'd hoped to emulate her success and take Fleet Street by storm when she arrived, fresh-faced, from a season as a chalet girl in Chamonix. But the months of waiting for her moment of glory to arrive had turned into years. Fresher-faced graduates arrived to pinch all the best leads, while she was left to deal with irate readers and do the Newsdesk's bidding, albeit with gusto.

She had been trying to persuade Barker to give her a tryout for a column about her single life, which – let's face it – was full of adventure and miles better than Marnie's boring cookery drivel. She had no problem with being a hack in the 21st century and was fully prepared for blogging, uploading, downloading, freeloading and generally sleeping with anyone who could help her get a proper job as a journalist.

But Barker had refused, making some unkind comments about promiscuity and family newspapers. To make matters worse, Athena Maldon was muscling in with her own column, so she was still stuck with the newslist. For now.

Marnie approached Barker's lair, The Bunker. The blinds were drawn, which meant she was in for a carpeting.

"Dwarf alpacas? Crumhorn Firkin?" was all he said, as she marched in and plonked her massive, squishy handbag right in the middle of his desk.

"Well, that is what she wrote," said Marnie, huffily.

"No, she didn't. I have got the original copy right here. I know this is difficult for you, but don't you dare pull anything like that again, do I make myself clear?"

"Yes, David," Marnie looked at the floor in shame. It had made her feel better at the time but in the cold light of day, it was rather juvenile. Maybe she should have started every sentence so that if you took all the capitals, it spelled ATHENA IS AN ARSE. That would have been harder to spot.

"What planet are you living on exactly?" said Barker, giving her his most piercing glare.

"What do you mean?"

"If you had turned CBeebies off this morning, Marnie, you would know that Vladimir Shustrov has just bought *The Sentinel.*"

Shustrov? Wasn't he a tennis player? Rather good. Nice legs.

Barker caught her vacant look and sighed, thrusting a copy of rival newspaper *The Globe*, with its gloating front page, at her: "Oligarch Shustrov Takes Stake in Fleet Street."

"I knew that!" said Marnie, a little hurriedly. "And, in any case, will Shustrov be offended by an article on goats and knitting and apples with funny names? I don't think so!"

Barker should sack her. It was only a bloody grand a month. She would find something else. Somehow.

Barker flicked up the blinds of his office.

There was Shustrov and there, oh my God, simpering by his side in a demure, high-necked dress and very smart heels, was Athena Maldon.

"Christ!" said Marnie, yanking the blind downwards. "She can't know I'm here."

"Relax," said Barker, grinning and pulling it back up as Athena's backside wiggled past: "She's on her way up to see the management on the sixth floor, they are just doing a victory tour. And, luckily for you, she's not interested in reading *Living the Dream*, or I really would have to terminate you. She's too busy riding the Russian Bear."

Barker went on: "But, from now on, you have got to keep your nose clean. No more tampering with her copy to make her look like the airhead diva that she actually is. You need to take one for the team, Marnie. Take one for the team."

Right now, Barker knew, deep down, that they all needed to stick together, more than ever.

CHAPTER FOURTEEN

Jonah was only going to LA, but as far as Belle and her baby routine were concerned, it might as well have been the moon.

Nothing he could say would persuade her to come with him. "I won't know anyone and they don't have parks and baby music and baby gym clubs just around the corner like they do here," she wailed. "What about the time difference and his routine? I've only just got him to drop one of his night-time feeds!"

Jonah hugged Belle and stroked her hair, which tumbled in loose waves over her shoulders.

"I hate leaving you. I'm supposed to be looking after you," he murmured.

She looked up at him with her adorable green eyes: "It cuts both ways, Jonah. How are you going cope without me burning your toast in the morning in LA?"

With a lump in his throat, he pulled a first class open return ticket out of his pocket and left it on the glossy white sideboard, next to the photograph of them kissing, in case she changed her mind.

He was only going for a couple of weeks. Just to lay down the rest of the tracks for the album and perfect a few of the lyrics.

The cab outside honked its horn.

Jonah took Gabriel from Belle's arms as they stood in the hallway and kissed him before enveloping her in a hug.

Another cab drew up outside and a trim little woman stepped out. She started to make her way up the steps to the front door.

"I couldn't leave you alone," said Jonah. "So, I've hired the best, the very best, to help you with Gabriel and make sure you get some rest."

If they were really pressed to admit it, so many of the Notting Hill mummies would reveal they had hired a live-in maternity consultant to help them through those difficult early months – but it had never been something Belle wanted to get in to.

Belle was open-mouthed, for standing in front of her, suitcase in hand, peacoat buttoned to the neck and raven hair cut short to reveal high cheekbones, a beaky nose and dark, beady little eyes, was baby guru Alexa Joy.

⚜ ⚜ ⚜

"I see you've got my book!" said Alexa Joy, surveying the spacious open-plan kitchen and settling herself at the dining table. "I hope you are following it to the letter?"

"Well, I'm trying," said Belle, sploshing some water into the kettle to make her a cup of tea. Alexa was very particular about her tea and had asked for Lapsang Souchong – which led Belle to scrabble frantically through her cupboards, to no avail.

"I'm afraid I've only got Earl Grey."

Alexa wrinkled her nose.

"It'll do. But you'll have to get me some Lapsang in the morning. I can't work without it!"

"Of course, sorry," murmured Belle.

"Now, I plan to observe you in your routine for 24 hours to see where you are going wrong."

"Wrong?"

"Sorry, my love," said Alexa. "I don't mean to sound bossy, but Mr Bevan said you were having some issues with little Gabriel's sleep and I am here to help. I am on your side. What we want is a happy Mummy and a happy baby! That is the Joy of Parenting!

"Plus, I will then be able to take over the nights so you can get proper rest and I will then take a nap during the day if I need to."

Alexa pulled out a shopping list.

"These are my required foods. Do you have a cook?"

"Err, no," said Belle.

"Never mind, I'm sure you'll manage. I don't eat much anyway but what I do eat needs to be high quality to keep my brain in tip-top working order."

She caught the look in Belle's eye and added: "I've confirmed it all with Mr Bevan, of course. It's in my contract. Now, would you mind showing me to my room?"

⚜ ⚜ ⚜

The baby's cries were growing more insistent over the monitor by her bed, rousing Belle from her half-sleep. She shuffled out of her bedroom and up the stairs to Gabriel's room to see what was wrong.

But someone else had got there first. And she was blocking the door.

"I knew you'd run to him, Belle!" said Alexa Joy, extending her arms across the doorframe, "That is the worst thing you can do for a baby. I know this is hard but it's best if I intervene now. I will deal with him. Let's just see if he can settle himself, shall we? As it says in my book."

In her half-awake state, Belle made to grab for the door handle but Alexa Joy shadowed her move. Belle caught a whiff of Alexa Joy's perfume – citrussy, bitter, with a top note almost like gin. It was quite an overpowering scent to wear near little babies but Alexa was an expert, so she must know best.

"We must stick to the book. I know it's hard. Turn your baby monitor off and go back to bed."

There was something in her tone that made Belle obey, but every fibre of her being wanted to reach out and hug her baby.

Dejected, she shuffled back down the stairs, switched off her monitor and lay back on the pillows.

Gabriel was screaming now.

Tears started to run down her face. She couldn't just ignore him. She wanted to pick him up.

She heard Alexa Joy open the door to the nursery above.

Gabriel wailed some more.

Belle tried to cover her ears with her pillow.

Then, ten minutes later, he stopped crying. Just like that.

She closed her eyes, guilt weighing heavily on her, and drifted into an uneasy sleep.

⚜ ⚜ ⚜

Daylight streamed through the Roman blinds.

Belle glanced at the clock. It was 7.30am.

Grabbing her robe, she scampered up to the nursery to check on Gabriel. He was still sound asleep and his first feed was overdue by...she checked her watch...47 minutes.

How could this be?

Gabriel's beautiful baby cheeks were slightly flushed and the strawberry blond curls at the back of his neck were matted with sweat.

She picked him up and kissed him.

Still he didn't wake, so she stroked his cheek and he yawned and his eyelids fluttered open.

He seemed rather groggy. He must have exhausted himself with all that crying.

She carried him downstairs.

Alexa was already dressed – in her gym kit.

"There, now!" she chimed. "Isn't that better for mummy and baby? A nice night's sleep. Now, I'm just off for my five mile run. I will be back later and I will need a lie down to recuperate after last night's tribulations.

"I think you should go out shopping with baby in the pram to ensure he gets some lovely fresh air and you get some exercise too." Alexa poked Belle in the stubborn bit of mummy-tummy above the waistband of her jeans.

"Then, you can cook me lunch – remember those foods on my list, please – and we will talk about where you went wrong. You let yourself down, rather, and that means you let your baby down. Unacceptable. OK?"

"Yes, Alexa," she mumbled.

Alexa tried to tickle Gabriel under the chin but he recoiled slightly and turned his face to Belle's shoulder.

"Oh, he's just a little grumpy booties!" she cooed.

"We also need to discuss the level of stimulation he is getting. I think you may need to order a few more toys from my website," she yelled, star-jumping down the hallway and out of the front door.

❧ ❧ ❧

It was spitting with rain as Belle settled Gabriel into the pram and set off to hunt down the items on Alexa Joy's list.

White truffles, some weird kind of Chinese mushrooms, beluga caviar, wild mountain strawberries, Kobe beef, foie gras, Lapsang Souchong tea in silk tea-pouches, and organic everything else.

Gabriel was dozing happily but Belle chatted away to him nonetheless. She still felt guilty about him crying so much last night. She couldn't wait to speak to Jonah about it – in fact she was desperate to hear his voice – but she'd have to wait until later with the time difference. It was still the middle of the night over in LA.

An hour later, she had covered a few of the items but even the delis of Notting Hill failed to stock Kobe beef, whatever that was.

Belle felt terrified of offending Alexa, so she trudged on through Kensington to Harrods Food Hall, with the rain lashing down on her face, to stock up on the most expensive and rare delicacies, in order to feed her house guest.

She really wanted to take a taxi home, but Alexa had implied she was overweight and needed the exercise so she found herself trailing home through Hyde Park, soaked to the skin. Still Gabriel slept.

By the time she got home, she was thoroughly exhausted, hair wet and matted to her head. She poured water out of her trainers as she sat on the front step, before heaving the pram and all the shopping up the stairs.

Alexa was sitting, like a praying mantis, at the dining table. She had a glint in her eye, rather like Belle's Great

Aunty Edna, when she'd been at the sherry on Christmas Day and was spoiling for a fight. Belle felt herself shrink under her glare.

"You're rather late!" said Alexa. "Where's my lunch?"

CHAPTER FIFTEEN

Could she really be enjoying it this much? She couldn't share it with Matt, he'd probably laugh at her for reading something so trashy. But *Harsh Winter* was a real page turner.

The gun hits the floor.

She counters with a well-placed kick, as my hands grasp her gown tightly, ripping it away to reveal a push-up bra, very tempting side-tie briefs and a body honed to perfection by years of martial arts training in Tibet. There is an undeniable stirring in my loins. I lose focus. She kicks again – extending a lean leg towards me, perfectly timed, right in my groin.

Winded and in agony, I fall to the floor, doubled up, like an amateur felled by a prize fighter. She runs, gazelle-like – even in her five-inch heels – through the French windows and on to the balcony, her hair swishing across her toned back.

I could roll over and clasp my gun once more. I'd have time. But I am mesmerized by her.

Out of nowhere, a chopper appears, a ladder is thrown down and she leaps on to it, without breaking so much as a scarlet fingernail, as she makes good her escape.

I rush outside, yelling into the cold night air: "You can run, Katya, but this isn't over."

The game is on.

The key turned in the lock and Marnie shoved her book into the kitchen drawer and pressed her weight against it. Matt didn't look particularly pleased to be home from work early.

"Shouldn't we be going soon?" he said.

The ensuing fracas of getting the boys through the bath and into bed while Dylan plonked himself in front of the telly meant they were five minutes late for their counselling at the Family Matters Centre.

"We have to keep to a tight schedule, Marnie," said Barbara, the therapist with the most wonderful hair in West London, giving her a hard stare. "I do have other clients, you know."

"Of course," said Marnie, fumbling with a tissue – she'd come prepared with her own this time. "Sorry."

"So," said Barbara, settling back in her comfy armchair, "I think Marnie is finally ready to say what the problem is."

"Well," Marnie began falteringly, "I want a third baby and I feel selfish for wanting it but Matt makes me feel useless and as if I don't have the right to want it because I don't earn as much as him. And, to be honest, I think he is bored by the kids."

She paused for a moment, before adding: "Sometimes, I think he would prefer it if it was just him, behaving like a teenager. He would rather drink and watch telly and flirt on Facebook with his ex-girlfriend Belinda."

"She's an environmental lawyer, Marnie, she just got in touch with me about some silly work thing she's coming over here for, that's all."

"Oh, yeah," spat Marnie. "The big court case with the smiley face and the 'Lol you are so hilarious and I love your picture of a cat on a pogo stick'. I'm not stupid! And when it's not her, it's Muffy the porn star because you don't fancy me!"

The colour drained from his face, he crumpled and began to cry.

"That's just not fair, Marnie!" he said between sobs. "I love you and the boys. I kill myself going to working all hours to provide for you and just when we are beginning to see the light at the end of the tunnel with the kids getting a bit more independent..."

"So you DO find them boring! It is boring to have to look after their every need. But, let's face it, I do that mostly," she spat.

"That's only because I am at work all day and then I can't do anything right, as far as you are concerned!" he shouted.

Barbara cut in: "I can see you feel very angry, Marnie. Do you think some of that anger is being misdirected at Matt because of your own frustrations with life? Matt works terribly, terribly hard all day to provide for you. Some women might be more grateful."

What? Marnie felt her self-esteem – which wasn't puffed up by anyone's standards – deflating.

Matt continued to sob and Barbara got up and put her arm around him.

Marnie shot out of her chair and tried to reach her husband but Barbara shooed her away: "No, Marnie. If you intervene it will stop the flow. Let him cry. He needs to do this."

Barbara was shoving his head dangerously close to her bosom.

"But, I can..."

"No, Marnie. I will handle it."

Not knowing what to do, Marnie sat back down and watched, powerless, as Barbara held his hand for a moment, patted him on the shoulder and sat quietly back in her chair, watching him intently until he was just snuffling a bit. "There," she said. "Does that feel better now?"

After what seemed like an eternity, he looked up at Marnie with red-rimmed eyes.

Before he could utter a single word, Barbara said: "I think you are suffering from Damsel in Distress Syndrome, Marnie."

"What on earth is that?"

"Oh, come now, you remember your fairytales, don't you? Rapunzel, Sleeping Beauty..." Barbara's eyes glinted.

Matt was listening intently as Marnie looked on, rendered dumb.

"The little princess, just waiting for the handsome prince to clip-clop up to the castle and whisk her away from all her troubles, to live happily ever after." Barbara almost spat those last three words out. "Well, Marnie, real life is not like that."

"I never said it was!" Marnie's hands clenched the arms of her little wooden chair.

"But you'd quite like it to be, wouldn't you? You are expecting Matt to just gallop up, like a handsome knight in shining armour, throw you over his steed and canter off into the sunset, granting your every wish. Quite a spoilt little princess really, expecting that of the poor prince, who is probably hot and tired under his armour and might need someone to give him a nice shoulder massage, at the very least."

"I most certainly am not expecting to be rescued!" said Marnie. She felt her cheeks burning with shame and rage. She did think of Matt as her protector in a way. And, although he was a bit rubbish at times, when push came to shove, he was on her side. At least, she used to think that. Right now, he was studying the carpet intently.

"No," said Barbara, "maybe not rescued. But you want the prince to provide you with another baby when you have already got two perfectly good ones and someone still has to pay for the upkeep of the castle!"

Barbara muttered under her breath as she returned to her comfy chair: "Quite selfish."

After what seemed like an eternity, Matt gazed up at her and said: "I love you so much, Marnie."

"I love you too, Matt." So why did she feel like strangling him? Why did he have to go and cry like that and let this woman hug him? Why wasn't he denouncing all this Damsel in Distress stuff as sheer nonsense? He didn't normally behave like a big girl's blouse. She thought counselling was meant to be about opening up and talking about her feelings. She hadn't thought for a minute what would happen once he got in touch with his.

Barbara smiled smugly to herself.

"It's good to see you are both ready to talk things over but I advise you should only do that here. With me. As your neutral facilitator."

And she shoved them both out of the door.

"What on earth did she mean about not discussing things," said Marnie, as Matt gazed into the middle distance.

"I have no idea but I am too tired to talk about it anymore," said Matt.

"Me too," she mumbled, aching to hold him close.

No, hang on, she wanted him to hold HER close. Oh God. She was a Damsel in Distress! Barbara was right.

"Didn't think much of Barbara's rant," she said, quietly.

"I thought she was quite good, on balance," said Matt, staring straight ahead, as they turned the corner into their street.

Marnie felt very foolish and very, very small, as if the blueprint for her whole life had been read to her, night after night as a child, somehow imprinting itself on her heart and soul, creating ridiculous expectations. Her life with Matt was a tall, tall tower built on weak foundations, which would now come crashing down around her ears and she would be left dangling precariously over the ruins by her long, swishy Rapunzel mane.

Desperate to change the subject from bloody Barbara, Marnie decided to take the bull – belatedly – by the horns and tell Matt about her new job.

"I got a new post at *The Sentinel*," she said.

"Great. How much are they paying you?"

"A thousand a month."

"Is that all? What are you doing? Making the tea?" He dug his hands deeper into his coat pockets.

"No, I'm just… " She couldn't quite tell the whole truth about ghost-writing for Athena Maldon, "I'm just doing a bit of work subbing."

He put his arm around her: "I know it's not your fault, it's a recession, but we really need you to try to earn more than that if you possibly can because I was relying on your salary to help with the mortgage. I've got a massive tax bill coming and I still have to pay chambers for this quarter."

He took his arm away.

"I will sort it," she said, not having a clue how she was going to do that with people being laid off left, right and centre from newspapers.

If only she could prick her finger and fall asleep for a hundred years.

CHAPTER SIXTEEN

Marnie was sitting in the kitchen replaying the record-ing of Maddox Wolfe failing to get it up with his wife that her soundman brother Dylan had won in a game of cards with the crew.

She'd listened over and over again to the bit where Maddox struggled to contain his upset about his problem in the bedroom department. He was so vulnerable. She had never realised he had such depth to his feelings. Behind the tough guy was a really sensitive character. If only she could give him a little hug.

There was a look of quiet satisfaction on her face as she mulled it all over.

She shouldn't really be feeling so pleased that he couldn't sleep with Cecily but this recording confirmed her suspicions: Cecily was rather horrid.

She was quite heartless to poor Maddox.

Marnie pressed play again.

It was delicious to hear his voice talking off-the-cuff and sounding just as sexy as in his films.

Plus, it was rather lovely to have the inside track on what Maddox was thinking and feeling, especially the bit where he put the boot into Byron Hunt. No, Marnie had never liked him either.

But God, her brother was a sneaky little sod. He'd

admitted he fixed the card deck in order to get his mitts on that recording. She never knew he had it in him.

Dylan wanted her to help him sell it to the nationals and was happy to split the proceeds.

She felt a bit sorry for Maddox, actually. It was rather intrusive. She could protect him from this tape ever being released. He would never know, of course, so he wouldn't be able to thank her personally, which was a crying shame.

Poor Maddox. He'd done a very good job of being extremely handsome, saving the world and flexing his muscles as superspy Seb Winter, in a way that just *did* something to her, while Matt was busy upstairs working on some legal case or other.

Was it his looks? Or was it the way he was so dominant when he needed to be, yet tender – and he was saving the world at the same time! He wasn't ever distracted by work, grumpy about his dinner (or lack of it), or too tired to bother with the kids yet still finding time to Facebook flirt with Belinda the whale-saver. He was too busy looking gorgeous in his suits, his swimwear, his underwear, his birthday suit. Mmmm.

Maybe she should watch another one of his films later, just to work out exactly *why* she liked him so much?

"I've seen a lady's boobies," said Rufus, running into the kitchen, giggling.

"Don't be silly," said Marnie chasing him back into the lounge. "Now, it's time for tea. Telly off!"

"Have too seen them!" shouted Rufus. "In Uncle Dylan's comic." And he pulled a well-thumbed copy of *Krazee* lads' magazine out from behind a grubby cushion on the sofa.

A pert blonde with gravity-defying breasts and a miniscule thong gazed out at her with a wanton expression.

"Boobies!" said his little brother Charlie, hopping from one foot to another, giggling.

"Right!" shouted Marnie, grabbing the magazine and rushing off to give that odious little brother of hers a piece of her mind, tripping over a half-empty can of lager that he had left by the sofa from the night before, as she did so.

Dylan was on the internet when she found him upstairs in the loft, looking at a woman with ginormous boobies doing something disgusting to herself with a can of squirty cream. And Matt was giggling beside him like a schoolboy.

"You two ought to be ashamed of yourselves," she yelled, throwing *Krazee* magazine at Matt and slapping her brother round the head.

"I will not have my sons raised to view women in this debasing manner."

Both of them looked at the carpet. That was also covered in discarded beer cans. And more copies of *Krazee*.

"It was just a silly bit of…" said Matt.

She was still furious with him for refusing to contemplate having another baby and for running her down as a mother. He hadn't apologised for that, or for those awful, tarty knickers he bought her as an apology. That was two lots of apologies he owed her!

Plus, she was still irked by the way he had let Barbara, the counsellor, comfort him the other day and brand her a spoilt little princess. It was just not fair or true.

Yes, Matt probably really wanted some tart in a teeny thong mincing around his kitchen in fuck-me shoes, serving him hot pies and lager, before getting down on her knees and giving him a blow job. Well, he could sod right off.

No wonder he didn't want another baby.

And Dylan? Well, he was just a bad influence and, right now, Matt didn't need any help in that department.

"Dylan, I want you to leave," said Marnie, drawing herself up to her full height of 5ft 2ins.

She was a giant next to these two pathetic excuses for men.

She folded her arms over her chest and had a steely glare to her eyes that neither of them had seen before.

"What?" said Dylan

"Don't be silly," said Matt.

"Silly, am I?" she yelled. "Silly? Will it be silly when Rufus tells the teacher he has seen boobies in a magazine, Matt? Will it? Will it be good for your career – which is, let's face it, all you really care about – when Social Services get involved and find you and my twit of a brother have been surfing the internet for porn with children in the house and letting them read unsuitable magazines?"

And God knows what their bloody counsellor would make of this latest debacle. Marnie felt strangely protective of their private life as far as Barbara was concerned. The last thing she wanted to do was to have to go and confess to yelling at her husband. Barbara would probably side with Matt.

"We're sorry," said Dylan, in that whiny voice he always used as a kid when mum told him off, which only made Marnie more furious.

"Darling, just let me take you out for a quiet meal together tonight. This won't happen again," said Matt, reaching his hands out to her arm, stroking it gently.

"I can babysit!" Dylan ventured, brightly.

Marnie gave him a look that could curdle milk.

"Too right it bloody well won't happen again, Matt," she said, brushing his conciliatory stroking hands off her arm.

"Because Dylan is leaving. As of now."

Dylan's mouth was hanging open.

"Pack your bags. And get out. I'm taking the boys out for tea. You and your sleazy magazines had better be gone by the time I get back."

She stomped off downstairs and didn't hear Dylan say to Matt: "But it was *your* copy of *Krazee*, wasn't it?"

⚜ ⚜ ⚜

The run around the park that Alexa Joy had prescribed to cure her sniffles hadn't worked. In fact, it had only made matters worse.

"I think I need to lie down," Belle mumbled apologetically, as her head pounded and she started to shiver again.

"Would you mind terribly watching Gabriel for me for a bit?"

Alexa sighed and flicked off the television.

She was watching a segment on *Naughty Tots! – How to Tame Your Terrors*, featuring herself, mostly.

She pushed her prim little feet into a pair of soft velvet slippers, stood up and checked the creases in her trousers before fixing Belle with a hard stare.

"OK," she said. "But you're on my time now, Mummy! So don't be too long. Does he need a feed?"

"Yes, in about half an hour. I'm so, so sorry. I don't know what is wrong with me, I ache everywhere."

Gabriel was gurgling in his bouncy chair.

"I'll have to get him out of there in a minute, I suppose," huffed Alexa. "Have you ordered those extra toys from my website yet? And we need to discuss weaning options. No jars or pre-made anything. You're going to have to puree from scratch, otherwise he might not achieve his milestones, Mummy!"

Belle had a horrible feeling that she was a total failure as a mother but she felt too sick to go there right now. If she could crawl out of her skin and inhabit someone else's she would – if only to leave behind the terrible guilt for disturbing Alexa's me-time, which seemed to stretch from 9 in the morning until tea-time.

Belle swirled the last dregs of an aspirin around her glass and glugged it back quickly, before the sediment caught her in the back of her sore throat. It was still a bit early to ring Jonah.

She'd been playing telephone tag with him for the last two days. The only time someone had picked up, it had been Marta, his PA, who had promised to pass a message on, but Jonah hadn't rung her back yet.

She climbed the stairs to her bedroom and clambered, fully clothed, under the duvet.

The air chilled her to the bone. Desperate to get warm, she buried herself deeper under the quilt, hugging her knees and shaking. Despite being freezing cold, her forehead was burning up.

She sat up to take a sip from a glass of water on the side. Her head was pounding and, oh dear, she was going to throw up.

She only just made it to the bathroom.

If she could just shout to Alexa to help her – but she was too weak.

The bed was drenched in sweat, she needed to vomit again but this time she found she could only crawl to the bathroom. Afterwards, she curled up in a ball on the floor, shaking.

She staggered back to bed to sleep. When she finally woke up, it was dark outside. She glanced at the clock – it was midnight in London which meant Jonah should be up and about in LA. She punched Jonah's number into the phone and it rang and rang and then went to answer-phone.

"Honey, I'm not well, please call me," she croaked. Her throat felt like razorblades and her tongue seemed to be swelling, her lips parched.

Even a tiny drop of water might help her. Just a drop. If she could keep that down.

She hadn't the energy to lift her head off the pillow now. Her lungs hurt. It was like a horrible weight pressing down on her chest.

Somewhere, Gabriel was crying. She couldn't reach him. Belle heard footsteps overhead. A door creaked open. The crying stopped.

She lay back as silent tears began to fall.

CHAPTER SEVENTEEN

As I watch Katya sleeping soundly beneath a mound of soft furs, the exhaustion of two days' trek through the snow to find her hide-out melts away.

"Were you expecting me this time?" I whisper in her ear.

Startled, she wakes and grabs for her gun. I am already holding it.

Our eyes meet.

"Get up."

She obeys, shrugging off the furs and standing before me. My eyes are drawn once more to her perfect figure, her pert breasts barely concealed beneath her silk nightdress.

"Take that off."

She shakes her head.

"Do it, Katya, or I will do it for you."

She peels the silk slip over her head and throws it to the floor, her mouth pushing itself into a pout.

"That's better. Put your hands behind your back."

I let her stand there for an instant, exposed, as I drink her in – I know that to her, it will feel like an eternity. Colour rises in her cheeks and she stares at the floor.

I put the gun down and, grabbing both her wrists, pull her briskly across my lap.

"First, I'm going to teach you a lesson you will never forget for taking an unauthorised look at my credentials

and then you are going to tell me where you have hidden the antidote."

"Screw you," she hisses, as I twist her arm behind her back, to secure her, face down, over my knee.

"I might even do that, if you ask me politely," I smile, bringing my hand down hard, in a satisfying slap, on her firm, round buttocks.

It is going to be a long night.

O h, poor Katya. That bit definitely made Marnie feel a warm glow of sympathy for the double agent. Seb had well and truly caught her. What further humiliation would he heap on her? He was so masterful.

Clasping the book to her bosom, she felt herself meandering off into another day-dream, with Maddox Wolfe as Seb Winter, punishing her for making him strip off.

She really ought to get on with some work, or some clearing up.

Marnie put down *Harsh Winter* for a second, wandered into the hallway and picked up the post, browsing through it.

No-one wrote letters any more. There were only bills and bank statements, which were best avoided.

There was a thick, cream envelope addressed to Matt. She flipped it over. It was embossed with One Aldwych on the back.

One Aldwych? Wasn't that the posh hotel just off The Strand?

Her heart was racing.

She sat down, as if she had been thumped.

Who was this man, who was ogling breasts in lads' mags, hooking up with exes on Facebook, watching porn on the internet and receiving personal letters from five-star hotels that she had never set foot in?

Just what was happening to her husband, exactly?

She'd never opened his post before. With every rip, she felt herself shredding the trust in their marriage.

It was a letter from the manager.

Dear Mr Martin,

We hope that you enjoyed your recent stay at One Aldwych. As a loyal customer, to tempt you back, we are offering 20 per cent off bookings for the next three months.

Please do not hesitate to get in touch if I can be of further assistance.

Loyal customer?

They'd never even been there!

She'd never been there.

It could only mean one thing.

Marnie, wife and mother, was reduced to a sobbing, snivelling wreck.

Wedding bells, two babies – and domestic drudgery – coming apart at the seams, and now this.

It was all her fault. She should have held on to her job. And her waistline. No wonder he was looking at other women – she'd really let herself go.

What a fool she had been, to think that being at home and raising the kids would be enough for him.

That wasn't the woman he had married, was it?

After a good ten minutes, she stopped crying, looked accusingly at the letter, and started to think.

From the depths of despair, her inner hack came running, with a large notepad and a very sharp pencil.

The journalist in her took over.

If she were writing a news story, she would have to get all the facts first, wouldn't she?

She rang the number for reservations, which was printed, rather helpfully, on the bottom of the letter.

"Hello," she said. "This is Matt Martin's head clerk from Zenith Chambers. He wants to book something special for his wife, as an anniversary treat. They had such a lovely stay last time. Could you remind me which room they had?"

"Certainly, I'll just look it up," said the voice. "Can you give me the home postcode and house number?"

The blood was rushing in her ears as she handed over their address.

"It was only two weeks ago," said the voice. "He had the junior deluxe suite."

"He's so busy!" said Marnie, her jaw clenching. "He hardly knows if he is coming, or going. But mostly coming, I think."

"Sorry?"

"Of course, I meant, could you remind me of the date?"

"It was March 28th."

That was the night of the Legal Eagle Awards. The utter swine. She clung on to the edge of the dining table for dear life.

"How much is it for the room again? I'm not sure if he will want to go for something more grand this time, as it is a very special occasion with his wonderful wife," her voice was wavering. She had to hold it together now.

"It was £800."

Eight hundred pounds! And she was worrying about whether they could afford to buy pesto.

"Thanks, I'll get back to you," said Marnie, wishing she hadn't made that call.

If ignorance was bliss, then knowledge was incandescent with rage.

❖   ❖   ❖

With her face set as hard as her granite worktop, she flicked open her recipe book; the book he had bought her last Christmas.

Only something very special would do.

Boeuf Bourguignon, thank you, Nigella!

She hurled a packet of frozen steak into the microwave to defrost and then began to violently chop one medium onion, two cloves of garlic, some mushrooms and some bacon.

Sadly, at such short notice, she did not have the two sprigs of fresh thyme that the recipe suggested, so half a teaspoon of the dried herb would have to do.

After heating the oil in her Le Creuset casserole dish, she chucked the steak in and it began to sizzle.

Once browned, she carefully removed it with a slotted spoon, fried off the onion and added the mushrooms and bacon. Now, she needed some red Burgundy.

Marnie laughed out loud as she located a bottle of Nuits Saint Georges Premier Cru that he had been saving for a special occasion. There would be no other special occasions for them.

To cut costs, the recipe advised, you could use cider. I don't think so, Nigella! She plunged the corkscrew in and pulled out the cork, which gave a satisfying "pop".

She was supposed to stir in the wine a little at a time, but sloshed in half a bottle with gay abandon, chuckling all the while.

After adding the chopped garlic and herbs she closed the casserole lid tightly and put it in the oven to cook for two hours.

She glanced at the clock.

There was still plenty of time for her to stew on his infidelity before the school run.

She ran herself a very deep bath, with bubbles in it.

Humming softly to herself, she slipped into the foam. Grabbing his razor from the side of the bath, she shaved her legs and – why not? – her armpits too.

Stepping out, she carefully dried every inch of herself (there were quite a few of those), before padding into the bedroom.

She opened her wardrobe and pulled out her party frock – the one she should have worn to the Legal Eagle Awards – carefully hooking the hanger over the wardrobe door.

It had a lovely V-neck with small, pearl buttons down the front; one was missing, of course, thanks to her mega-bust.

It didn't matter that she was too fat to wear it. She had every right to wear that dress and she was bloody well going to.

It was supposed to skim the body. It clung to hers like glue, showing every lump and bump, but Marnie didn't care.

Pulling open the drawer on her bedside cabinet, she located her make-up bag and unzipped it.

This called for a full face: foundation, eyeliner, mascara, blusher and lipstick. Red lipstick. Matt loved it when she wore red lipstick.

A solitary tear threatened to spill down her perfectly made-up cheek as she wondered if Georgina, the Courtroom Cutie, wore red lipstick too.

She spoke to her reflection: "You deserve better than this, Marnie."

Then, she went downstairs and set off for the school gates, looking, scarily, like a mother who meant business.

❧   ❧   ❧

With the boys fast asleep upstairs – thank you, Piriton, for making bed-time that little bit easier, for once – Marnie took a deep breath as she heard Matt's key turn in the lock. Then, she strutted into the hallway.

"You look nice," he said, unable to hide his surprise at finding his wife dressed to the nines, never mind on a week day evening. "Going somewhere?"

"No, just making dinner for my wonderful husband," she smiled. "Let me take your coat, you must be so very tired after a long day."

He looked a bit puzzled, but shrugged off his jacket and handed it to her. She hung it up for him and gestured for him to come through to the kitchen, her high heels clicking on the spotlessly clean tiles.

"Why don't you sit down and have some wine? I've opened a bottle," she said, with a glint in her eye.

She motioned to the table, laid out with her best, white damask cloth and silver cutlery that only saw the light of day at Christmas.

"There's no need to go to all this fuss for me, Marnie," he said, sitting down. "I might get used to it."

"Oh, I doubt that," she gave a hollow laugh, which ricocheted around the kitchen like gunfire.

"So," said Marnie, as he sipped his wine. "Why don't you tell me all about your day. Every last detail. Don't miss anything out. I want to hear everything – *exactly* what you have been up to."

He shot her a look of concern. This was followed by horror as, inspecting the bottle, he realised that his finest wine had been opened and half of it was already gone.

"Are we celebrating something?" he spluttered.

She gave him a weak smile, before carefully ladling her Boeuf Bourguignon on to their best bone china dinner plates.

He cleared his throat: "Well, it was just run of the mill stuff. There was a court appearance this morning, a conference with clients this afternoon."

She laid the dinner plate in front of him, flicked open the linen napkin and placed it across his lap.

"Do go on," she said.

"Then I came home, of course."

"What?" said Marnie, her face twisting into a sneer. "That's it? It sounds very respectable. What a hard-working husband! Didn't you even go for a drink after work?"

"Marnie," said Matt. "Are you feeling all right? Don't take this the wrong way, because all this food looks so lovely and you have made a real effort with..." He paused and looked at her dress, "...with everything. But you are acting a bit strangely."

He almost whispered the last word.

"Strangely?" said Marnie. "Shall I tell you what is strange, Matt? The fact that you think it is OK to spend £800 on a luxury hotel suite for you and Georgina, the Courtroom Cutie, while I am fretting over my shopping bills and running myself ragged looking after the kids!"

She pulled the letter from One Aldwych out of the kitchen drawer and threw it at him.

His mouth fell open.

"Marnie, I can explain," he said, holding his hands up. "It was just an after-party for the awards. I've been working so hard, it was just a bit of a treat; some fun with my work colleagues on a big night out. I didn't sleep with her."

"You expect me to believe that?" she screamed. "You've spent time chatting to Muffy the porn-star and when you are not doing that you are ogling women's breasts in some stupid lads' mag. You spent our money on a hotel room on the same night that you are out with a 20-something hottie and you expect me to believe you? I am just the good little wife at home, aren't I? Cooking and cleaning and ironing, looking after your children and worrying about my household bills."

All the colour had drained from his face.

"It should have been me!" she yelled.

She took hold of his glass and filled it to the brim with red wine.

"Here," she said, "you look like you could use another drink."

And she picked up his glass and slowly emptied it over his head.

He sat there, speechless, with red wine dripping down his face.

"What's the matter?" she said. "Not hungry?"

She picked up his dinner, the tender meat swimming in a delicious red wine sauce, and tipped it into his lap, making him leap to his feet with a yelp.

"Now," she said, "Get out of my house. And leave me your credit card."

CHAPTER EIGHTEEN

"Trust," said Barbara, the counsellor, "is the foundation stone of any union. Without it, the walls will come crashing down."

Sunlight played on the leaves of a tree just outside the window.

Marnie shifted on her wooden chair and Matt stared at the floor.

"Perhaps," said Barbara, "Marnie would like to explain why she doesn't trust you any more, Matt?"

No, she bloody well didn't want to explain it. It was so hurtful. She wasn't invited to the awards do and a long-legged lovely, voted number one in the Courtroom Cuties hotlist, went in her place, while she was left at home in her jogging bottoms and grubby T-shirt. He had the night of his life – without her – and then he booked a hotel suite. You didn't have to be Sherlock Holmes to work it out.

"No," said Marnie. "I can't."

"I see," sighed Barbara, twisting some hair around her fingers. "Communication has completely broken down. Oh dear. But, what about you, Matt?" She gave him a brief smile.

He looked up and his eyes met Marnie's. There was such a hollow, haunted look to his face and the bags under his eyes were evidence of the sleepless night he had spent at the Premier Inn, after she had thrown him out.

Something twisted inside Marnie like a knife to see him looking like that.

"I feel hurt that she doesn't trust me," he said, falteringly. "I work so hard, my life is nothing but work and I do it all for you and the boys, Marnie. Can't you see?" A tear threatened to spill down his cheek and he brushed it away with the back of his hand.

"Stop playing the victim," said Marnie, stiffening in her chair. "You are the one who is in the wrong."

"Is he?" Barbara interjected.

"Yes, because he spent money we haven't got on a hotel room for an after-party for his work colleagues and I think he slept with someone while he was there."

She'd said it.

"And did you?" there was a glint in Barbara's eyes as she spoke.

"No, I did not," said Matt. "But what is the point if she doesn't believe me. The trust has gone."

"The trust has indeed gone," said Barbara. "The trust has departed, vanished, skiddaddled." She almost sounded as if she was relishing those words. "Marnie, trust is crucial. Your husband says he hasn't done anything wrong. A good wife would believe her husband. Perhaps you should think about that before you rush to ... "

A great tidal wave of grief and anger threatened to engulf her as Barbara spoke. But before it could consume her, she got up and sprinted to the door, pushing down hard on the handle and stepping into the corridor.

Marnie could hear Matt's voice calling her name, but her legs carried her away, through the entrance to the Family Matters Centre, down the street, across the pedestrian crossing, past the shops and houses, with cars zooming past.

She didn't stop until she reached her front door.

She pushed the key in the lock and stepped inside, sobbing.

Everything was broken. She couldn't trust him. She was such a bad wife. Barbara had said so, and she was an expert, so she must be right, mustn't she?

✤ ✤ ✤

The next day, after a sleepless night of her own, Marnie gathered her thoughts and decided to take action.

She always knew that in arguments, she would crumble first. For all she could shout like a banshee, she hated conflict and just wanted a world in which everyone got along together.

She didn't hate Matt, she loved him.

She was just so angry about being taken for granted and left at home. She was furious that he had looked at stupid, laddish porn, while ignoring her.

Her demands for a third child hadn't helped. That was probably hormonal. She was over 40 and it was her demonic ovaries driving her, in some final gasp of fertility, towards that one last baby. Barbara's talk about her being a Damsel in Distress had rattled her.

Everything about Barbara had rattled her.

They just needed to talk, without Barbara getting in the way.

Maybe going to counselling hadn't been such a great idea, after all?

He had done something very stupid by booking that hotel suite without telling her, but maybe – just maybe – they could talk about it and work it all out? If he said he hadn't betrayed her, perhaps she should trust him?

Matt had never given her any reason to doubt him before, but he needed to do more to make her feel special. Their marriage couldn't afford to miss out on lovely evenings out together in luxury hotel rooms.

She was still working out how to say all of that, without losing her rag, as she pushed open the doors to his favourite pub on Fleet Street. She'd be bound to find him here. It was his regular haunt after work.

There was Matt at the table in the corner, with his back to her. Oh, thank God, she'd found him. They could talk things through, try to make sense of it all somehow. Marnie started to walk across the pub, thinking of all the things she needed to say, the things she wanted to say to him. How on earth would she manage to get the words out? She wouldn't shout. No, she'd keep her temper and maybe they could just have a little drink and a chat for starters, on neutral ground.

But as she came closer, she realised he wasn't drinking alone tonight. There, by his side, her beautifully blowdried locks almost touching the side of his head as they talked, was Belinda, his old flame.

Marnie froze.

In that split second, Matt put his hand up and started to play with her hair and then he kissed her cheek and murmured something. She laughed and he moved in closer and kissed her. Properly kissed her. With tongues and everything.

Matt, her Matt.

Marnie's whole life with Matt flashed before her – seeing him leaning on the student union bar, fancying him just from the back of his neck, pretending to have the best night out ever with her girlfriends while surreptitiously checking him out.

He did the same to her of course, laughing a bit too loudly with his mates and shooting glances in her direction.

Eventually, he came over to her table and she had to feign looking for something in her handbag because she could feel herself blushing.

As he sat down beside her, his fingers brushed against her hand. The moment he touched her, it was as if her past, present and future merged into one.

They could barely keep their hands off each other after that and sloped away for a night of passion under his grubby duvet.

Their nickname at college was Mattress – because they were rarely out of his bed.

Now, her knight in shining armour was snogging the wicked witch.

Blinded by tears, she span around and ran back out of the pub without him even noticing she was there.

CHAPTER NINETEEN

Marnie gazed at the empty space in the wardrobe, where Matt's clothes used to hang.

Right now, she would usually be ironing his shirts, swearing under her breath that he didn't do his own.

An awful, empty ache sat inside her.

But she had caught him – caught him! – snogging Belinda, who he had only gone out with for three months in the first year at university, for God's sake.

Matt wasn't returning her calls or texts, which were a bit on the sweary side, to be honest. She never knew there were so many ways to say fuck you.

It was a damn good job that none of his clothes were hanging there. She might just take a pair of scissors to the lot.

Marnie felt a knot of anger twisting in her stomach but took a deep breath. She couldn't just stay here all day, staring at an empty cupboard.

She had work to do.

Athena's latest column on the joys of springtime had to be subbed – or rather, rewritten – and there could be no funny business or Barker would fire her for sure. Now, more than ever, she needed the money.

Marnie went into her little office, which used to be the baby's room. Both of her boys had slept in here as babies. Then they got big enough to share a bedroom and bunk beds.

LIVING THE DREAM!

Today, Ladies, I am going to treat you to a picture of myself – I am such an inspiration to you all!

Here I am, painting Easter eggs (free range, organic, obviously) in eco-paints, to entertain the little ones, wearing a beautiful, ethically-sourced, day dress – hand-stitched by poor people. I just love to support them in their work, don't you?

As I look out on my well-stocked borders and think about those homely jobs to be done – polishing the grouting, deseeding pomegranates with a fine needle, before hand-pressing juice – I feel all is right with the world because I am wearing kitten heels, as well as matching lip and nail colour.

Easter, such a wonderful time for us mothers. We will stroll out across my ten acres and roll those little painted eggs gaily down the hill, laughing together in the sunshine. What fun. Then I will return to the kitchen and bake a Simnel cake for us all to share, with organic flour ground at the local mill. Lovely.

And knowing things are ethically-sourced – especially the diamonds that my Russian boyfriend likes to shower me with – really is so important. I could practically devote myself to that, if I weren't so busy, busy, busy being a super-duper do-it-all mother!

Why don't you send me some pictures of yourselves, living the dream, dressed in your finery, baking a soufflé or a nice quiche for your husband's tea?

Next week: advanced embroidery techniques.

Until then, Mummies, keep Living the Dream!

Marnie sighed.

Here she was, writing in the room that was supposed to contain the cot that would hold her third baby. The baby that would never be. Was she selfish for wanting it so much? The tears returned.

She could not pull herself together, no matter how hard she tried. How would she manage later on, when she picked up the boys from school and nursery? Their smiles were heartbreaking because they were just like Matt's.

Seized by the sudden desire to tell the truth, warts and all, about her life, she went to her blog.

It was anonymous, she hardly had any readers, so she could use it to get things off her chest.

No-one would ever know it was her. In fact, nobody would probably even bother to read it, but just knowing that she had put her thoughts down might make things easier.

If she was going to have to write lies about motherhood, on behalf of Athena Maldon, to earn a living then it somehow balanced things to tell the other side of the story.

The truth, in fact.

She'd had enough of fantasy.

As it turned out, her so-called happy marriage had been nothing but make believe, in any case.

Mrs Make Believe

THE TRUTH ABOUT MY MARRIAGE.

I am Mrs Make Believe.

I'm not the most brilliant stay-at-home mum – in fact, I'm rubbish at it. If I could, I would sack myself. I hate cooking with a passion. I'd rather have a take away and a bottle of wine than bake a bloody cake; mine are so awful my children only eat them out of pity. I often feed my boys oven chips and fish fingers and in my world, ketchup counts as one of their five-a-day. In fact, we're lucky if we manage two a day. Do chips count as a vegetable?

Anyway, while I was busy daydreaming about the fantasy of how life was supposed to be, starring my movie hero crush, the reality with my husband turned sour.

I wanted a third child so badly, I forced him into counselling.

I longed to wear maternity bras, he expected me to dress up in pole-dancer pants. I discovered he had booked a hotel suite on a night out when I was NFI – Not Flipping Invited – and a 23-year-old sex siren went in my place. I think he probably did use it as a chance to have a fling with a woman who doesn't look like a burst mattress.

Now it turns out he has been harbouring some secret fantasies of his own, involving an ex-girlfriend from his university days, of all people.

Yesterday I caught him holding hands with her in the pub before giving her a tongue sandwich.

I married him for better, for worse, but no-one warned me it would get this bad.

I did consider ending it all, but then I thought of my kids – and the fact that I had a load of laundry to do and still had to empty the dishwasher. Plus, there is the matter of the socks that have yet to be paired.

That's the reality of life as Mrs Make Believe.

She smiled ruefully to herself.

There, somehow, that felt a bit better.

❧   ❧   ❧

It was time to face facts.

It was a brand new day, a new beginning, just her against the world.

He had probably cheated on her with his pupil and he had definitely cheated on her with his ex-girlfriend. And the most crushing thing was, she couldn't go to pieces, because of the children.

She had to be strong. Marnie simply did not have time to fall apart. Sadness enveloped her the moment she dropped Charlie off at nursery and Rufus at school, but she knew it was a strictly time-limited wallow. With this in mind, she determined to find some kind of inner strength and make some changes for the better.

Was she so ugly that her husband could not remain faithful? Was it all her fault?

She'd walked past the dance studio on the High Road so many times but always thought it was not for someone like her, mainly because it was filled with yummy mummies clad in neon lycra dancewear. Some of them even had visible hip bones.

She just had hip fat.

Plus, she usually felt guilty spending time doing things for herself but that was when Matt was around; Matt, who was now thinking only of himself. Exercise was good for depression, she had written about that.

Plus, a body could be reshaped and not just by surgery. She was beginning a programme of reinvention. She was Marnie-lite, a yummy mummy in the making.

The studio was a bit daunting – full of women whose bodies were already perfect and definitely did not need reshaping.

Never mind, she would be one of them soon enough.

An impossibly lithe teacher unfurled herself from the chair behind the desk as Marnie signed up for the ballet barre class, which was, apparently, better than Pilates for toning up.

The teacher was just like the ballerina from inside Marnie's jewellery box when she was a little girl, except this one was wearing a headset and had hard, scary little eyes to match her hard, scary little body.

"New?" she said, eyeing Marnie with suspicion.

"Yes, it's my first time, sorry," said Marnie, who felt the need to apologise for ruining the air of sleek beauty with her lumpen body, baggy T-shirt and black leggings, sagging at the knees.

Women waiting for the class to start, in their zingy little Capri pants and matching vests, sipped from water bottles. A few were doing stretches. Marnie just stood there, not knowing what to do. It would normally be latte and cake o'clock in her house.

"Just do your best to keep up," said the teacher, as the gaggle of beauties crowded into the dance studio behind her.

Keep up? Ballet was all about slow, graceful movements, wasn't it?

A thudding beat filled the air and the yummy mummies started to march in time to the music like an army of robotic Barbie dolls, swinging their arms and raising their knees to ridiculous heights.

Marnie tried to keep up, honestly she did, but after a minute of it she was bloody exhausted and this was only the warm up.

"Now, to the barre!" ordered the teacher.

The yummy mummies positioned their long legs in turn-out, standing dutifully, yet gracefully, in a line, one hand upon the ballet barre.

They plied downwards. Marnie followed. They got back up. She got stuck in an ugly squat.

They turned and placed a lean leg each upon the barre, with ease.

Marnie couldn't quite get her leg up there to join them.

Was there a height restriction on this class?

"There is a barre for the vertically challenged, over here," said the teacher with sigh, pointing to a lower barre, for midget ballerinas.

"Sorry," said Marnie.

She picked up her handbag and heard her phone go "ping", signalling the arrival of an email.

Marnie surreptitiously checked it – her blog had 30 likes on Twitter! People had tweeted and retweeted her post about Matt and his betrayal.

She felt suffused with a warm glow, which had nothing to do with the fact that she was sweating like a pig in here.

"One, two and three!" shouted the teacher. "Point your toes. Up, up and down."

The yummies each extended a leg gracefully behind them and lifted and lowered it unison.

"This is where change happens. Exhaust your leg muscles. Feel the burn. Please try to keep up," said the teacher, giving Marnie's leg a little slap.

"Sorry," she said, sweat trickling down her temples. Her leg felt like it was going to drop off.

Ping, ping, ping.

Her phone was chiming like Buddhist bells.

"Who has left their phone on in class? It had better be Hollywood calling!"

Several heads swivelled around to look at Marnie and she saw disdain register before they swivelled back again.

"Now, let us find our inner calm," said the teacher, giving Marnie a particularly hard stare.

Searching for inner calm involved Marnie lying, head forward over the barre, one foot on the floor and the other leg lifted out behind her at a crazy angle. How was this calming exactly? It was painful for a start.

"I think you are going to have to find me an ambulance," groaned Marnie, whose phone was still pinging and had now started ringing as well.

Ballet Barbie-with-a-headset tapped her on the shoulder: "I expect one hundred per cent dedication to my class. I'm sorry that you have not been able to find that special place within yourself today. Your inner calm is lacking. It's time for you to continue your journey without us."

She could feel herself turning the colour of beetroot. It took a few seconds for her to register that she was, in fact, being booted out. "Of course, I'm so sorry," said Marnie, who was secretly quite relieved that the ordeal was over. This was not exercise. It was torture.

She could have sworn that one of the yummy mummies muttered "fatso", as she exited the studio on wobbly legs, hanging her head in shame.

She was never going to cut it at the ballet barre but at least the Twitter support for *Mrs Make Believe* called for a coffee shop celebration!

Dipping her finger into the cream of her hot chocolate was the best kind of exercise for her.

As she munched on a muffin – she had definitely earned it with all that hard ballet graft – Marnie started to read through the comments on her blog, mostly very supportive, a few truly bonkers.

"Honey, what a jerk! Thank God you threw him out before he hurt you any more!"

"You could learn to love baking! Don't give up hope. Or why not try gardening? Knitting is also such great fun!

Sometimes when my husband stays out all night, I knit him a really long scarf to get over the fact that he is probably having an affair."

"Ring him to talk it through? You have two kids. It has got to be worth saving."

"KILL the ex. KILL HER! And throw away the mismatching socks. You will never, EVER, find the right ones to pair them with once separated. Drink a bottle of gin instead. It helps."

"I like your blog but I label and colour code all my socks to prevent such disasters."

Marnie pulled her laptop out of her bag and blogged again, with renewed fervour.

Women liked what she was writing. That gave her hope.

Mrs Make Believe

CAN HE?

Dear readers,

May I just thank you all for your support, particularly the advice on sock pairing. Sadly, I think my cookery skills are beyond help.

I would love to talk to him but he refuses to answer my calls or texts.

Of course, when he finally rings me I might just be too busy with the laundry and the washing up.

Just because he goes to work all day and has adult conversations, doesn't give him the right to treat me like this.

I gave up a very good career to have his kids and, bit by bit, I have found myself and my confidence eroded.

Work treats me like a half-person, I am working on reduced pay and he doesn't treat me with the respect I deserve. Why? Because I am a mother and society treats mothers like half-wits despite the fact that we are raising the next generation. We do what Nature intended us to do and are rewarded with pay-cuts and redundancies, topped off with complete disinterest from our partners. To make matters worse, as women, we all judge each other on how brilliant we are at it, don't we? There's more competition at the school gates than your average city bank and I have had enough of it.

Yes, he might be out there making multi-million pound deals but can he name all the baddies in Adventure Time? *I think not. Can he build a Lego Hero Factory in under two minutes?*

Can he negotiate the political minefield that is the mother and toddler group, not to mention gym club and fun music for the under-fives? Nope!

Can he keep body and soul together whilst removing a truculent two-year-old (with a very full nappy) – scream-ing "push me, push me!" – from a swing when it is time to leave the playground. Can he?

Can he take the kids to the park just once at the weekend and at least pretend to enjoy it?

Can he cook a meal from scratch, have the children say "yuk" and throw most of it on the floor and not lose his temper?

And, last but not least, can he name Bob the Builder's best (female) friend? Ha!

By lunchtime the next day, she'd been approached by not one, but three, blogging communities and she had amassed nearly 1,000 followers.

"We love your brutal honesty. Your life sucks but it makes great reading! Would you like to guest on a discussion tonight about being an imperfect mum and failed wife?"

Marnie's anger seemed to have hit a raw nerve and her feed was full to bursting with supportive comments from fed-up mums and housewives revealing their horror stories of being treated like second-class citizens by their work, their partners and each other.

And, best of all, one of her new followers was a presenter on lunchtime television's *ChitChat*!

Marnie skipped around the kitchen when she saw that.

The next day, the presenter had retweeted Marnie's blog to her 12,000 followers. The likes for her posts were in their thousands by lunchtime and her own following had swelled by more than 1,000. It was strange, really, because she didn't know these people from Adam and she'd always been a bit mystified by all the fuss about Twitter. But there was something which made her feel all warm and fuzzy about having so much public affection heaped on her, when she was feeling at such a low ebb.

Tuning in to *ChitChat* at lunchtime, she was amazed to see a discussion about confessional blogs on social media, featuring her most recent posts.

"As *Mrs Make Believe* shows, this kind of airing your dirty linen seems to provide a forum for women to support each other and to get things off their chest but will it do their relationships any good in the long run?" intoned the psychologist. "Can they translate that level of honesty into their relationship or will their anger just be used to forge new friendships with like-minded women? I'm not saying that is a bad thing in itself but who knows what the end result will be? That said, *Mrs Make Believe* does seem to have touched a nerve with other mothers."

The plastic-faced *ChitChat* presenter nodded in the nearest thing to solemn agreement that her surgically-altered features could muster.

"Yes," she said, turning to camera.

"My husband won't mind me saying he is absolutely useless! And I personally have terrible trouble getting my cleaner to pair all my socks correctly. Where DO they all go?"

Marnie's phone rang.

It was Barker.

"I don't suppose you've picked up on this *Mrs Make Believe* thing, between doing the dishes and wiping your kids' noses, have you?"

Gulp.

"No," she lied. "But I think I've just seen something about it on *Chitchat*."

"Good. You will be delighted to hear that *Living the Dream* is going down about as well as a cold cup of sick with the readership. I need to find something else that women out there really want. It pains me to say it, but women moaning about their husbands seems to be the topic du jour. I want you to get hold of Mrs Make Believe and get her to write for us. Exclusively."

"Write for us?"

"*The Sentinel*. You do still work for us, don't you?"

"Yes."

"Well, get on it then. I know it's not going to be easy, Mrs Make Believe is anonymous and hasn't broken cover. I want to find out who she is, get her to be named and photographed and then we can go to town on this bastard of a husband of hers."

Marnie experienced a wave of nausea. That wasn't what she had intended! Her confessional blog was meant to be something personal … which she had then shared with millions of other people worldwide.

Oh, God. What had she done?

One minute she was just a nobody, with a crap husband. Now she was somebody – because of her crap husband.

She wasn't ready to be a celebrity because her marriage had broken up, was she?

"OK," she squeaked.

"I will make it worth your while. Failure is not an option. The Editor is very keen on it. Exclusives, not excuses." It had been a while since she had heard him say that. Oh, dear.

Surely no amount of money would be worth invading her own privacy for, even if it meant getting her own, brilliant, witty, column, would it?

Marnie picked her way through the ruins of her career – the soul-destroying task of rewriting Athena Maldon's column, week in, week out – and was unable to answer that question.

Just then a text landed from Barker: "SORT IT, SLUMMY MUMMY!"

She was just trying to work out how to disentangle herself from this disastrous situation when she received another text, which stopped her in her tracks.

It was from Belle and said: "Help me."

CHAPTER TWENTY

Marnie wanted to speed out of the house to rescue her friend. However, the reality of having two little children clinging to her legs slowed her progress somewhat. Charlie had a meltdown about wanting to wear his wellies and Rufus needed the loo after she had shut the front door.

Eventually, she bunged the boys in their car seats, throwing them a bag of crisps to keep them quiet, topped off with an electronic game each.

Then, she drove at a reasonably safe speed (Baby on Board!) in her little Mini with its cherished numberplate MARN1E that Matt had bought her (bastard) to Belle and Jonah's house in Notting Hill. She hoped to God it wasn't the baby. And not blood. She could deal with anything but blood.

Huffing up the front steps, with Rufus at her feet and Charlie in her arms, she hammered on the door. Then, she looked down and realised she was still wearing her pyjama bottoms with her Ugg boots, but there was no time to worry about that now.

The house stood silent.

Marnie rapped again.

Footsteps pattered down the hall and the door swung open to reveal a strange, bird-like, dark-haired woman, whose breath smelled distinctly of spirits.

"Yesh?"

"Where is she?" said Marnie, pushing past her.

"Who?"

"Belle. I just got a text."

"Sheesh in bed, lazy trollop. Leaving me to look after baby!"

"What did you just call my friend?" said Marnie.

"Jusht look at the shtate of you! Call yourshelf a Mummy!"

Charlie had a finger up his nose, which was rather runny, and Rufus was spitting bits of crisp out all over the front doorstep.

"Your brats are a disgrash!"

At this point, Rufus took an instant dislike to Alexa Joy and bit her leg, quite hard, causing Alexa to scream and retreat into the kitchen.

With Charlie still in her arms, Marnie shouted: "Well done Ruf! Follow me!" and charged up the stairs to find Belle.

She was lying on her side in the bed and her breathing was quite laboured.

Marnie called her name softly, as the boys climbed on to the bed and, mercifully for once, didn't use it as a trampoline.

"I think I'm dying, Marnie," said Belle, rolling over to face her.

She looked as if she had lost a stone in weight since Marnie last saw her. Her green eyes seemed to be eating up her face, and she had the most awful pallor.

Marnie knew Jonah was going away to LA but why hadn't he flown back to help? Her friend was doing a very good impression of a Bronte sister.

"How long have you been like this?" she said, stroking her friend's face.

"Days, I think," Belle croaked.

"We need to get you to hospital. I'm going to call an ambulance now. Where's the baby?"

Belle started to cry.

⚜ ⚜ ⚜

Marnie found him in the nursery, fast asleep, in a very dirty nappy, with half finished bottles of milk littering his cot. She took a picture of the horrible scene on her camera phone to show Jonah – the bloody idiot – the full extent of what he had allowed to happen by jetting off to America.

Then she spotted a half empty bottle of sedative on the side and felt herself struggling to control the desire to knock the woman downstairs into the middle of next week.

She took a picture of the bottle as well, before picking Gabriel out of the cot and taking him to lie by Belle's side.

"It's OK, honey," she said, as Belle sobbed. "He's OK, just in need of a change and a cuddle from you. He'll be fine, I promise."

Then she stomped downstairs to give this bitch – whoever she was – a piece of her mind.

Alexa was slugging from a bottle of vodka, hugging a photograph of Jonah. Well, it was half a photograph – she had taken Belle's favourite picture out of its frame on the sideboard and ripped it in half.

"I don't know who the hell you think you are," Marnie began, feeling her temper about to erupt, Vesuvius-style.

"Who I think I am? I'm Alexa Joy, the world's besht baby guru and let me tell you, thish woman doesn't deserve to have his baby. It should be me!" she said, leaping unsteadily to her feet.

Signed records of Jonah's band Destroy lay scattered across the floor. And, oh my God, she was wearing one of his tour T-shirts!

She turned on her heel and ran back upstairs to Alexa Joy's room. The bed was covered with a treasure trove of Destroy memorabilia, most of it nicked from around the house. Next to the bed, in a little silver frame – the one from the sideboard downstairs – was a picture of a much, much younger Alexa Joy at a Destroy concert, with her arms around Jonah.

Marnie started flinging Alexa's belongings into her monogrammed Louis Vuitton suitcase.

She heaved it downstairs into the hall.

Rufus appeared at her side as Alexa swayed into view, still clutching her vodka.

Marnie took a snap of the sozzled baby guru as Rufus bared his teeth.

"Get out of this house," said Marnie, opening the front door and pushing her out: "Before I set my children on you."

⚜   ⚜   ⚜

She is limp in my arms after her punishment, crying softly.

I pick her up and carry her over to the fur rug by the blazing log fire.

Outside the wind is howling and a blizzard of snow-flakes sweeps across the window panes.

As I lay her down, she tries to kiss me, leaning forward, pushing her lips to mine.

I pull away a little, raising myself up on my elbows, giving her a better view of my honed torso, while denying her the kiss she craves.

"First, you must tell me where the antidote is."

The beating has made her hungry for me. I can see it in her eyes.

She hesitates for an instant, biting her lip, before touching the amethyst pendant around her neck.

I hold up the gem in the firelight and realise it has liquid inside.

"My bosses will kill me for this," she whispers, trembling.

Our lips touch and I hold her close, pushing her legs further apart, before sliding into her, forcing a sigh of delight from her beautiful mouth. Her fingers trace their way down my back, coming to rest on my muscular behind.

"I will die happy, Seb," she murmurs.

I kiss her eyes as they close in ecstasy and she melts into my arms.

Flipping her over, running my hands once more over her perfect little rump, I whisper: "They will have to kill me first, Katya, now you are mine."

Belle laughed so hard she set off another coughing fit, just as Marnie poked her head around the door of her hospital room.

"I like your clit-lit Marnie," she giggled, waving *Harsh Winter* at her.

"Don't be silly," said Marnie, covering baby Gabriel's ears. "It's a perfectly respectable spy thriller."

She'd only let Belle borrow the book to give her something to read whilst convalescing. Belle had failed to see its significance as a commentary on the power relationship between men and women. That was what she was planning to discuss with the girls at the book club, in any case.

"I'd better take it back," she said, blushing bright red. Reading it on the iPhone was one thing, but it was more delicious to be able to hold the book in her hands and flick to the mucky – sorry – the most challenging bits.

"Now, how's my lovely baby?" said Belle. "Is he behaving himself?"

Gabriel reached out his arms to Belle.

"Yes," said Marnie, handing him over. "He's such a sweetie. The boys absolutely adore having him stay with us."

"What about Matt?"

Marnie turned and looked out of the window: "Oh, he's been really busy working away, so he hasn't seen him yet. But he will be thrilled."

"Are you sure it's not too much of an imposition?"

Marnie seemed to have something in her eyes. She was rubbing them a little as she turned back round to face Belle.

"No, of course not! I love having all three of them. Just take your time and get better."

"I'll be well enough to go home tomorrow, so it's not for much longer."

Marnie sat on the bed, disappointment etched on her fine features: "I do love having the baby to stay. You can leave him with me any time you like."

"Jonah's coming home at the end of the week," said Belle, grinning at the thought of it.

"Belle, don't take this the wrong way but will you be alright on your own with the baby?" said Marnie.

"Yes," said Belle, hugging her baby. "We are going to muddle through, aren't' we, Gabe?"

Marnie looked a bit crestfallen.

"You know I'll call you the minute I need anything," said Belle. "Don't suppose you've heard any more from Alexa Joy?"

"No," said Marnie, brightening. "I don't think we'll need to worry about her again for a long time."

"I still can't believe I allowed that awful woman to take advantage of me," said Belle.

"Don't beat yourself up," said Marnie. "For a start, she was a bunny boiler and you were exhausted and sleep deprived. You couldn't think straight. It's a form of torture for a good reason."

"Does it get any better?" Belle asked, hopefully.

"Err, I don't really know," said Marnie, who had only this morning absent-mindedly put the sugar in the fridge and shoved a pair of children's shoes into the dishwasher, "But by the time they're teenagers, I hope it will. Then you spend your life trying to get them out of bed, not to stay in it."

✣ ✣ ✣

Mrs Make Believe's blog caused a sensation with her pictures of Alexa Joy swigging vodka straight from the bottle, dressed in a grubby old Destroy tour t-shirt – not to mention allegations that she had drugged a baby to get it to sleep through the night.

"Alexa discovers the true Joy of Parenting! It's 40 per cent proof and she swigs it straight from the bottle ... " Fleet Street went into a feeding frenzy.

Efforts to trace Alexa, through her agent, had failed but rumour had it that Alexa had checked in to The Convent, the Surrey-based facility favoured by the stars, to recuperate.

When *The Sentinel* managed to confirm the fact that she was in The Convent, her agent released a statement:

"Alexa was very distressed by the recent photographs of her drinking vodka. She works tirelessly to help mothers and babies everywhere have a happier life. Millions worldwide have enjoyed the Joy of Parenting (Registered Trademark) thanks to Alexa. All her efforts to help others have left her suffering nervous exhaustion and in this fragile state, she turned to drink in a moment of madness.

"She denies absolutely that she has ever drugged a baby to get them to sleep. The sedative was hers, to help her rest. But she is a very big fan of Destroy and so was happy to be pictured wearing a tour T-shirt."

Chapter Twenty-One

M arnie was considering what tissue of lies she could possibly tell Barker about Mrs Make Believe to get him off her back.

He was pushing her hard to get Mrs Make Believe to sign with *The Sentinel*, especially after her Alexa Joy coup.

"Whoever she is, she played a blinder with that," he said. "Are you sure she isn't a man?"

"Positive," said Marnie, curtly, flicking croissant crumbs off her top, as she sat at the dining table in her little kitchen. "I have spoken to her. She is just very, very shy and not sure she wants to be identified."

Besides, she'd had a long chat with her conscience, off the record. No amount of money would persuade her to do it. No, never, never, never.

"The Editor wants her. Do you think she would do it for a hundred?"

"A hundred quid! You must be joking!"

She knew times were hard at *The Sentinel* but that was what she normally got paid for a bloody tip-off. At that rate, he could sod off.

"I meant a hundred grand a year, Marnie. The Editor is keen, very keen."

Marnie was speechless.

Bugger her conscience. That was an absolute fortune!

"I thought you were hard-up!" she spat. "I was only paid half that amount!"

"Oh, not that again," groaned Barker. "I will make sure you get a hefty finder's fee Marnie. To be honest, with Shustrov and his cronies going over the books, I am not sure how much budget I am going to have left, so I thought I'd better get in and spend some of it quick. Now please get on to her and let me have an answer. Soon."

The doorbell rang.

With her head reeling from the prospect of earning a humungous salary – which she surely could afford to pay a third set of school fees with! – she didn't quite register the sight that stood before her at first.

It was her sister-in-law, Iona, but instead of a glossy black sheet of hair, protein-treated into submission, there was a haystack. In place of a Chanel suit stood a grubby pair of jeans and a sweat top – a sweat top! No Jimmy Choos, but trainers. Oh dear. Iona was looking less like herself and more like a real mother.

Trixie, her beautiful daughter, was covered in snot and tears.

"Help me, Marnie!" she wailed. "The nanny has walked out. You have to help me!"

Marnie sighed.

"Come in, Iona... Let's have a cup of tea."

While Trixie watched telly with Charlie, Iona recounted her tale of woe. It was just typical of Matt to run off to her eldest brother Ethan's house. And Dylan, well, if there was a cat flap he could squeeze through, he would probably sleep anywhere.

"Dylan insisted on leaving copies of *Krazee* magazine lying around in the nanny's bathroom and she found it too distressing. Ethan is insisting he can stay because blood is thicker than water, apparently. Help me, Marnie, please! I can't find any nannies willing to work with him in the house, lounging around in his boxer shorts and . . . "

"Think yourself lucky," said Marnie. "He went through a phase of going commando when I refused to wash his pants for him."

"I'm begging you," said Iona, falling to her knees, a flicker of emotion registering on her smooth, frozen features. "Take him back!"

"Hmmm," said Marnie. "What about Matt?"

"What about him?" Marnie couldn't wait to hear what Iona made of Matt's inability to load or unload a dishwasher or do any laundry or make a bed. Ha! The list was endless. "He hasn't been living with us since last week. I really haven't a clue where he is, sorry."

Marnie felt a large stab of longing. Perhaps he had got himself a nice little flat on his own and wouldn't ever want to come back to her and the boys. Or, perhaps he had moved in with blow-dried Belinda. Longing was replaced with an angry feeling, right in the pit of her stomach.

"Look, I will help put a roof over Dylan's head but he will have to promise to help me with the boys," she said.

"Oh, thank you! Thank you!" cried Iona. "I don't know how to thank you."

She took in Marnie's bedraggled form – scruffy hair, not a scrap of make-up, laughter lines, uneven skintone, sloppy T-shirt, and – surely not? – pyjama bottoms with assorted stains on them. Not to mention the tatty Converse, which were too distressing for words.

Iona said: "Actually, yes I do. I can help you, Marnie. I am going to make you an appointment with my favourite beauticians and skin specialist. I have a block-booking for myself, so I will have no trouble getting you in."

"No need, Iona, I can't really afford it just now."

Matt's credit card was almost up to its limit and her meagre earnings from subbing Athena's column weren't paying for much – which made the prospect of a *Mrs Make Believe* payday quite alluring.

"No, no, I am paying. I would love to do this for you. It will make you feel like a million dollars."

"As long as it doesn't cost me a million dollars!" said Marnie, with a tight little smile. Iona had no clue about financial realities as the wife of a banker, adept at spending her husband's bonuses on her appearance. Marnie touched her on the shoulder as she was turning to leave.

"And if Matt should call, by any chance, or if Ethan knows where he is, please tell him…" She almost said that she missed him but he had treated her appallingly. What on earth was she thinking?

Iona's plastic face softened as she gave Marnie a look of sympathy. "Tell him that the boys miss him," said Marnie.

❧ ❧ ❧

Dr Tolko's clinic in Harley Street was possibly the most daunting building Marnie had ever had to enter – and she'd entered a few in her time: ministers' offices, Number Ten, press conferences at which she knew she would get a pasting.

But this was something else because it was all about sheer perfection; the walls, the chairs, the art, the staff. Especially the staff.

"Hi, I'm Storm," said a woman with impeccable everything. Her hair was tied back in a neat little bun and her nails, lips and teeth all gleamed, as if she had spent hours buffing them with chamois leather.

Marnie glanced at the beauty therapist's feet. Yes, even her little ballet pumps were polished to perfection.

"And how are we helping you today, Marnie?"

Marnie wiped the last of her complimentary mango and orange smoothie from around her lips. God, that was yummy.

"I think I'm having some, erm, waxing?" she whispered.

"Brazilian?" said Storm, louder than was necessary in the waiting room, which did have other women in it, for goodness' sake.

What had she let herself in for? Iona insisted it would make her feel like a new woman. Marnie feared it would make her feel as if she had been napalmed somewhere quite essential.

But it was too late to back out now.

Storm was gliding down the white corridor to a room where music tinkled softly, white towels lay on the therapy bed and a scary, scratchy, miniscule paper thong lurked.

"Just get changed into these knickers – unless you prefer to leave everything off."

Marnie was rather hoping she could leave everything on. Including her coat.

She whipped off her dress and her pants and squeezed herself into the paper knickers, which barely covered anything.

Marnie hardly dared to look. She was quite, well, overgrown, really. It was a bit embarrassing.

Storm came back in and started humming softly to the music as Marnie lay back on the bed.

"Just try to relax your legs," she said, pulling Marnie into what can only be described as the gynaecology exam position.

"Jesus!"

"Is it a bit too warm?" said Storm, as gloopy wax was smoothed into areas Marnie was not all that familiar with – and it was her body.

"No, it's fine, just not done this before. Reminds me of doctors having to look at you before you give birth, you know."

How could Storm know that? She was practically just out of school! Look at her smooth skin.

"Yes, I do know. Got one myself!"

That was reassuring. She was a mother.

That was something to talk about, as her nether regions were rendered hairless.

"Yowch!"

"Just breathe as I pull the wax away, it helps," said Storm.

"Yes, my little girl is at school now, Year One," added Storm, as a horrible ripping sound echoed around the room.

"Oh, my eldest son is too!" said Marnie, through watering eyes.

"Turn over. Would you like me to do round the back?"

Round the back? She sounded scarily like her gardener offering to trim her wayward leylandii.

Oh, God. What to say?

"Errr, yes?"

Marnie found herself clambering on all fours onto the bed and sticking her bottom in the air.

As the hot wax was applied somewhere that no man had gone before, Storm cried: "I recognise you now! You're Rufus Martin's mother aren't you? Year One, Astral Prep!"

❧ ❧ ❧

Her cheeks still burning with humiliation, Marnie was only slightly mollified to be wrapped in the fluffiest white robe before being sent upstairs to see Dr Tolko.

Iona had booked her in for a total body consultation and so she was still in the scary paper thong but had at least managed to sneak her bra back on.

Storm showed her to the white leather examination chair, stripped off the lovely robe and then left her twiddling her thumbs.

Out of nowhere, Dr Tolko appeared at her side – silently and suddenly – with his cadaverous, sunken cheeks and wide eyes.

Marnie checked his feet in case he was on castors.

"There are no ugly women, Marnie," he whispered, caressing her face with his fine fingers and appraising her doughy body and plump thighs. "Just lazy ones."

"I don't have much time for myself," she muttered. She wanted to flee.

He smiled warmly: "Don't be afraid, I can help you. Lots of women who come to see me need help. Let's start with something simple. What about some extract of bee-sting to relax some of those lines?"

"Is it safe?"

"Very."

"Maybe just a little, then." Was this a good idea? Matt hated anything to do with cosmetic surgery. It was for vain, silly women, with mouths like inflatable rafts and breasts like barrage balloons.

What did she care what he thought anyway? He hadn't bothered to ring or even ask after the boys!

"Go for it!" she told the doctor, who was already preparing the needle.

"It might hurt a little, but afterwards you will look like a new woman. If this doesn't work I sometimes use snake venom for deeper wrinkles. We shall see."

An eye-watering minute later, Dr Tolko had injected the bee-sting extract into laughter lines around her eyes and

mouth and the worry lines on her forehead, which had mul-
tiplied since Matt left.

"I will leave you for ten minutes to see how it has taken.
Just relax."

And with that, he rolled out of the room – to see another
patient, presumably.

Marnie could hear the faint hum of the computer on
his desk.

Bet he treats loads of celebrities. I wonder what they
have done?

She shouldn't, she really shouldn't, but Marnie was a
journalist first and foremost and just couldn't help it.

Besides, it was getting chilly in just her paper thong and
bra. She needed to stretch her legs a bit.

So she did. In the general direction of his computer. His
email inbox was helpfully on the screen. Who would have
thought she was having cosmetic treatments! And him! And
even the leaders of some of the political parties were email-
ing asking for appointments.

Something else caught her eye.

An email marked "Potential problems: threat high".

She opened it and her eyes scanned the page. A drug
called Obduro. Some tests in Russia and South America.
Unwanted side effects and potential problems with the reg-
ulator. Tests being carried out in UK on willing volunteers –
results as yet unknown.

God almighty. It was a proper story! She hadn't had one
of those in ages!

Quickly, she pressed print and the machine in the corner started to spew paper. Then she closed the email and
returned to the inbox, heart pounding.

She ran across the room and, grabbing her huge handbag, stuffed the print-outs inside. As casually as she could,

she strolled back towards the examination chair, with the bag slung over her shoulder, just as Dr Tolko slipped back into the room.

"Leaving already?"

"No, no, just seeing how I'm going to feel in real life, carrying my handbag and feeling like a new woman!" she blurted, edging sideways towards the examination chair, pulling the bag around to cover her backside, which must have looked quite enormous in the scary little thong.

She was too terrified of being caught nicking his secret emails to even blush.

He looked quizzical.

"Lie back down for a minute, Marnie. Let me see ... "

He appraised her face, which was feeling a bit tight and numb where the needles had gone in.

"Yes, it all seems fine. You may get a bit of swelling but that should settle and you will notice fewer lines and a fresher look. You must come back for a top up in three months' time."

Marnie attempted to smile but found she couldn't.

"And don't worry about the bill, your sister-in-law has settled that."

On the tube on the way home, Marnie noticed that people were staring at her.

By the time she had reached Turnham Green, she'd had sniggers, smirks and a small group of children blatantly laughing at her.

When she got through the front door, she stared in the hallway mirror and let out a scream, which frightened the neighbour's dog into a barking attack.

Her face had swollen where the needles had gone in, giving her the appearance of an extra-terrestrial with a lumpy forehead and face.

It was then she remembered: she was allergic to bee-stings.

CHAPTER TWENTY-TWO

Barker would normally be going through his newslist, shouting at reporters for being low-fliers and, maybe, slurping his fourth or fifth double-shot latte by now.

Instead, he was sipping tea in Marnie Martin's open-plan kitchen diner as she busied herself with the dishwasher.

The walls were adorned with children's artwork and the noticeboard seemed to contain every bit of paper that had ever emerged from her kids' school, art class or backpacks.

"Well, when is she getting here?" he said, glancing at his watch.

"Oh, she'll be along in a minute," said Marnie, smiling as she clanked cutlery into the kitchen drawer.

"In fact, would you mind if I just have a look at the contract?"

"Be my guest," said Barker. "It's a standard one but obviously, more money than you were on." His eyes glinted. He couldn't resist goading her. She always rose to the bait.

This time she didn't. Marnie merely raised an eyebrow, pulled out a chair – covered in grubby children's pawprints – and sat down.

She scanned the page in front of her.

"Her own weekly column for a hundred grand. She can decide the subject matter but will have to be open to suggestions from you and the Editor. Will she have copy approval?"

Barker sneered. "Who are you, then? Her bloody agent?"

"Well, we are quite close. I feel kind of protective of her, particularly if she is going to give up her anonymity. She has kids to think about, you know."

"I am sure copy approval will not be a problem. We just want to sign her. This has all been a total ball ache. I am sick to death of getting bollocked by the Editor for not getting this sorted. Where the bloody hell is she?"

He stood up.

Marnie stood up too and rifled through a box of children's crayons on the kitchen island.

She grabbed the chunkiest crayon she could find, took the contract, and quickly signed it.

"What the hell are you doing?" yelled Barker. "I haven't got another contract with me! I'll have to go all the way back to the office now."

"Don't worry," said Marnie, handing him the paper. "That won't be necessary, David. I'm Mrs Make Believe. Time for another cup of tea or would you prefer something stronger? I think congratulations are in order, don't you?"

Belle and Gabriel arrived just in time to see a thunderstruck Barker departing. "Mother and baby club, great," he muttered under his breath as he stomped up the garden path. "She'd better not be late with her copy."

❧   ❧   ❧

Despite her new job as a *Sentinel* columnist, Marnie seemed to have lost her sparkle. There were dark circles under her eyes and her chestnut hair had lost its sheen.

"I bet you can't wait to tell Matt the good news news!" said Belle.

Marnie couldn't speak but started to cry, big, fat, salty tears coursing down her cheeks.

"He's gone," said Marnie.

"Why didn't you tell me?" said Belle, completely taken aback. Matt without Marnie was like cheese without pickle or eggs without bacon. They had history, they had two kids – they'd have to work it out somehow. "What happened?"

"I threw him out and then he got back with an ex from a long time ago," said Marnie. "It all got too complicated and I didn't want to bother you with it while you were ill. Then things with *Mrs Make Believe* just took off…"

"But you are still going to try to get back together, aren't you?"

Marnie fumbled with the fraying edge of her T-shirt. "I'm not sure that there is anything worth saving and anyway, I have the new job to think about now, so I guess I won't have as much time to spend dwelling on the past," she said, ignoring the look of complete disbelief on her best friend's face.

⚜ ⚜ ⚜

Mrs Make Believe

A RECIPE FOR HEARTBREAK

1. *Take one marriage – the older the better, although this recipe can work for unions that are still quite green.*
2. *Sprinkle with disinterest and season with lies.*
3. *Leave your wife to stew in her own juices.*
4. *Select fresh meat. Tender breast or firm rump are good choices. Why not try both?*
5. *Remember, timing is crucial to keep several dishes on the go at once.*

6. *Turn up the heat and toss your tasty morsel.*
7. *Meanwhile, your wife should be simmering nicely.*
8. *Reduce to tears.*
9. *Put her to one side.*
10. *Whip into a frenzy (this should be quite easy).*
11. *Separate.*

Her first column for *The Sentinel* was a massive success. She held the phone close to her ear, as the radio presenter read out her recipe for heartbreak to millions of listeners across the nation.

Marnie had never done a radio interview before but Barker had organised it all so that she could call in from her new office – and he could loom large in the background.

"That's quite a recipe to launch your first column as Mrs Make Believe, Marnie," said the radio presenter. "Things must be quite angry in your kitchen."

"Yes, well if you can't stand the heat, keep the hell out of my kitchen," she said, triumphantly.

"You seem to be a voice for cheated, heartbroken wives everywhere, is that a role you relish?" the presenter said.

"Well, let's just say it was thrust upon me, because my husband was thrusting elsewhere," she said, glancing down at the newspaper, with its massive headline "Happy Families – It's All a Sham".

"And it's all thanks to *The Sentinel* for giving me this brilliant opportunity. You can read all about me in today's edition," she added.

Barker was quite literally breathing down her neck as she did the interview. He took a step back and grinned at her for the plug. It was as if a show-room dummy had just developed feelings.

"Well, we hope you'll come back and join us soon, but perhaps not as our agony aunt. You're just too scary. Remind me not to introduce you to my wife," said the presenter.

"Behave yourself, and you will have nothing to fear from me," she laughed.

She really was Mrs Make Believe.

The vitriol flowed so easily and she'd hardly had a moment to even think about Maddox Wolfe or her silly daydreams. Her obsession with her hunky Mr Make Believe seemed to be taking over her life at one point.

Well, now Mrs Make Believe had the upper hand!

But, strangely, despite the excitement of it and the elation that the world was actually listening to what she had to say, there was something hollow inside her, something the money and the column couldn't quite fill.

It was early days, wasn't it? Just like when she first started the blog and it had hardly any readers. It would just take a bit of time to get used to being famous for being Mrs Make Believe, that's all.

She closed the newspaper. She didn't want to look at their wedding picture any more, in any case. It had Matt's face blotted out, so he wouldn't sue, but seeing it in print made her feel quite sick. It was probably just nerves. From now on, in her column, he was just known as The Husband. Belinda the blow-dried eco-lawyer was The Wicked Witch. Matt had made no attempt to get in touch with her or the children, so he could hardly complain of unfair treatment, could he?

"There are a couple more interviews lined up for this morning and *Vision* magazine want to do an interview with you too," said Barker, rubbing his hands together. "You need to make sure you stick the knife into your husband at every opportunity. And mention *The Sentinel*. OK?"

"Yes, David."

She swallowed hard and returned to her computer screen.

Her inbox was full to bursting with emails from heart-broken women everywhere.

"I'm not sure I know how to solve all their problems," she said, as Barker peered over her shoulder.

"You don't have to," said Barker. "Just give them to Bryher and she will write a nice little letter on your behalf." Sales were massively up because of the *Mrs Make Believe* column, which brightened his life, no end.

But he hadn't seen much of Bryher, the Newsdesk secretary, for the past hour. Where the hell was she? It was time for his pre-conference triple shot latte. If he was going to get a monstering from the Editor – and that was a dead cert – he needed caffeine to gee him up a bit first.

He marched into The Bunker, his office lair, and heard snivelling coming from beneath his desk.

He peered underneath.

"Bryher! What on earth are you doing under there?"

"Hiding," she sniffed. "I'm not coming out!"

Barker's tough outer shell cracked. Well, temporarily, at least.

"Come on," he said, extending a hand to her and pulling her up, "What's the matter? You can tell me."

Her mascara was running in rivulets down her cheeks and even her nose was red from crying. It was not a pretty sight.

"It's my career, or lack of it," she said. "I'm never going to be a proper journalist. I have been stuck with the news-list for years and now even Marnie Martin has got her own column…"

Barker fished a tissue out from the box on his desk.

"Blow," he said.

She slumped into a chair and buried her face in the tissue.

"Ambition is nothing to cry about," he said, in his most avuncular air. "It's just, I don't think I ever realised that you had any burning ambitions at this newspaper."

That wasn't strictly true. It hadn't escaped his notice that she was ruthless and successful when it came to sleeping with other people's boyfriends and the occasional husband. Her limpid eyes were expert at picking out her prey; worn-down husbands, who enjoyed her company a little too much. Tom, the Deputy Editor, was a particular favourite.

"Well, I do," she said, looking up at him. "I want to show everyone I'm a great reporter, I'm serious about issues and things."

"Yes," said Barker. It was a bit of a stretch to imagine Bryher as a giant on the political stage but he didn't want to be unkind.

Human resources had warned him he needed to have more of a listening ear to his staff's woes. Besides, Bryher always worked Christmas and bank holidays without complaint, so he knew he could rely on her to give it 110 per cent. There was no-one she wanted to spend time with at home, as all the family men she dated were busy covering the tracks of their affairs with her, spending time with their wives and kids and praying Bryher wouldn't send them a sexy text message.

"I'll tell you what. You put together some ideas for a news exclusive or even your own column and I can see what we will do about it. We could even get you shadowing that idiot Harry Hedgeson on a story next week. How about that?"

"Really?" said Bryher, brightening. "That's brilliant! I will be totally one hundred per cent dedicated to the job, you will see."

"Ok," he said, sitting down and his desk and sucking in his cheeks. Who cares if Bryher was only writing for the spike? As long as she was busy. "Now, let's get on with this bloody newslist or the Editor will have us both on the ducking stool before lunch."

❧ ❧ ❧

After lunch, Bryher stomped around to Marnie's office to hand deliver an invite to an award's bash. Ordinarily, she would have chucked it straight in the bin in a fit of pique that she hadn't been invited, but it had gone to Barker first, so there was no chance of getting away with filing it in the wastepaper basket.

Never mind, she planned to throw it into the chaotic pile of papers in Marnie's office, in the hope that it would lay undiscovered until it was too late.

Office – yes, Marnie had one of her very own. It was more of a broom-cupboard really but, at *The Sentinel*, being a columnist and having an office in the corridor of power meant she was someone to be feared and envied in equal measure. Loathed and envied in Bryher's case.

Marnie was, unfortunately, already ensconced at her desk.

"Top Chick Awards have invited you, for some reason," said Bryher, wrinkling her nose in distaste at the picture of two little blonde boys that Marnie had placed next to her computer screen – they must be her kids, how totally inappropriate for a working environment.

"I expect you won't have a thing to wear. It will be quite a young crowd. It's tonight, by the way," she smirked.

"Thanks, Bryher," said Marnie, ignoring the hateful secretary's barbed comments, which were worse than ever since Marnie got her new job.

Marnie sighed as she perused the invite, which was in the shape of a high-heeled, glittery shoe.

She'd never been invited to a glamorous awards evening before. It was at the Kensington Roof Gardens. Matt had been to a work do there once. There were flamingos wandering about in amazingly lush shrubbery, that's what he said.

The thought of him gave her a pang of something horrid, right in her chest. She concentrated on the glittery shoe invite to get rid of it. Top Chick Awards – that sounded wonderfully A-list. She couldn't actually go, could she?

The phone rang.

"Dah-ling, it's Maeve from *Sentinel Woman*. David tells me you've got a little party later?"

"Err, yes I have, I suppose," said Marnie.

"Has someone died?"

"No?"

"Well, don't sound so miserable then!" cried Maeve. Marnie could hear laughter in the background. *Sentinel Woman* was always such fun; the promised land of freebies and fabulous fashion, where happiness and handbags reigned supreme and everyone was coated in lashings of lipstick and loveliness.

"I've got some samples in the fashion cupboard for you to try."

The door to the promised land swung open. Then, as Marnie grabbed hold of her roll of tummy fat, it clanged shut again.

"But samples are size 8!" she cried. Her muffin top was developing a life of its own, bulging uninvited over her waistbands. If it got much bigger, it would require its own postcode. There was no way she'd get away with squidging it into a size 8.

"These samples are from a before and after weight-loss shoot, dah-ling," soothed Maeve. "You're the before dresses, no offence."

"None taken," said Marnie.

"I can throw in hair and make-up too, as you are representing the newspaper."

She was getting her own stylist! It was just like being a real celebrity.

"Well, in that case, I think it would be churlish not to go," said Marnie, with barely disguised over-excitement.

"You go, girl!" said Maeve. "Pop round later on this afternoon."

Bryher's chipped nails crept around the doorframe of Marnie's office.

Had she been there the whole time, the nosy cow?

"I forgot to give you this," she said, leaning over and slapping a yellow post-it note right in the middle of Marnie's computer screen.

"The reporter formerly known as Belle Devine rang you three times this morning but you were too busy blabbing about yourself on the radio," she said.

Belle! Oh my God. It was her birthday today and they were supposed to be going out for a drink tonight to celebrate!

Marnie had totally forgotten.

She'd have to ring her and explain about the awards thing cropping up. She'd just pop in to the Top Chick Awards for half an hour to show her face. She was representing *The Sentinel* as a top columnist now and Belle would be bound to understand if she was a bit delayed.

Bryher added, for good measure: "Oh, and someone on Twitter has some very interesting thoughts about your new column. Someone called Caveman. I think he described it as 'mediocre, sub-post feminist crap'."

Then, she turned on her heel to leave – Marnie's office was satisfyingly titchy.

Marnie sighed.

She would ring Belle in a minute but she'd just check Twitter first, to see what this Caveman bloke was saying about her.

"Blame the guys, Mrs Make Believe, your whining might take the feminist cause further #notverylikely."

A horde of manspreading morons had torn themselves away from their beer, football and Xboxes long enough to post some replies, which were rather unkind, to say the least.

Caveman added: "Do we open the door for you or will you slam it in our faces? #confusedandemasculated."

Marnie felt steam coming out of her ears.

She tweeted him: "The truth hurts Caveman. Grow up #patheticmale."

He tweeted her straight back: "You can dish it out but you can't take it #testosteronehater."

This was so juvenile!

It reminded her of a book she'd read when she was in her late teens and desperate to understand what made men tick.

What was it called, again?

Men are From Mars, Women Prefer Shopping?

No, that wasn't quite right.

Men Are From Mars, Women Are From Venus – that was it!

Blokes went into caves when they were in a bad mood and women went somewhere called "the well".

The injustice of that had always rankled and she'd even had a few arguments with Matt about that at university.

Why should men get a cool den, with bear-skins and fires and handprints on the walls and women get a dank hole in the ground? Furthermore, women could only get in and out of the hole via a bucket, tied to a piece of rope. Bitter experience had taught her she usually ended up hauling herself out of that well. Women were not supposed to follow men into their cave for fear of provoking them. Men were supposed to be like rubber bands, with an innate need to pull away and be alone for a while because they would always come back anyway.

Well, sod that. We'd all like some me-time!

She'd lost count of the times she'd followed Matt into his cave, wiped her muddy feet all over his bearskins and poured cold water on his fire.

She tweeted again: "Shouldn't you be lighting a fire in your cave? #neanderthalpeabrain."

He replied: "Go and sulk in your well, like a good girl #yourwhininggivesmeaheadache."

A-ha! So Caveman had read at least one book in his lifetime, which judging by his tweets, was a big achievement.

"You tore yourself away from the football long enough to read a book! #welldonesexistpig."

"You clearly haven't read it. Let men take charge. #getbacktothekitchensink."

How bloody dare he tweet her like that!

Marnie didn't have time to formulate a reply to Caveman's stupid last comment because Bryher's spiteful face reappeared: "Oh, and Barker says you are late with your copy. File it or die."

Marnie heard Bryher sniggering to herself as she stomped her way back down the corridor to the newsroom to shower scorn over some other poor, unfortunate journalist, no doubt.

Marnie glanced at the clock. There was no time to waste.

She removed the sticky note from her computer screen. Marnie still had half a page to fill for her *Mrs Make Believe* column and she needed to leave time for a decent blow-dry if she was going to look her best at the Top Chick Awards.

She kept getting distracted by thoughts of Caveman, the internet troll. Eventually, she imagined herself driving Caveman off the edge of a cliff with his spear to be rid of him.

Time was running out.

From the murky depths of her journalistic brain, there came a glimmer of hope.

There was one story she had yet to write about: Maddox Wolfe's impotence problem.

Plus, there was the bit where he slagged off his co-star, Byron Hunt.

It was a genuine exclusive and she still had the recording won by her half-wit brother to back it up.

Hmm, that was good. It would definitely make half a page. In fact, it could be her lead story. It really was top-notch gossip.

Just then, her conscience decided to dust off its boxing gloves and give the journalist in her an almighty thump, leaving her inner hack sagging on the ropes. Maddox was Mr Make Believe! He was her secret and most precious fantasy. She couldn't hurt him like this. Imagine what it would do to his pride.

Plus, there was a public interest aspect to all of this; women the world over would mourn the loss of his virility and be unable to have nice dreams about him, knowing that at the key moment, Maddox wouldn't actually be able to deliver what they so desperately needed.

She could shatter his image as a sexy, hunky, potent, thrusting hero with a stroke of her pen. It was a massive responsibility, finally holding that kind of power over the fantasy which had consumed so many of her thoughts.

The thrill of it sat in a knot in her stomach as she pondered her next move.

The phone rang.

It was Barker.

"Where the hell is your copy?"

She began to type.

Chapter Twenty-Three

Was there an unwritten rule on how to dress at a glam event?

As Marnie surveyed the gaggle of endless, bronzed limbs attached to perfect bodies, she decided the rule must go something like this:

- A clingy dress should always have stupidly thin spaghetti straps, making a bra an impossibility.
- A cocktail dress must be so short that at least a year's worth of daily gym work outs are required to wear it.
- An evening gown with plunging neckline should be matched by a dramatic thigh slash – do not attempt unless legs are like matchsticks, coated with Cuprinol.

Marnie had been fully upholstered by *Sentinel Woman* in an enormous body shaper, the colour of a sticking plaster, to suck in her fat, before being crammed into a black dress – "So slimming, dahling!" – giving her the most impressive bust she'd ever had.

The skirt was nice – quite full and swishy to disguise her chunky thighs – but next to the high-fashion mavens from the world of television, music and magazines, she felt like a total frump. Her hair had been tonged into ringlets, making her look like Shirley Temple's older, fatter sister.

Lots of people had made an effort to talk to her about the success of her column, though, which was very gratifying. Most did have an annoying habit of peering over the top of her head after about a minute, in search of someone more interesting, but it was her first personal invite to a glamorous occasion, so things would get easier, she was sure of that.

She was just racking her brain for some top gossip – no mean feat when your life is spent at home with two small kids – when a tray of cheese straws was wafted under her nose.

She picked one up. It looked delicious – excellent crumbly pastry. She raised it to her lips.

"You are not seriously thinking of eating that, are you?"

An immaculately dressed little pixie, with a sleek bob, appeared at her elbow.

"I'm Zoe, stylist to the stars," she said, thrusting her card into Marnie's hand and removing the cheese straw from her grasp.

"You are going places and I think you could use my help. But we have got to start with the diet. There is no point cramming in more calories than you need."

Marnie checked the stylist's feet. She wasn't wearing pointy, elven boots, but towering, chunky platforms, which must be twice this strange, ethereal creature's bodyweight. Her gloriously tanned legs protruded from sparkly hot-pants, quite at odds with the prim little blouse, complete with Peter Pan collar, she was wearing on her top half. It was not a look Marnie could pull off in a million years, but she had to admit it, Zoe did look rather good.

Zoe deposited the cheese straw onto the tray of a passing waiter, and seized two glasses of champagne, offering one to Marnie.

"But there are loads of calories in drink!"

"Not as many as canapés and, anyway, if you are missing meals you can afford to make up for it with a few bubbles, because they make you more interesting to chat to," said Zoe, with a grin. "How would you describe your signature look?"

"My what?"

"The key pieces in your wardrobe. What do they say about you?"

"Faded, baggy, several sizes larger than I would like?"

"No, no, no!" said Zoe. "You really do need my help. We have got to start to think about your image. Mrs Make Believe is approachable, but stylish and smart. She might even be a bit edgy at times. How do you feel about leather?"

"Very useful on a sofa, makes it easy to clean," said Marnie.

"I meant on you."

"Oh, desperate!" said Marnie. "I couldn't wear a leather skirt or trousers. It would be a crime against fashion."

Zoe looked her up and down, thoughtfully.

"OK, to be honest, in your current state, maybe not your best look. But skip a few lunches, lose half a stone and hey presto! You will look hot, I promise."

"Really?"

"I'll come and edit your wardrobe, just to show you what we can achieve, how about that?"

"That sounds very generous of you, I'm not sure I could..."

"Yes, of course you can. Now, get that down your neck, I think they have got some really interesting cocktails at the bar, before they start handing out the awards. I want to know more about what makes you tick."

Marnie did as she was told and felt herself starting to blush a bit from the drink. She felt warm inside, though, and more witty than she had in ages.

Zoe linked her little arm through Marnie's as they tottered to the bar together to meet Zoe's fashiony pals who all had silly names, sillier hair and a-mazing jobs in the industry.

✤   ✤   ✤

Zoe made sure she sat next to Marnie during the awards dinner. It consisted of a series of teensy portions: this was a fashion event, after all.

Marnie met hedge fund managers, bankers and artists who lived, not in houses, but in spaces, somewhere in the East End. It was a world away from her little life in Chiswick but everyone was terribly nice about her scribblings. The wine kept flowing and Zoe kept refilling her glass.

Marnie was working out why anyone would cover a perfectly decent chocolate cheesecake with salt and call it pudding – never mind, she would eat it anyway – when she heard someone call out her name.

A twiglet on the podium was signalling for her to come up, and the headlines from her Mrs Make Believe column were flashing up on a big screen at the back of the little stage.

"Top Chick Newcomer of the Year, for her out-there views on motherhood and marriage, telling it like it is, in the most in-your-face way imaginable – Marnie Martin!"

Marnie clung to the backs of chairs as she made her way to the stage. It was like being on an ocean liner, listing gently from side to side.

She made it to the twiglet, who appeared to be wearing a mini-dress made of tinfoil. Marnie steadied herself on the twiglet's arm, praying it wouldn't snap.

The twig handed her a statuette.

This was like the Oscars! It was all too much.

"Thank you, so much!" she said to a sea of expectant faces. "I'm so…shocked. Thank you, for liking Mrs Make Believe."

There were a few murmurs from the assembled guests and then people started talking, quite loudly, amongst themselves.

The twiglet spoke: "Thank you, Marnie. Obviously wittier in print than you are in person. Have a great night!"

Marnie was too drunk to care, clutching her little Top Chick Award, as she staggered back to the table.

❧ ❧ ❧

Clubbing wasn't really her thing but Marnie was thrilled to find, after a few cocktails, that she knew all the latest moves and was a big hit on the dance-floor at Funky Buddha or it could have been Luxx, she wasn't sure which one came first.

Some of the things Zoe said were hilarious – well, they probably were. It was hard to tell above the racket that passed for music but, anyway, she had such a thrillingly amusing evening, it made her feel totally up for anything.

Marnie was still bopping as Zoe poured her into a cab back to Chiswick. She had a bit of trouble getting the key in the front door, which appeared to be moving of its own accord. That made her laugh quite a lot as she bowled into the kitchen to find Dylan sipping tea at the dining table.

"Whassamarra?" said Marnie.

"Where the hell have you been!" said Dylan. "I've been worried sick!"

"I'm jush fine, I've been with Zoe and her homies. They are my new bee eff effs."

"Well, you could have called. I was worried about you," said Dylan, folding his arms across his chest and looking just like their father.

Marnie pulled a face.

"Belle rang quite a few times, she thought you were going out for her birthday," he said, quietly, stirring his tea.

Marnie's hands flew up to her face: "Oh, God! I'm sorreeee!"

"She was really looking forward to going out with you, but I guess you are going to be too busy with your new BFFs now. You can tell her yourself in the morning. I'm going to bed."

"Don't be like that," said Marnie, slapping him on the shoulder playfully with her award. Apparently, it was a touch too hard as the little plastic figurine detached itself from its plinth. "Oh, shit," said Marnie. "I've broken it."

"Yes," said Dylan, getting up to leave. "I'm sure you can glue it together in the morning."

Oh, don't be such a meanie," said Marnie. "I think you are jealoush of my…"

But she didn't finish the sentence because, at that point, Marnie threw up on the table and passed out on the floor.

⚜   ⚜   ⚜

Could her head hurt this much? Her mouth felt like the bottom of the hamster's cage. Marnie opened one eye and reached for the glass of water on the bedside table. Dylan must have put her to bed. God knows, she'd covered for his drunken antics more times than she'd care to remember when they were teenagers so he owed her, but this was still very sweet. He'd even left two paracetamol and a little note: "Don't worry, I have taken the kids to school, you old drunkard."

Oh, God. She'd really let Belle down as well as being too hungover even to do the school run. She was too old to be behaving like some feckless teenager.

She glanced around the bedroom. There was a mark on the wall where a picture of her and Matt used to hang. She'd have to redecorate.

Marnie picked up the phone to her best friend.

"Yes?" Belle answered, curtly.

"I'm so, so sorry," said Marnie. "I got outrageously pissed and forgot our date. It was this stylist, Zoe, she started talking to me and then I had drink after drink. I got in a real mess, I'm so sorry I forgot your birthday."

There was silence at the other end of the line.

Marnie started to cry: "I'm an obese, out of control, drunk columnist!"

Belle sighed: "Oh, stop the pity party. I forgive you. It's just I was so looking forward to our night out and Jonah was all ready for a boys' night in with Gabe, so it was a bit of a let down."

"I'll make it up to you."

"Don't be daft."

"I'll bake you a birthday cake."

"Please don't do that!" said Belle, rather too quickly. "We'll go out another time. Your story about Maddox Wolfe seems to have provoked a bit of a reaction, though."

"Has it?" Marnie had completely forgotten about that.

She checked Twitter and fought the urge to throw up. Caveman had gone and done it again. Marnie might have known he'd get the wrong end of the stick and try to beat her with it.

"Mrs Make Believe laughs at men with impotence #thatisjustcruel."

Twitter was alive with men calling for her to be sacked over her Mrs Make Believe column featuring Maddox Wolfe.

"Make a menopause joke and the sisterhood will chop your bollocks off #oneruleforthegirls."

But she hadn't been a laughing at Maddox Wolfe! She was just filling a space with valid gossip and it was quite interesting that even movie stars suffer from impotence problems, wasn't it?

Just because he was an A-lister (who she fancied) didn't mean he would get special treatment from Mrs Make Believe! She had her readers to think about now, and her image. She needed to pull in some top-notch gossip to justify the plaudits she was winning, didn't she?

Besides, Maddox had such broad shoulders. He could take it.

Heading off to work, still nursing the hangover from hell, she tweeted back to Caveman: "It was just a showbiz story #youaresounreasonable."

He didn't reply.

She'd obviously hit home with that tweet!

It was a relief when no-one looked at her as she made her way down Kensington High Street to the office. She turned up late and logged on to find her inbox overflowing. Emails from her readers should have come with a warning from Weightwatchers. Why couldn't she have a heartbreak diet like other women? Losing Matt had made her not only dejected, but chubbier than ever, and her fans and followers weren't helping.

She needed that layer of gooey stuff and cream, or chocolate sprinkles on the top, just to be able to digest some of the truly sorrowful tales of rejection and betrayal they told her day in, day out.

Marnie closed the email, sighed and pinned her hair back behind her ears, just as Bryher strutted in.

"There's someone important to see you in reception," she said, turning on her heel before Marnie could make further inquiries about the visitor. Marnie wasn't looking her best – not that it mattered – because the reader's tale of woe had made her cry quite a lot. She did up the waistband of her skirt as she stood up, before making her way to the lifts.

As she got out, she stopped dead in her tracks.

Standing there in the atrium of *The Sentinel*, glowering at her, was Maddox Wolfe. All 6ft of him. Like a movie poster. But breathing.

"Hello, Marnie," he said, stalking over and clasping her hand tightly – rather more tightly than she was comfortable with, actually.

"How do you know my name?" she gasped. The blood was rushing to her face.

"Picture byline," he said drily, as he towered over her.

Journalists and sub-editors in the work cafe stopped drinking their cups of tea and coffee and were nudging each other and murmuring. This was a newspaper and they were used to seeing minor celebrities, but a genuine film star was something else.

"What on earth are you doing here?" she said.

They started to walk together towards the escalator. She had no choice. He had his hand closed tightly around her wrist now and was almost pulling her in his wake.

When he spoke, his voice was slow and deliberate.

"I thought I would drop by and see how you were doing, seeing as you have been eavesdropping on some very private conversations of mine," he said, his eyes blazing as he turned to face her.

Marnie wanted to run and hide. But she couldn't. He had hold of her and he wasn't letting go.

"I did consider putting you over my knee in the middle of the office because, frankly, you need to learn some manners," he bent his head forward and spoke almost in a whisper. Marnie's mouth fell open in shock. She blushed bright red. He couldn't talk to her like that!

Maddox smirked. He was enjoying getting his own back. She had made him look like a bloody fool in front of the studio bosses.

"Yes, imagine the headlines, Marnie," he said, pausing for a second, for effect.

She was dumbstruck.

"But I decided it would be better to take you out to lunch and find out who in my camp has been spilling the beans."

"I always protect my sources," she squeaked, as he pulled her through the front doors of *The Sentinel* and into his waiting limo.

"Do you, now? We'll see about that."

And he slammed the door shut, trapping her inside.

❧   ❧   ❧

People stopped talking in hushed tones and stared as Maddox Wolfe led a curvaceous woman, who was definitely not his wife Cecily Haywood, to a table and ordered her to sit down. Then they remembered they were dining in Claridges and pretended to talk to each other again, straining to hear what the movie star and this woman were saying.

A waiter, with slicked back hair and a fawning smile, appeared with the wine list.

"I don't really drink at lunch," said Marnie, who was only just getting over her hangover from the Top Chick Awards.

"She'll have champagne," said Maddox, in a voice that suggested he was not to be argued with.

"You can't force me," said Marnie, who was feeling rather flustered. Whatever was he going to do next? Spoon feed her? And why, oh why had she worn this stupid too-tight blouse this morning? She could have recycled the wrap dress. It only had a few grubby children-related stains on it. But no, she had plumped for the sheer number, which used to look quite prim before kids but now looked almost indecent with the buttons straining to contain her bust.

"Just have a drink and don't be silly," said Maddox, his face softening. "I'm taking you out for a lovely lunch. You might even enjoy it."

And he winked at her. Was that a funny, fluttery feeling in her stomach? He was supposed to be mad at her, so why was he smiling now?

"But I might get drunk and giggly. It doesn't take much, you know," she protested.

"Good," he said, "I am hoping to loosen your tongue, one way or another."

What other way? This was going to an excruciatingly long lunch. Couldn't they just call a truce? She glanced around at the other diners, who seem to ooze luxury, perched on their purple velvet-backed chairs, chatting as they took teeny mouthfuls of their very expensive meals.

Maddox was watching her intently. There was something about the way he looked at her that made her feel almost naked.

The waiter arrived with their drinks. She took rather a large glug. Dutch courage.

"I can't possibly tell you how I found out about your, your personal problem," she said, unable to look him in the eye and fumbling with her heavy white napkin, which was almost as big as a tablecloth itself. She couldn't bring herself to say it to his face: erectile dysfunction. For some reason, she pictured a deflated elephant, flopping about in the corner of the room. It was quite disturbing.

"Someone might lose their job. I couldn't have that on my conscience," she said.

"I see," said Maddox, sipping slowly, "but what about me losing my dignity? Did you stop to think about that for a millisecond? Never mind losing my job for criticising my co-star."

"You haven't, have you?" she gasped. "I'm so sorry."

"No. I haven't lost my job. Only because I am a big enough name to still throw my weight around," he said. "Just. But as for my dignity..."

"I am so sorry. I could write a really positive piece about men dealing with, erm, that sort of problem? Sometimes just brazening it out is the best way to stop the gossip," she ventured. This was like trying to extinguish the Great Fire of London with a watering can and she knew it, but it was worth a try. Needs must.

Maddox didn't bother to respond but gave her the most withering look. She was frozen to the spot, unable to say anything to make him feel better about what she had done. This just wasn't right! Mr Make Believe would never dream of making her feel this way. He would be kind and understanding, reach over, stroke her face and whisper his forgiveness.

Maddox sat, those broad shoulders hunched, like some brooding giant. His anger was room-filling, one hundred per cent red-blooded male and it was not very nice to be around. Mercifully, the fawning waiter reappeared and hovered expectantly at Marnie's side, pen poised.

She was so nervous, she took another large sip of champagne and felt the bubbles exploding on her tongue. She was too miserable to enjoy it. Marnie glanced down at the menu. It didn't appear to have any prices on it.

She was terrified of asking for something too expensive in case Maddox thought she had done it deliberately, given that he was paying. The memory of Matt going through her weekly shopping list and questioning her inability to make economies was still fresh in her mind.

"I'll just have a salad please," she said. She had been meaning to start her diet. There was no time like the present. Lettuce was bound to be reasonably cheap, even somewhere jaw-droppingly expensive like this.

Maddox flicked his eyes upwards and sighed audibly. It was bad enough with Cecily fussing about her figure morning, noon and night. He would be damned if he was going to let this beautiful, curvy, sexy example of a woman starve herself too.

"Vegetarian?" he asked.

"No."

"That's the most sensible thing you have said to me all day," he said. He turned to the waiter: "We'll both have oysters to start, followed by the steak."

He looked at Marnie and said menacingly: "Make it bloody."

She shifted uncomfortably. He looked furious again.

"It disturbs me that you were able to find out about my falling out with my co-star, as well as my ... personal health issues," the first signs of a blush were creeping up above his collar, and he had two tell-tale circles of pink on the apples of each cheek, which were a dead giveaway of his discomfort, try as he might to contain it.

He ploughed on, regardless – years of acting training taught him to keep going and the blush would subside: "If you had bothered to try to speak to me in person ... "

"You'd never have taken my call!" she scoffed, determined to put up some kind of a fight.

"And how do you know that?" he said, gently, flicking her one of his lady-killer looks. "I'm enjoying speaking to you now. I might well have spoken to you, especially once I'd looked up your picture online. There's a nice one of you on Facebook too."

Oh, mortifying. He was pretending to like her and she couldn't stop herself going all squishy.

"I might have called round to the office in person and been rather less cross, for a start," he said.

It was an Oscar-winning performance designed to get the groin vote and persuade her to spill the beans. But he was finding it surprisingly easy. Those breasts looked very tempting. What would she be like in bed?

Marnie was blushing like a schoolgirl. She glanced around the room. All the lonely evenings she had spent in front of the telly while Matt worked late. All the Maddox Wolfe films she'd been rather pleased to watch on her own; especially the Seb Winter ones, when his shirt got shredded and his face was covered in sweat and grime. That usually meant a shower scene and a peek of his backside. Swoon.

And there he was in front of her now. It was all too much. She mustn't let on that she was his biggest fan ever. Ever.

"Ok. Apology accepted. Almost. I still really think you owe it to me to come clean about your source," he said, turning his big, dark blue eyes on her.

She was a rabbit caught in the headlights.

Her brother Dylan was a royal pain in the bum but he didn't deserve to lose his job. She was the one who had written the story. She was trying to justify her humungous salary from *The Sentinel* by writing top-notch gossip, not upset Maddox.

"No, no I can't, I'm sorry," she said, looking downcast.

"Can't blame me for trying," he said, with a resigned sigh. "Give me your mobile."

He held out a hand.

"What for?"

"I'm going to give you my number so that next time, there are absolutely no excuses. And if you cross me again, I really will give you that hiding."

Marnie pressed her legs together. She could feel herself getting turned on by the very thought and willed her traitorous body to stop it. It was like *Harsh Winter*, only better.

Maddox was oblivious to the scenes being played out in her mind and smiled as he punched his number into her contacts list and spotted her screen saver of the kids grinning on a day out at the park.

"Are these your little monkeys?"

"Yes," she said whilst thinking, please don't ask about my husband or I will cry.

"Handsome boys. What does your husband do?"

Maddox obviously wasn't one of her regular readers then.

"We've separated, actually," she said, studying her knife and fork closely.

He swallowed hard. "I'm sorry. What happened?"

Oh, Christ. Where to start? She couldn't bore him with the whole story. And she didn't want him siding with Matt about the baby thing because she might be tempted to thump him, even if he was an A-list film star.

"We had some issues, went to counselling, he snogged his long-lost girlfriend from Australia, quite unreasonably. End of. End of marriage, actually."

She added rather too quickly, in an attempt to salve her battered ego. "But I threw him out first, anyway. So I suppose I finished it."

"Oh dear," said Maddox. "That sounds complicated. What a silly boy. But not irrevocable. He will get bored and come home." He made it sound so easy, so simple to resolve. And how come he was interested in her emotional life in any case? He was probably just looking for ammunition, to get his own back on her for the impotence story. Marnie cleared her throat and did her damnedest to focus and behave like a proper journalist. After about ten seconds, she realised that this was not going to work. Maddox Wolfe was just too gorgeous. He could recite the alphabet backwards, over and over, and she would still being hanging on to every word he said, gazing into those blue eyes and thinking about... Oh, stop it!

"And what if I don't t want him home?" People stopped eating and looked at her. She had cranked up the volume without meaning to. "I mean," she said in a whisper, "what if I am not going to forgive him?"

"You are angry with him, which means you still love him," said Maddox, stage-whispering back and taking a sip of his drink. "In my experience, people fall in and out of love in marriage. They might have affairs, they might just dream about having affairs. If you still love him – and I think you do – there is still hope."

"I'm not sure I even like him," said Marnie. "And, anyway, he booked a very expensive hotel suite on a work night out, without me."

"Did he?" said Maddox, raising an eyebrow. "What for?"

Marnie hesitated. She wasn't going to give him the full tragic details about Georgina the Courtroom Cutie. It was too demeaning.

"He says it was just a work party after he won an award. I'm not sure whether to believe him."

"It sounds like he got carried away with his ego, but remember, Marnie, he has you at home and I doubt he would have wanted to jeopardise that. I know I wouldn't." He flicked her a little smile.

"*Had* me," said Marnie, pursing her lips, as her insides did somersaults. "More fool me. I caught him looking at internet porn as well. I happen to think he is just a sexist pig."

Maddox stifled a laugh.

"Oh, come on, that's a bit hard on him. Men just, well, do that kind of thing sometimes. It doesn't mean anything. Women can find that stuff entertaining too." Some of the best sex he and Cecily ever had was with a blue movie playing in the background, so he could speak from experience, but he wasn't going to reveal the full details to Marnie. She'd probably put a headline on it.

Marnie shot him a withering glance. He really was just a towering hunk of machismo, like Seb Winter, hell-bent on dominating women. She had thoroughly enjoyed reading about Seb's exploits, of course, and watching Maddox in that role, but that was not the point.

Maddox continued: "But even if there are periods when you can't be together, it doesn't necessarily mean your marriage is over."

"Doesn't it?" she said, examining the tablecloth even more closely, and tracing a few breadcrumbs around with her fingers. "He hasn't made any effort to even contact his sons."

"That's odd," said Maddox. "Maybe he's afraid to make the first move?"

It was a bit like listening to Cecily but she was a proper ball-breaker compared to this specimen, who was not relishing the crisis.

Cecily. Now there was a complex problem he had yet to solve. He probably never would. It just so happened she was playing away at the moment. The flirty texts he had found on her phone from that little shit Byron Hunt had confirmed his suspicions that he was sleeping with his wife.

And that was before he got on to Cecily's demands for another child. Marnie would probably side with his bloody wife. You know what women are like. This one was clearly having a sisterhood moment. Better leave it at that.

When it was time for them to leave, Maddox picked up the bill. He placed one hand gently but firmly on Marnie's waist as he kissed her on the cheek, pretending not to notice as she coloured up. With any other lunch date, he would have congratulated himself, safe in the knowledge that he hadn't lost his touch. Feeling the warmth of her body through her dress, there was something else, which took him by surprise. He almost found it hard to pull away from her.

On her return to the office, Marnie found herself coyly batting away questions from the reporters about her lunch with a film star.

"Come on," said Harry Hedgeson. "Give us some dirt at least! Are you going out for dinner next time?"

"There really is nothing to say," she said, smiling to herself. "He was the perfect gentleman. I just put him right on a few things to do with my story about him, that's all."

As she took the tube home that evening, she kept replaying their conversation in her head and stopping at the bits when he appeared to have flirted with her. She could be imagining it but when they said goodbye, he had actually seemed a bit disappointed to see her go. Had that been real, or was it just make believe?

Chapter Twenty-Four

Two blue lines on the test!

This was the best news since her agent told her she didn't look a day over 35 – and that was in daylight with minimal make-up.

Cecily Haywood skipped around her spotless kitchen, avoiding the housekeeper, who was having a second go at mopping the floor after she had pointed out a few smear marks on the wet tiles.

She couldn't wait to tell him the joyful news. He needed to be the first to know.

"Dr Tolko? Yes, it's Cecily Haywood. I'm pregnant! I know – really quick wasn't it? Only eight months to go before I get to try your new Baby Facial. I can hardly wait!"

Now, with that matter resolved, it was on to the next thing on her little to-do list. Byron had been bombarding her with flirty texts. It was best to take action quick, before she started showing. She quite fancied a trip to Shilling Hall Hotel and Spa for one of those lovely warm mud massages – for two. If she asked him really nicely, he might even screw her in character.

⚜ ⚜ ⚜

Zoe, the stylist, was determined to be Marnie's new BFF.

She wafted into Marnie's little kitchen with armfuls of clothes, which she laid on the table with great reverence.

"Now, Marnie," she said with a steely glare, looking her up and down, "you must let me do my job. You are badly in need of a make-over."

"Of course," said Marnie, pulling her stripy T-shirt down to cover the coffee stain on her jeans. "You know best, Zoe."

"Once we have cleared out your rubbish – sorry, clothes – we can have a look at these lovely things I've got for you to consider, from One boutique in Notting Hill."

"OK," said Marnie, but Zoe was already off, marching up the stairs to find her wardrobe.

She flung open the doors and started to pull dresses, skirts, tops and blouses off their hangers, chucking them into a pile on the bed.

"Do you have any bin-bags?"

"Yes," said Marnie, who was starting to lose enthusiasm for this editing exercise. Would Zoe let her keep anything?

She returned to find Zoe had created three piles of things on the bed.

"This is to throw away, what the hell possessed you in the first place?" she said pointing to the biggest pile, which appeared to have most of her day-to-day clothes in it. "These are possible keepers, but frankly you could do better," she said, gesticulating towards the middle-sized pile. "And this," she said, holding up a couple of designer frocks from her pre-baby days, "is the well-done pile. You can keep them."

"But they don't fit!" said Marnie.

"Yet," said Zoe darkly. "You need to think about skipping a few meals, or at least going to the gym a bit more. Fashion is not about feasting. Fabulous doesn't mind if it is hungry. Make that your mantra. How many fat supermodels do you know, Marnie?"

"I don't want to be a supermodel."

"Fair enough, but you need to at least be slim enough to try to wear something on-trend," said Zoe, holding up a handful of printed smocks. "Are these your pregnancy wear?"

Marnie winced. "They are my day-wear, mostly."

"Not any more," said Zoe, tossing them into the black plastic bag.

Zoe picked up a silk blouse from the "possible keepers" pile on the bed. It was fraying at the seams, probably too small, and several buttons had come off, but she loved that blouse because she had worn it in the Maldives with Matt, nearly ten years ago.

"I think we should bin this," said Zoe.

"No!" screamed Marnie, lunging forward and grabbing the blouse.

Zoe held on to it, with a grip that was surprisingly vice-like, for an elf.

"Let it go, Marnie," she said, through gritted teeth.

"I can't," said Marnie, pulling quite hard. They were so carefree then. Her heart fluttered, as she remembered walking barefoot with Matt to the restaurant, right on the beach of their little island, wearing that blouse and a linen skirt. They'd chatted about having kids, their dreams for their life together and how happy they'd be.

She would be damned if she was going to let go of that blouse. She realised, with astonishment, she wasn't ready to let go of those dreams either.

There was a ripping sound as the sleeve came away in Marnie's hand.

"OK, you win," said Zoe, coldly, throwing the rest of the blouse at her. "But you will have to mend it."

Marnie held the torn garment, feeling the softness of

the silk between her fingers. How could she even begin to explain what it meant to her?

But Zoe wasn't remotely interested.

"I'll bring some of the best designer dresses from One upstairs for you try as a reward for parting with so many things," she said, tying the top of the bin-bag.

"Will you be able to pay me cash for my help today?" Zoe shouted over her shoulder, as she left the room. "Three hundred quid should cover it and we can discuss payment for the One frocks after that."

❧ ❧ ❧

Belle called around with Gabriel just in time to catch sight of Zoe as she departed down the garden path, a bin-bag slung over her shoulder.

"Off you go, back to Rivendell," muttered Belle under her breath. She still hadn't forgiven Zoe for leading her best friend astray on the night of the Top Chick Awards.

Marnie opened the door, wearing one of her new dresses from the long-awaited wardrobe edit.

"What do you think?" she said, giving Belle a self-conscious little twirl.

"It's very…colourful," said Belle, hoping the obvious pause hadn't been too tactless.

The frock featured enormous stripes in neon pink, yellow and orange. They made Marnie look like a fairground attraction.

"Oh, God," said Marnie. "It's hideous, isn't it?"

"I've seen better," said Belle, taking Gabriel out of his baby sling and strapping him into Charlie's stained old bouncy chair. His Babygro was covered in his lunch – which Marnie regarded as progress. At least Belle had stopped changing his outfit for every speck of dirt, which made parenting a lot less stressful.

Charlie and Rufus were chasing each other around the kitchen island and Dylan had the laundry basket on his head, pretending to be a Dalek. He took it off, took one look at Marnie, and burst out laughing.

"Sofaland," he said, matter-of-factly. "Exactly the same pattern as your dress. I saw it on the adverts yesterday, after *ChitChat*. They're selling them off, clearance, I think."

"I've spent £500 quid on a dress that makes me look like a sofa!" wailed Marnie.

"Maybe not a sofa," said Dylan, with a grin, "more like one of those big armchairs, you know, for two people."

"Never mind," said Belle, steering Marnie out of the kitchen and away from Dylan's hurtful comments. "Why don't you show me the edited wardrobe? Did you get anything else?"

Marnie swallowed hard: "Yes."

Like a condemned woman, she climbed the stairs to the bedroom and pulled open the wardrobe doors.

"There's hardly anything in it!" said Belle. "Where have all your clothes gone?"

A skirt suit, a couple of blouses, a pair of trousers and one pair of jeans hung rather forlornly in the wardrobe. Plus some designer dresses in a size 10 and a lovely printed sun-dress – at least Zoe hadn't chucked that out.

"Zoe binned most of them," said Marnie, staring at the floor. She brightened: "I have managed to save some stuff, though, because it was in the laundry and she didn't look in there."

Belle bit her lip to stop her true feelings about the stylist from spilling out.

Marnie's "new image" seemed to consist of the sofa dress and a worrying pair of shorts. Leather shorts. They were horrid, shiny and very short. Belle held them up.

"What on earth are these?"

"They are my on-trend piece. I'm supposed to look edgy," said Marnie.

"I think you might look insane if you go out in these," said Belle.

Marnie was a bit crestfallen.

"Sorry," said Belle, "it's just, as your friend, I don't think these will suit you. Can you take them back?"

"I don't think so," said Marnie. "Zoe said the shop only did credit notes for very exceptional customers. She's already told me I am not yet a VEC."

"Can't she sprinkle some fairy dust and magic your old wardrobe back?" said Belle, with a little grin.

Marnie burst out laughing but she really wanted to cry. She'd spent over £1,000 on the most awful dress and ridiculous pair of shorts, and all because she felt insecure about the way she looked.

"Marnie, I love the way you dress. As long as you are comfortable, who gives a stuff what anyone else thinks?" said Belle.

"It's just because of *Mrs Make Believe*," said Marnie, twiddling with her hair. "I thought I should try and look the part."

"What part? The column is about your life. It's you people love, not some Zoe-bot."

Marnie knew it, deep down, but didn't say it. The only person she wanted to look good for, who didn't used to mind that she was fat, because he loved her, was Matt. And now he was too busy looking at someone else.

Her phone rang.

It was Barker.

"There's good news and there's bad news," he said. "No, hang on, thinking about it, there's bad news and there's bad news. Which would you like first?"

"I'll have the bad news, please," said Marnie, grimacing at Belle.

"I need you to do an interview with Athena Maldon, to make up for us ditching her *Living the Dream* column."

"But you know she can't stand me and now she probably hates my guts more than ever!"

"Which is why you are going to do a lovely puff piece about the new kids' clothing line she's planning to set up."

"Backed by her sugar daddy, of course," added Marnie.

"You see, your attitude is all wrong," said Barker. "It's because she is a multi-talented actress and home-maker and now a budding fashion designer that we are giving her a double page spread and you, as our star columnist and mother, will write about how bloody brilliant she is."

"As well as the fact that her boyfriend owns the paper," said Marnie.

"I'll ignore that comment. You will get a free trip to the South of France out of it, because she is busy schmoozing with Shustrov down in Cannes. I think you should show a bit more enthusiasm, or I might have to send someone else."

Cannes! How exciting. She was actually getting sent off on a foreign expedition.

Marnie back pedalled: "OK, I'm sorry, I am really keen and I will be really nice to Athena, I promise. So what's the other bad news?"

"Rumour has it that they're planning to make another Seb Winter spy film based on the latest book, *Harsh Winter*, which is apparently the steamiest one to date. Are you familiar with it?"

"Erm, no, yes, well, perhaps – I think I have heard of it," said Marnie, blushing to her greying roots. She hadn't had time to read much of it lately, so that was almost true.

"My wife can't put it down, can't think why," said Barker. "Anyway, as you are in Cannes, why don't you try and get alongside Maddox Wolfe and see if you can pick up some gossip about it. I'd like to have an exclusive along the lines of 'Why I'm still fit enough at 50 to play sexy superspy Seb'. It might help him get over that piece you wrote about him the other day."

"But he doesn't like me very much," whispered Marnie, her insides churning at the thought of having to doorstep Maddox or even, in fact, see him again after their lunch.

"I am not running a bloody helpline, Marnie. Get on it. Exclusives not excuses."

And he hung up.

CHAPTER TWENTY-FIVE

The warm breeze ruffled the palm trees along La Croisette as women glided along, with their hair slicked into neat chignons, a lap dog peeking out here and there from a designer handbag.

It was only May but their limbs were effortlessly bronzed. They were dressed in crisp linens or little shirt dresses, belted at the waist, feet shod in wedge espadrilles, tied to emphasise their slim ankles.

All except for one woman: puce in the midday heat, squished into her only remaining skirt suit, scurrying like a mad thing to find the Martinez Hotel. Marnie hurried past the red carpet of the Palais des Festivals where, later on, a host of A-listers would tread lightly in their impossibly high heels, smiling and posing for a wall of camera lenses from around the world, in jaw-droppingly beautiful dresses.

She wanted to enjoy the moment, the thrill of being here at the Cannes Film Festival. She really did, but she felt guilty about leaving Dylan with the kids and she was dreading her interview with Athena.

The Art Deco facade of the Martinez hotel lay before her, just as her feet began to blister. She had a pair of sandals back at the hotel but they'd seen a few summers and were rather tatty so thought it best to dress up in her best court shoes. She looked like a stuffed sausage in her black jacket and light wool skirt, straining at the waistband, but her feet did look smart – although, totally wrong for the country and the climate.

Marnie had sweat trickling down her armpits as she stepped into the hotel lobby, all marble, muted tones and clean lines, feeling the air conditioning envelope her in the most delicious breeze.

"You're late," said a tall, thin woman with cropped blonde hair and dazzling white teeth. She stretched out a hand, fingers bedecked with chunky rings: "I'm Donna, assistant to Miss Maldon."

Marnie followed her to the lifts, which took them to the penthouse suite on the seventh floor, down dizzying corridors with black and white tiled floors and striped walls. It was enough to induce a migraine. Donna only spoke just before she opened the door with her swipe card: "Miss Maldon cannot abide lateness."

And she fairly shoved her inside.

Athena was perched on the taupe, square sofa.

A vast round glass coffee table lay between her and Marnie, who was obviously supposed to sit on the very low pouffe positioned opposite Athena, but about six feet away.

It was a good job Marnie wasn't hard of hearing.

Athena's eyes were concealed behind the most enormous designer shades, mirrored ones, so that all Marnie could see was her own reflection, which was even more flustered than she had feared.

Athena leaned forward, her small breasts jiggling slightly in her teal silk halter-neck jumpsuit, and very slowly picked up the glass of iced water in front of her.

"Hot outside, isn't it?" said Athena, swallowing slowly.

There was no glass set out for Marnie.

"Water," said Athena, glancing over the top of her sunglasses, "not gin, in case you were wondering."

"I wasn't wondering, honestly," said Marnie. Should she mention the Boozy Britain article? Athena was obviously still seething. It hadn't been meant in a personal way. She just happened to be the most trollied celeb snapped that week, falling out of a nightclub, clutching a bottle of spirits.

Marnie cleared her throat.

"I want to apologise for anything I have written that might have upset you," she said, heart thumping ten to the dozen. She had only been doing her job! The Picture Editor had suggested it. But it was pointless trying to explain that to Athena. It was better to just say sorry.

"If I caused you any grief…"

"Caused me any grief!" Athena shrieked, tearing off her sunglasses. "Oh no, how could an article in a best-selling newspaper, seen by millions on the internet, have affected ME in any way?"

Her eyes were shark-like as they appraised Marnie, who was squirming on her pouffe and wringing her hands.

Athena stood up and began to strut about, spindly Jimmy Choo heels doing God knows what damage to the highly-polished wood floor, the silk of her jumpsuit clinging to her perky posterior. Her beautifully tanned back made Marnie feel as attractive as a lump of lard.

"You have my permission to make up the quotes for the feature about my new clothing line, just send them over to Donna for copy approval, I am bored by this interview. I am bored by you," said Athena, with a wave of her hand.

"Oh, thank you," Marnie gasped, gratefully accepting this insult and feeling she had been spared the guillotine. She rose to leave.

"But I haven't finished yet, so make yourself comfortable," said Athena, gazing out to the sea through the floor-to-ceiling windows.

Marnie sat back down.

"In fact, I really ought to thank you for ruining my career, because that is what you did, Marnie. Without falling so low I wouldn't have picked myself back up again. I was really beginning to find myself as a writer and a mother with my *Living the Dream* blog and column. But, once again, you managed to ruin that, just as I was beginning to get some recognition, didn't you?"

"I didn't set out to do that, I was just writing about my rubbish life and *Mrs Make Believe* seemed to strike a chord with real women."

Athena span round and picked up a glass paperweight in the shape of the globe from the marquetry inlay sideboard, which was stuffed with bouquets of sunflowers.

"Yes, your rubbish life. Are you suggesting for a minute that my column wasn't liked by the readers?"

"No, no, of course not. It was definitely really … good."

Marnie hoped that her pause wouldn't be taken as an insult. She was just struggling to find the right words to describe *Living the Dream*.

"Well, I can't understand why anyone would prefer to read about your life instead of mine but Vladi – that's Mr Shushtrov to you – said I'm not allowed to question those kind of commercial decisions."

"Well, that's a relief," said Marnie, before she could stop herself.

"You may think so," said Athena. "But luckily, I have persuaded my darling Vladi to allow me a little editorial input from time to time."

Athena sat back down and started to pass the globe from one hand to another.

"I can't have your job, Marnie, but I still own your considerably large ass," she said, with a cackle. "Especially since Vladimir is making me Head of Content for *Sentinel Woman*."

Marnie fought the urge to gag. Her throat was parched with fear. Athena had an editorial role! Barker hadn't mentioned that. She wondered if he even knew about it. With the Russian in charge, anything was possible. Marnie wanted to flee but she couldn't. She put her head down and pretended to make notes.

"Yes, you'd better make a note of it," said Athena. "You aren't about to cry are you?"

Marnie did not speak, but started to examine her shiny shoes. The mantra "utter cow" was running through her head.

"I've already emailed your News Editor with my first idea. It's a fashion feature," her lip was curling, "about big knickers. Sort of thing you wear, I imagine."

"Not really," said Marnie. She was not going to give away her underwear choices to this bitch.

"Well you're going to have to start," said Athena. "Mrs Make Believe is going to road test big pants. Double page spread, featuring lots and lots of lovely pictures of you wearing... not very much. It could be quite embarrassing. I hope. You might be Mrs Make Believe but I'm still pulling the strings. Let's see how you like living in my world, Marnie."

Marnie emitted a small squeak of anguish, like a mouse that had just been speared by one of Athena's five-inch heels.

Athena snarled: "Now, get out. And if I ever lay eyes on you again in person, you're fired."

❧ ❧ ❧

Marnie sloped back to her hotel and tore off her stupid suit. She lay on the bed, allowing the cooling air conditioning to waft over her. Athena was probably just making idle threats. If she really was Head of Content for *Sentinel Woman* Barker would have mentioned it before, surely?

Her phone buzzed with an incoming text from the devil himself: "Get me some gossip on Seb Winter movie, soonest."

The more immediate problem was how on earth she was going to get an exclusive out of Maddox Wolfe. Scrolling through her contacts, his number was there, where he had keyed it in the other day in the restaurant.

Her hands shaking, she typed out a text to him: "Hi, it's Marnie. I'm in Cannes for work. Might you be around for a quick chat?"

To her amazement she received an instant reply: "Sure! Come along to the Quatre Hotel party later, we can have a catch up. Maddox."

She checked Twitter and discovered that the Quatre Hotel party was the pop-up event of the film festival. There were pictures all over Instagram of models, actresses and whatevers in a never-ending round of jaw-droppingly beautiful floor-length designer gowns getting caught in the revolving doors of the hippest hotel in town. After a refreshing shower, a spritz of her favourite perfume and a slick of lipstick, she pulled on her best sun dress. It had a fifties-style nipped in waist and full skirt which hid a multitude of sins. She glanced at herself in the mirror and was pleasantly surprised to see a reasonably pulled-together woman in her early forties looking back at her. "I can do this," she said to her reflection.

A gaggle of scantily clad girls and gorgeous blokes were already fuelled by killer cocktails and groping each other on the banquettes in reception by the time she arrived at the hotel. She was about to mingle her way through into the party when her path was blocked by a spiky blonde brandishing a clipboard, who towered at least two feet above her head.

"I know for a fact your name is not on the guest list," said Donna, assistant to Athena Maldon. "This party is paid for by Mr Shushtrov and Miss Maldon does not wish to have your personage on the premises."

"Might I just pop in for a little bit?" she whispered, in the hope that the growing queue of guests waiting to get in behind her wouldn't hear.

"Look, darling," said Donna, putting her hand on her scrawny hip, rings lining up like a knuckle duster. "She doesn't like you, so best scram before her bodyguards find out you are here."

"Please," said Marnie. "I just need to get a teeny bit of gossip." She made to take some money out of her purse.

"No!" said Donna, pointing to Marnie's frock. "And, anyway, this isn't the Boden family carnival. Look around you. You're totally outclassed, darling."

It was worse than not being cool enough to get into the youth club at school. She had to do the walk of shame the length of the queue, past designer suits, slinky sheath dresses, up-dos, swishy tresses – every last one of them laughing at her.

Her phone rang.

It was Barker.

"I don't give a shit about you having the wrong outfit!" he screamed. "Get your arse back in there and get me some gossip. Shin up a drainpipe. Use your initiative. You are supposed to be our top columnist, for fuck's sake."

And he hung up.

Marnie sat down in the alleyway at the side of the Quatre Hotel, which despite being a boutique establishment, still smelt of garbage rotting in the heat. There was a drainpipe. Could she shin up it?

She smoothed her hands over the folds of her printed halter-neck sundress. It was her favourite; so many happy days in the sun with Matt and the kids before ... before this. It had looked quite nice in the late afternoon when she left the hotel but now, in the evening, with everyone else making such an effort, she looked about as sophisticated as a Kiss Me Quick hat. And that was before she got on to her little Hobbit feet. She hadn't had time for a proper pedicure so had done her best with the nail varnish but, frankly, one of her boys could have done better.

She stood up and turned to go but was held back by someone who grabbed her by the arm. She span around and came face to face with Maddox Wolfe, dressed, dashingly, in a black dinner jacket. His crisp, white shirt, fastened at the neck by a bow tie, framed his tanned face, his hair greying at the temples. He was so handsome, Marnie nearly fainted.

"Leaving so soon?" he said, staring straight into her eyes, which started to fill with tears.

"Please," she said. "Please, let me go."

"Hey, I'm sorry," he said. "I didn't mean to upset you. I was rather hoping you'd come and have a drink with me. Can't stand these bashes."

He untied the bow tie and undid the top button of his shirt, making him look even more raffish: "I've just sneaked out of the back door."

"I ... I can't get in," said Marnie, miserably. "In fact, I am banned."

"Oh dear, have you been writing nasty things in that column of yours again?" he smiled.

"No … yes … I don't know," she mumbled.

"Come on," said Maddox, leading her gently by the arm to his waiting limo, "Let me take you somewhere for a quiet drink and then you can tell me all about it."

She gave him a weak smile.

"You look lovely in that dress," he added.

She floated into the car.

⚜ ⚜ ⚜

The scent of lavender filled the evening air as she stepped out of the limo at Maddox Wolfe's villa, overlooking the bay of Cannes. Water gushed from a terracotta wall fountain in the shape of a woman's head and cicadas were still busy chirruping away in the lush gardens, which bordered the most beautiful infinity swimming pool that Marnie had ever seen, with loungers that probably cost as much as her family car. What on earth was she even doing here?

Maddox held the heavy front door open for her and they stepped inside, footsteps echoing on the marble floor.

"You've been very kind bringing me here, Maddox, but it's getting late and I'm sure your wife will be back soon and be tired after the party," said Marnie who, in her misery, had almost forgotten that Maddox Wolfe was very much married to the gorgeous Cecily Hayward.

"She's screwing Byron Hunt, so no, I don't think she will mind," said Maddox, matter-of-factly.

"Oh, I'm so sorry … I didn't mean to … " There was an exclusive. But she couldn't betray him by writing about it. He looked totally crestfallen.

"It's a hazard of the profession, Marnie," said Maddox, chewing his lip. "I will probably bump into her at some point but she's pretending to be in the States. I know she's at his villa down in St Tropez."

"How do you know?"

"Word gets around," he said, drily. "Now, we have more important matters to attend to than the state of my marriage. When's your deadline?"

"About half an hour," she said, glancing at her watch. She was done for. "My bosses want me to write something about the new Seb Winter film, *Harsh Winter*," she said, miserably.

"Do they? Well, I couldn't possibly comment on the fact that I may have been approached to play Seb Winter in the new film but I'm sure I could have told my friends that," he said, as he led her into the drawing room with the most enormous cream sofas and cushions arranged so neatly that Marnie did not dare to sit.

"Oooh, that's perfect gossip!" she cried, almost dislodging a crystal vase from the sideboard as she swung her handbag around to get at her notebook.

Marnie started to make notes.

"Of course there are younger actors such as Byron Hunt in the frame but they lack my experience, at least, that is what sources close to me would say."

Marnie nodded.

"But what about your fitness regime?"

"I box three times a week and have a personal trainer putting me through my paces. I've also taken up Pilates recently – I was persuaded to do that by some Premier League footballers who are friends of mine."

"But what about the sex scenes?" said Marnie, feeling the beginnings of a blush. "Isn't the plot a bit raunchy, even for Seb Winter?"

"Oh, I'm sure I'm up to the challenge, in fact I would relish it," he said, smiling at her in a way that made her go weak at the knees.

"Brilliant!" said Marnie. Yes, just enough titillation for a family newspaper, without crossing the line into all-out smut. She was saved! "Could I just borrow your computer for a minute?"

"Through there," he pointed to a large room on the right. "I'll fix us some drinks."

❧ ❧ ❧

It was just a little peek at his email inbox. She shouldn't, really shouldn't, but it was there and she had filed her story so it couldn't hurt, could it? Besides, she had already perfected the art of snooping at Dr Tolko's clinic. It was becoming quite a habit.

Marnie called up his last email from Cecily.

Was he really telling the truth about her shagging Byron Hunt?

Maddox darling,

I'm planning to stay over here in LA for a bit longer, having such fun with the girls.

Are you remembering to take your magic pills from Dr Tolko like I told you? Please DO NOT FORGET. You said Obduro was making a real difference and I want to feel that difference when I get back.

Kiss Kiss,
C

Obduro – wasn't that the name of that drug she'd read about in Dr Tolko's email, the one with the side-effects? Marnie still had the print outs about that somewhere at home – unless the boys had turned them into paper aeroplanes. She'd been meaning to look into it but then *Mrs Make Believe* took off and she had, well, forgotten about being a proper investigative journalist.

"Find what you were looking for?"

Maddox was standing right behind her, holding two gin and tonics, watching her scrolling through his private emails. And making notes in her notepad.

He'd changed into some chinos and a white linen shirt, which hinted at the muscular torso beneath it.

Marnie stepped away from the desk, colour rising in her cheeks. "I'm really sorry," she said holding up her hands in apology. "I didn't mean to be nosy. It was just there and I sort of had a glance. But I didn't find anything much…"

Her voice trailed away to nothing as he gave her the hardest stare.

"Never trust a journalist," she ventured, her arms hanging limply by her side.

God, he was scary.

"I suppose I shouldn't have left you in temptation's way," he said, putting the drinks on the desk and turning the computer screen off, his face softening slightly.

Then he turned and caught her by the wrist: "I warned you what I would do to you if you crossed me again."

All the kindness had gone.

Marnie felt herself blushing furiously but her insides were turning to mush.

He was threatening to punish her like a naughty child, which was humiliating, so why was the prospect of his hands on her body so thrilling?

She was teetering on the edge of a cliff. But she recovered herself enough to look him straight in the eye and say: "You'll have to catch me first."

He looked at her darkly.

Oh, dear. What the hell was she thinking? She was in no position to issue challenges.

"I've already done that, Marnie," he said closing his hand more tightly around her wrist. "And I always keep my promises."

Her heart was pounding.

In a split second, he pulled her to him and she was in his arms, looking up into his big, dark blue eyes.

She was falling now.

His lips met hers, their tongues mingling as the ground beneath her feet disappeared.

Still kissing, Maddox picked her up very gently and carried her across the hallway and into the master bedroom overlooking the pool where, to her absolute horror, instead of taking things further in the way she had hoped, Marnie then found herself hauled, unceremoniously, across his lap.

His sheer size and strength meant fighting was useless, but she balled her hands into fists and blurted out: "You can't do this!"

"Yes, I can," he said, with a laugh, "and I'm going to. You know you've had it coming."

"I'm sorry!"

"Too late."

He wrapped his right leg around both of hers, to prevent her from lashing out, pulled up her dress and landed the first heavy slap on her upturned backside. She let out a shriek of protest as the stinging smack registered on her behind and she tried to wriggle herself free.

He caught her around her waist to keep her still as he sat on the bed, his arm placed firmly between her shoulder blades to prevent her from rearing up.

"There's more where that came from. The harder you struggle, the harder I am going to spank you. Those are the rules."

What rules? Was this a game?

A second slap landed, harder than then first. She tried to kick. Another smack. He spread his fingers to make it sting more.

"You bastard!"

"The same goes for swearing," he said sternly, delivering another firm slap, making her howl.

He smiled to himself as he did so, for despite her protests, she hadn't asked him to stop.

She took a sharp breath and pondered his words. Her mind was focused not on running away any more but on the effect it was having on her, not being in control. She willed herself not to cry out. Every time he smacked her, she had to fight the urge to wriggle on his knee. It was such a reflex, she couldn't stop herself entirely. And there was something else rather surprising: a deep pull of desire inside her.

He varied the pace and target so she never knew when or where the next blow would fall: left, right, or – oh, that hurt the most – the back of her bare legs. She heard her voice crying out with every slap when he smacked her thighs like that.

"I'll be good!"

He chuckled: "Of course you will." And delivered another smack.

The tingling inside her was mounting.

He started to caress her. She gave a little sigh, flexing her hips against his thigh.

She wasn't struggling any more.

The surging throb of desire inside her was almost overwhelming. What was happening to her?

"These are very nice, but they are getting in the way and they're going to have to come off, is that OK?" he murmured, putting his thumbs inside the edges of her lace pants, tugging gently to gauge her response.

She was mute, heart pounding in anticipation, willing him to continue to undress her, but too terrified to speak. Would he see her arousal? Could he feel it?

He got the message from her silence.

"Sweetheart, you have such a beautiful bottom," he said, stroking, as he gently pulled off her underwear.

He was actually treating the bit of herself she hated the most with reverence. The bit she tried to tame down at the gym or hide under baggy jumpers. She felt herself getting wetter.

Maddox stroked every inch of her, relishing her curves, the softness of her skin. It was lovely to have a woman with some flesh on her for a change, rather than Cecily's hard, gym-tortured body. And this one seemed to be enjoying his little game rather more than he expected.

He pulled her up, so she was sitting on his knee. Marnie put her arms around his neck, blushing and still smarting, too embarrassed to look at him. He tilted her chin upwards. Slowly, their eyes met. It ignited something deep inside her.

She pounced, knocking him backwards onto the silk quilt, frantically pulling off his shirt and undoing his trousers to get to him.

He didn't stop her – what a fantastic result! – and, anyway, he was too busy unzipping her dress, on a mission to free those breasts from her lacy bra.

She straddled him, his hands cupping her bottom, which was radiating warmth. He needed to possess her now. All that squirming on his lap had given him an erection which could support a marquee.

She eased onto him and started to ride him, leaning forward to kiss his lips as he fondled her amazing, full breasts, gently tugging her nipples, making her squeeze harder with her thighs in response.

Her hair fell on his face. She was flushed and breathless, dress hitched up around her waist, wanton and wobbling in all the right places, as he stepped up his rhythm to match hers.

"Have you learned your lesson?" he said, eyes molten, as he lightly tapped her backside a couple of times with the flat of his palm, reminding her of her chastisement.

His words were her undoing.

The pull of desire became a tidal wave, crashing deliciously, as she yielded to him.

⚜ ⚜ ⚜

Maddox was gazing at her body – her entire, naked body – as he lay propped on his elbow next to her in bed. She grabbed the sheet and started to cover herself. Why was she so bloody fat?

He stopped her.

"Marnie, what are you doing?"

"You don't really want to look at me. My body is not up to much," she mumbled, suddenly wishing she was fully clothed.

"Oh, but I do want to look at you. All of you," he said, stroking her face gently. "You are a very beautiful woman."

He ran his fingers over her breasts, her stomach and down to her hips and she felt herself responding to his expert touch, as he pulled the sheet away from her.

"Curvy and soft, like a woman should be."

Marnie blushed.

"Besides," he said with a half-smile, "you don't want to make me cross again do you?"

He ran his fingers lightly across her bottom, which was still smarting slightly. His touch made her tingle all over. She found herself quite unable to speak from a heady mix of embarrassment and desire.

"Now what can I do to make you feel good about yourself?" he murmured.

"Again?" she looked shocked. Once a week, yes, once a day, maybe, but twice in one evening?

He started to tease her nipples with his tongue. Just until she squirmed. Then he stopped.

"Enough?"

"No," she moaned.

He kissed down her belly until his lips were hovering at the apex of her thighs.

She was quivering with excitement. She silently thanked God for the visit to Dr Tolko's clinic. The nightmare waxing had at least made her look presentable.

He nudged her legs further apart.

"Ask me," he said, looking up at her with his deep, blue eyes.

She felt herself getting so turned on by the very thought of him. Down there.

"Ask me," he said again more firmly, his eyes searching her face.

"Kiss me," she whispered.

"Where?" He looked quizzical. It was completely beguiling.

He really was going to make her beg.

"There," she moaned, but he had already begun and took her breath away.

She was climbing higher now and he was guiding her with his wicked tongue.

"Don't stop," she gasped, as he took her over the edge.

"What do you want now?" He was drinking in her every movement, relishing what he had done to her.

"You," she said, before she could stop herself.

"My pleasure."

Suddenly, he was inside her.

He. Was. So. Big.

Every thrust was almost too much but her body wanted him more.

Her hips jolted forward to meet his, making him groan.

He looked for a moment as if he was concentrating, trying to stop himself, but she pushed harder against him, forcing him to give in, shouting her name as he came.

❧ ❧ ❧

Sunlight streamed through the gauzy curtains and on to the crisp white sheets of the bed, stirring Marnie from the most delicious sleep.

Then, realising where she was, she sat bolt upright.

Oh my God. She'd slept with Maddox Wolfe. She'd stayed the night. She was a total harlot and she had probably snored or made little hamster noises in her sleep at the very least.

Mercifully, he was nowhere to be seen. He had probably left early in the hope that she would just disappear. How totally embarrassing. She grabbed a robe laid across a sumptuous armchair and dashed into the bathroom.

He was in the water, waiting for her, his hair wet and brushed back from his face, knees raised so he could fit himself into the bathtub.

"Aren't you going to say good morning?" His eyes lit up.

"Good morning," she mumbled, unable to meet his gaze. "May I use your toothbrush?"

"Be my guest," he laughed. "Then, why don't you get in here with me?"

"You want me to stay?" she said, catching sight of her hair, which was sticking up all over the place, and her shoulders which had got a bit sunburned yesterday because she forgot to pack suncream.

"Yes, I want you to stay – unless you want to leave?"

He watched her intently, as she inched the fluffy towelling robe over her shoulders, fumbled with the belt and then, with agonising slowness, let it drop to the floor.

There was no way on God's green earth she was going to turn around and hang it up on that little peg on the back of the door. At least lying down, gravity was not so cruel, but standing?

The most delicious scent of lime and mandarin bath oil filled the air. Marnie crossed her hands in front of her plump thighs as she shuffled towards the bath.

"There's no need to hide from me," Maddox said softly. "You are lovely. Come and get in."

He extended his hand to steady her. She stepped into the bath, water sploshing over the sides, and lay back on his chest, relieved to be partially camouflaged. He enfolded her in his arms. She could feel the hardness of him pushing against her back, as his hands deftly worked their way across her breasts and downwards, under the water.

She closed her eyes and his fingers began a gently pleasing rhythm, which she echoed with her breath. He nuzzled her neck and kissed her ears, whispering his intentions, making her arch her back and forget herself.

"But first I am going to have you here," he said, in that voice which gave her butterflies.

"Turn around, let me see you," he murmured and she swiftly found him, pushing down, making the water churn, as they clung to each other, her hands on his broad shoulders, slipping down his oiled torso. He kissed her deeply, cradling her head in his hands, her hair soaking and clinging to her neck.

She placed one hand behind her and felt down between his legs, grinding against him, stroking insistently until he gave himself to her, his eyes burning with desire.

All the fantasy faded away. This was real. It was just her and him: Maddox and Marnie.

CHAPTER TWENTY-SIX

B arker was late for work.

That had never happened before. Bryher flicked through *Vision* magazine, rang her mates, checked and updated her Facebook page. Then, she started to get worried.

Suddenly, at 10.30am, Barker arrived. He looked ashen.

"Shut the door," he said.

"Where have you been?" said Bryher. She caught the look in his eye and added, hurriedly: "I mean, it's not like you to be late. Is everything alright?"

He sat down behind his desk and pulled a letter out of his briefcase. He left the paper on the desk and pointed to it.

Bryher read the words in front of her but she couldn't take them in.

It was from Shustrov to the Editor and Barker. *The Sentinel* was to close in three months' time.

Just ten per cent of the staff would remain to work on the new-look *Sentinel* – a celebrity news website and online TV channel. Shustrov was planning to concentrate his business interests on acquiring the major satellite TV station *Future News* – because it was the only future that news had, as far as he was concerned.

Bryher gasped and covered her mouth with her hands. She hated her job but now it was under threat, all of a sudden, she loved it more than anything. The security of coming in day after day, of having something to aim for – usually someone else's husband or job – gave meaning to her life, which was otherwise just a round of late nights and empty wine bottles.

"What are you going to do?" said Bryher.

Barker's eyes glinted.

"Well, I have done a little research on our new owner. The comrade's version of history seems to have a few crucial missing years, when he was back in the USSR. I need someone unstoppable who will do the unthinkable to save *The Sentinel*. Do you still have a burning ambition to be a real reporter, Bryher?"

She looked perplexed. She had been reading the paper every day and not just the horoscopes. Plus, she'd been out on a job with Harry Hedgeson, although they did spend three hours in the pub...

Barker printed out a couple of pages of background briefing for her and an address in Russia.

"I've got a proper reporting job for you but I am sending you because you and you alone have a set of skills, special skills, Bryher, which you have honed over many nights of drinking Chardonnay with other people's partners."

Bryher blushed: "You can't talk to me like that!"

"I'm afraid the gloves are off, Bryher, to save *The Sentinel*. You are the only one I know who can do it."

"Really?" she said, puffing out her chest. "So, *The Sentinel* needs me? Me, just doing what I know best?"

"Yes, now more than ever. God help us all," he said, with a sigh.

He opened the safe and gave her five grand in cash.

"Do not spend this on drink, shoes or nail varnish. Clear?"

"Clear," she said.

"There is a flight for Moscow leaving in three hours. The Newsdesk driver will take you to the airport. Have you got your passport?"

She had waited for this moment for so long! Of course, she had her passport, tucked safely in her desk drawer, just like all the real reporters.

But before she left, she span around and fixed Barker with a steely glare. "What's in it for me?" she said. This was her big moment and she intended to profit from it.

He smiled a big smile: "How would you fancy your own weekly column? Maybe you could pen something amusing about your life as a sad singleton, like you were suggesting. I'd just have to edit it carefully to suit the readership."

She took the paper, read the name and address and flicked her lank hair over her shoulders.

"Deal," she said. "Put your offer of a column in writing and you will find I will be fully prepared for all eventualities."

CHAPTER TWENTY-SEVEN

Bryher's eyes darted around the little bathroom. The threadbare curtains of dark orange and brown floral cotton looked like they had been sewn in the late 1960s.

There was a little pedestal mat underneath a salmon pink washbasin and a bath of matching hue, with another little mat in matching pink.

But where, oh where, was the bloody loo?

Her bladder was beyond aching now. A four hour train ride from Moscow to get here and there was no way she was going to relieve herself in that shit-covered hole in the floor on the train that passed for a khazi, so she had hung on. And on. And on.

She'd spent the afternoon loitering outside the Zhukovsky Camp 17 prison and chatting up the guards as they left. That was easy-peasy. Talking to strangers and flashing her cleavage were her two top talents.

The prison staff had tipped her off about Ivan, the guard, who – Barker reckoned – could hold the key to Shustrov's past.

Then, it was simply a case of waiting for him to come off shift, batting her eyelashes at him, overcoming the language barrier quite brilliantly – and coming home to meet his parents.

She had a bladder of steel but the rivets were about to ping off with disastrous consequences. She couldn't face the embarrassment of coming out of the bathroom and having to ask for the lavatory. What if it was one of those wooden ones shared with the whole village? She couldn't go there.

No, she would just have to pull her knickers down and hoick herself, somehow, into the sink. It was only a quick wee. And she was a British national and a member of Her Majesty's Press. She would thoroughly wash the sink out afterwards.

She hoisted herself up onto the edge of the salmon pink sink. Relief was just seconds away. But there was an awful crunching sound as the sink came away from the wall and the last thing Bryher saw was the smooth salmon pink side of the bath rushing towards her face.

⚜ ⚜ ⚜

"Breeyerrrrr," the voice purred.

She felt a hand stroking her hair. "Beautiful Breeyeerrr."

It was Ivan. He was sitting next to her on the bed. She looked down under the patchwork quilt. She was starkers. What the hell was going on?

"You hurt your head in bathroom," he smiled at her as he stroked her hair some more.

She put her hands up to her head and felt an egg-sized bump on her forehead. Ouch. That was really sore.

Then she remembered trying to do a wee in the sink and it coming away from the wall, and she wanted the ground to swallow her up.

"It is OK Breeyerr. Your clothes vere – how you say? – vet. I took zem off."

She nodded.

This was worse than getting plastered and throwing up on someone's carpet – which she had done a few times in the past, to be honest.

"I may have wrecked your parents' bathroom. I'm so sorry. *The Sentinel* will pay for the damage," she said looking around for her handbag.

"Don't worry, Breeyerrr."

Suddenly she remembered why she was here. She needed more details about why Shustrov had been imprisoned in one of the toughest jails in Russia, all those years ago, before he made his millions. And why had his criminal past been so carefully airbrushed from history?

She looked up at Ivan imploringly with those big, clear blue eyes as he swept her hair away from her face.

"The thing is, Ivan," she said, flashing her best gappy-toothed smile, "I am actually rather chilly. Do you think you could hop in here and keep me warm for a bit? Then you could tell me a bit more about your extra special prisoner Vladimir Shustrov."

CHAPTER TWENTY-EIGHT

Marnie spotted his curls first of all. They were dark brown and pushing through at the nape of his neck.

Hurrying along Chiswick High Road on her way to pick up the boys, Marnie froze as she saw Matt about a hundred yards ahead of her. He was walking along as if he hadn't a care in the world – or an abandoned wife and two kids a few streets away.

She couldn't bear to let him pass, to let him get away with being in Chiswick and not bothering to even speak to his children.

But then, she'd cheated on him with Maddox Wolfe, so did that make her any better than him?

She quickened her pace. He was heading for the bus stop. What would she say to him? It might be quite a mouthful.

So many thoughts were whizzing through her head and she was almost running now, determined to catch him. He always walked so much more quickly than she did, which only infuriated her more.

The bus drew up and the doors opened.

Matt was about to get on.

Marnie pushed herself to the front of the queue and seized his arm.

He span around and looked straight through her.

"Sorry? Do I know you?"

Her mouth formed a silent "O".

It wasn't Matt.

"I thought you were someone else," she said. It was as if someone had punctured her and she was slowly deflating.

"Of course you did," he said. "Now, can I have my arm back?"

She loosened her grip. People behind her in the queue started jostling, annoyed that they were being delayed.

As the bus pulled away, with faces staring at her from the windows, she sat down in the shelter, numb with the stupidity of her mistake. She was hallucinating imaginary Matts in the street and accosting them at bus-stops. The dreadful guilt of sleeping with Maddox Wolfe pressed down on her as she watched people scurrying along, getting on with their busy lives.

She hadn't told Belle about it. How could she? She was so ashamed of cheating on Matt, particularly because she had enjoyed it so much. And she was a mother!

It was a chapter of her life which would have to remain hidden forever, especially as he had been so masterful in the bedroom. Something fluttered in her groin as she replayed Maddox taking her in hand for sneaking a look at his emails. Oh, it was like Seb Winter, but for real. She couldn't imagine Matt dominating her like that. No chance.

Would she even want him to?

The very thought of them exploring power-play in the bedroom gave her a strange, twisty feeling in her stomach. She couldn't ask him to do that to her. They had barely had the energy for sex as it was. She was so boring and unadventurous in her marriage. No wonder he had hooked up with Belinda, who was probably walking over him in spiky heels at this very moment while telling him about her exploits with Greenpeace.

Why was she even thinking about sex with Matt? Matt wasn't speaking to her. He didn't even have the decency to be the guy at the bus-stop just now.

She wiped her eyes and stood up.

What was the point of thinking about fantasies if you were still in love with the flawed reality and it didn't want you in any case?

❧   ❧   ❧

The hubbub of the school gates, for once, came as a relief from the knot of Maddox and Matt thoughts in her head.

As Charlie zoomed ahead of her into the playground on his scooter, Marnie spied Felicity Harper-Bilge, queen of the alpha mums of Astral Prep, brandishing a clipboard. She was like a general surveying her troops.

"Now, ladies," she said to the assembled crowd of Mummies, "I am expecting a good show on the baking front tomorrow for the cake sale. I've already drawn up an Excel spreadsheet for the rota, covering chocolate cupcakes and brownies, butterfly cakes, Smartie cakes, shortbreads and pastries. Millicent has promised us her spectacular ginger-bread men, dressed in school colours."

There were murmurs of appreciation at this last piece of news.

"We do not want to be outdone by Year Three!" said Felicity. "Their macaroons, at the school carol concert, were mentioned in the headmistress's last parents' briefing – a whole three months after the event!"

She lowered her voice to a conspiratorial whisper: "I have heard they may be planning a profiterole mountain."

There were several gasps of horror.

"Don't worry, girls, if they do, I will personally ensure it comes crashing down," said Felicity, with a glint in her eye.

She turned to Marnie: "What are you going to bring?"

Oh, Lord. She hadn't even thought about it. Marnie opened and closed her mouth. Felicity and her culinary demands had a horrid way of rendering her speechless.

"I will expect a Victoria sponge from you," said Felicity. "Nothing too complicated, especially now you are so busy being a celebrity columnist." There were a few snorts of laughter.

Marnie's heart sank.

Her phone bleeped at her.

Vision magazine were due at her house in less than an hour for a photoshoot! Honestly, she'd forget her head if it wasn't screwed on. Could she still blame baby brain when her kids were at school and nursery?

There was no time to bake. She'd have to pop into the supermarket and grab a sponge cake. She could distress it with a fork later and make it look home-made.

Reading her thoughts, Felicity tutted: "And no cheating, Marnie! We need home-made, not shop-bought."

Just then, Rufus zoomed out of the school and into the playground on his scooter, nearly squashing Felicity's toes, which was rather pleasing.

He presented Marnie with a painting.

There were two little stick people with big heads and blonde hair, a taller, smiley woman with long brown hair, and a triangle for a dress and a stick man, also with blonde hair, standing near her.

"Who's that, Ruf?" said Marnie, pointing to blonde stick man.

"It's Uncle Dylan. Daddy is not in the picture because he is at work. When can I speak to him?"

Marnie felt those words prick her heart. "Soon, darling. He rings me every night when you are fast asleep and tells me how much he loves you and Charlie."

She was going straight to hell for that lie, but needs must.

"Why can't I speak to him?"

"Oh, you will, all in good time."

"When?"

"Soon."

There was no answer to that one.

"Shall we count red cars on the way home?" said Marnie, chirpily.

"Where's Uncle Dylan?" said Rufus, who seemed to be having a male role model moment. God help her, Dylan was the best she could manage.

"He's busy."

"Want Dylan!" cried Charlie, hanging off Marnie's arm, like a dead-weight.

"Yes, darling, but he had to go to work."

"Mummy, can we have sweets?"

"Not today, darling. We're late for something important for Mummy's work."

"But Uncle Dylan always ... " they whined.

"Not today!" she snapped. A couple of people turned to look at her.

It wasn't like her to be so snappy but she just felt more stressed than usual. The imaginary Matt had rattled her and now Rufus was showing signs of desperately missing his father. She was running out of excuses about Matt's work.

And she didn't really want to do a magazine spread about her life as Mrs Make Believe but Barker said she had to. Writing the column was OK because she controlled it but having a magazine photographer and journalist in her house, taking pictures of her with the children just made her uncomfortable. *Vision* would definitely start asking personal questions.

"Don't like you," said Charlie.

"Mummy, you hurt my feelings," said Rufus. "I think you need to think carefully about your behaviour or there might be consequences." He practically sang the last word.

"I'm sorry, sweetheart. That was very silly of Mummy."

Good grief. What on earth were they teaching them at school these days? UN peacekeeping skills?

❧   ❧   ❧

Peter, the portly photographer from *Vision* magazine, barrelled through Marnie's front door with piles of equipment and set up camp in the open-plan kitchen.

He started to unfurl reflectors, yanking flash meters, gaffer tape and tripods from black kit bags, fiddling endlessly with his camera lenses as he spoke.

"So, Marnie, I need you to put on a nice, colourful dress and we will need a high heel and a nude tight, OK?"

Marnie nodded.

Charlie was posting Cheerios down the gaps in the floorboards and Rufus was under the table with him, building Helm's Deep out of Lego – it was a long-term construction project, mainly because Charlie kept breaking bits off and hiding them under the sofa cushions in the living room.

Or in shoes. That was a memorably painful experience.

"The boys will need to be in something smart. Shirts and little trousers?" he said, hopefully. "And their hair must be brushed a bit."

Hmm, that was not going to go down very well.

Marnie plodded upstairs and pulled her circus-stripe, hideous frock on. It was colourful, there was no doubt about that. She rummaged in the knicker drawer and found a nude pair of tights left over from her cousin's wedding last year and some cream high heels.

The boys would have to put on their wedding shirts and some chinos that they had been forced into on the day. Marnie winced at the memory of how much they had whined and fiddled with their outfits throughout the ceremony, ripping off their shirts at the reception and running about bare-chested, like Lord of the Flies, to the horror of the other guests.

A pile of soft toys fell on her head as she opened the boys' wardrobe.

Venturing into the darkest recesses, she found the nasty loafers her cousin had bought for the boys to wear. They made them look like miniature bankers.

"Here goes," she said, under her breath as she stepped lightly downstairs in her high heels.

"Not wearing them!" said Rufus.

"I want my Crocs!" cried Charlie.

There was a knock at the door.

As Marnie opened it, a dead-eyed, rail thin young woman thrust her hand forward to greet her.

"Portia," she said, stepping into the hallway and gazing in wonder at the ordinariness of suburbia, as she tucked her bleached blonde, very funky graduated bob, behind one ear.

"Brilliant to meet you," she lied. "I am dying to know all about your thrilling life as Mrs Make Believe out here in the suburbs. I don't usually stray far from W11.

The look of disdain on her face said it all, really.

"Oh, I used to love going out in Notting Hill before I had the kids!" said Marnie, sounding so gushy she just wanted to kick herself. Portia gave her the coolest nod, which could have been approval but was more likely to be disbelief.

"Err, thanks Portia, I'm just getting the pictures out of the way first," said Peter, cutting in. "The kids are getting tired already."

He gestured to two pairs of feet, wearing little loafers, sticking out from under the table.

Portia scowled and checked her emails.

"Can we get a nice family, cuddly shot first?" said Peter, as Marnie pulled the boys out, one at a time.

They stuck their tongues out at the photographer.

He fired off a few shots.

"OK, can we maybe have you doing something really motherly, like stirring up some ingredients in a mixing bowl?"

"OK," said Marnie, going over to the cupboards and pulling out some flour and sugar and a glass bowl. She could get on with her cake-mix for the school sale tomorrow.

She broke two eggs into the mix and brought it over to the table, where Charlie and Rufus stuck their fingers in it as she stirred with a wooden spoon, grinning at the camera.

This was going rather well.

"Can I just ask a few teensy questions, as we go along?" said Portia, who was bored rigid and couldn't wait to get back to Notting Hill for cocktails with her pals Flossie and Cassandra who had been clean-eating only edamame beans and kale for the last week and were now up for a massive re-tox before their next purge.

She pulled out her digital voice recorder.

"Sure," said Marnie, mixing like crazy.

"So, is your life really like your column?"

"Well, as you can see, it is quite similar. Rufus, please don't put the mixture in Charlie's hair."

Portia smiled but her eyes were as cold as cod on the fishmonger's slab.

"Do you think other mothers secretly hate you?"

"I hate them, mostly!" she laughed. "I mean, all that trying to pretend you're perfect nonsense. It is total betrayal of our sex. We are all failures, aren't we? I'm just better at it than most."

What on earth was she even saying? She didn't hate anyone – except perhaps her News Editor and Belinda the husband stealer. She was waffling on, just desperate to get this bloody cake in the oven.

Portia smiled to herself.

"What about your husband?"

"Can I answer that in a minute?" she said, herding the boys into the living room and putting the telly on.

"OK," she said, returning and splodging cake mixture into a baking tin, "I don't think I can put into words how I feel about him."

"Don't you want him to come back?"

Marnie felt herself being speared by that question, right through the heart.

She'd be damned if she was going to give Matt the satisfaction of reading about how she was missing him, while he was off living the life of Riley with his fancy woman.

"Ha! No!" she said. "We are managing just fine without him. In fact, we are better off. I don't need any man because I'm Mrs Make Believe."

❀ ❀ ❀

It was gone midnight by the time Marnie fell into bed.

The cake was a total disaster: uncooked in the middle, burnt at the edges. She'd tried again, mixing up a storm once the kids were tucked up, but that had turned out even worse.

Marnie drifted into an uneasy sleep.

He was smiling down at her as she pulled him close. Then, he was inside her, moving slowly and she was stroking the back of his neck, their bodies so warm and familiar together. Marnie could almost hear his heart beating.

He started to push harder and somewhere inside she felt him touching the very core of her. She wanted to give herself to him totally. They weren't having sex, they were making love.

She called out his name: "Matt."

She woke up. It was still dark. The bed beside her was cold. She was alone.

All alone, except for the guilt of what she had done with Maddox Wolfe.

Chapter Twenty-Nine

M att Martin had the haunted look of a man who had lost everything dear to him and knew he was never likely to get it back.

He had worked out exactly what he wanted to say but he was worried that she would take it badly.

Sitting, hunched on a little bar stool chair in the pub around the corner from work, he addressed his comments to the carpet.

"It's over between us, Belinda, it never should have happened in the first place," he murmured.

"But what about our dreams?" said Belinda, with a look of anguish. "I thought you were going to take a sabbatical and come to Australia to be with me, to find out who you really are."

"I know who I am, Belinda," he said. "I'm the idiot who hasn't been begging my wife to take me back."

She clasped his hand and looked deep into his eyes.

"Matt, I thought we'd talked about this. Marriage is a form of brain washing. She's trapped you with the kids, that's all. You've lost who you really are. What about the footloose young man I first knew at uni; the one who said marriage was like a ball and chain?"

"He's long gone," said Matt. "He grew up – with Marnie. God knows how she ever put up with me. I'm so sorry

Belinda, to have led you on and got you mixed up in all of this but I love my wife."

Belinda brushed a silky strand of hair behind her ear and reached inside her jute shopping bag, pulling out a magazine, which she then held, rolled up, in her hands.

"You know Marnie isn't right for you. She has her own journey, she's got too many problems and her issues are making you lose sight of yourself. It's not fair on you."

"I don't care about all that," said Matt, his big, brown eyes filling with tears. "I love her and I need to go back and say I'm sorry and see if we can work it out. I want to see my children. I don't want anyone but her."

Belinda's mouth twisted into a sneer: "Well, Matt, she doesn't seem to want you! Look at this!"

She threw a copy of *Vision* magazine at him, open at picture of Marnie hugging the boys, headlined: "MRS MAKE BELIEVE – WHY I HATE ALL MOTHERS, BUT MY HUSBAND MOST OF ALL."

The strap line, across the bottom of the double page spread, read: "We are better off without him, I never want him back."

The colour drained from Matt's face.

"Well?" she said, her eyes glittering. "I'm ready to hear your apology. Then, you can find a way to make it up to me – in bed."

"I only want Marnie," he said, standing up. "It's over, Belinda."

"You'll never make it with anyone, Matt, because you don't know who you really are! You've never taken the time to really explore yourself. You're trapped in the role of husband and father!"

Matt looked at her for a moment.

She clutched at his arm: "Yes, you can see it now, can't you? You are always droning on about your children and how Charlie is great at building blocks or Rufus won't go anywhere without his special teddy even though he is too old for that now. Honestly, Matt, it is boring, but I know there is so much more to you than just your kids and we can find that together."

Matt smiled at her: "I need to thank you, Belinda, really I do. You're right. I am boring. I am a boring dad to the most beautiful children in the world and I will still be talking about them with my very last breath."

He turned on his heel and walked through the door and out of her life.

❧ ❧ ❧

As PR exercises go, the *Vision* magazine feature on Mrs Make Believe was widely agreed to be a total disaster.

"That's all we bleeding well need," said Barker, as he deleted yet another hate mail from an angry mother, who had cancelled her subscription to *The Sentinel* in protest at Marnie's comments.

Marnie clasped her hands behind her back as she stood in The Bunker.

Caveman, of course, was stoking the fire with his horrid internet tweets about her: "Mrs Make Believe hates all mothers #whatiswrongwiththispicture."

And: "Some sisterhood – she hates you all! #feelletdown."

Marnie couldn't bear to respond to him.

She was such a fool.

Portia was only doing her job, really. Marnie should have known better than to open her big mouth. The magazine had taken things out of context, seized on the juiciest quote and used it to grab a headline.

"I'm sorry," she whispered. "It all came out wrong. I was so busy trying to bake a cake."

Barker flicked his eyes upwards: "Lame excuse."

"I know, but it happens to be true," she said.

"The readers didn't like that either. Mrs Make Believe is supposed to be a chaotic mother who doesn't like cooking, not Mary sodding Berry."

He pointed to the picture of her, beaming proudly as she stirred her cake mix, her two little blonde boys looking angelic, for once.

"Well, my cake was a big flop," she ventured. "I will write an apology column to the readers explaining what happened. I am a rubbish cook."

"Oh, spare me," said Barker. He sucked his hollow cheeks in, making him look even more skeletal than usual. "You might as well know, we're all for the chop anyway."

"What?"

"Shustrov is closing us down in a couple of months. *The Sentinel* is being turned into an internet celebrity news channel on a skeleton staff."

"No!" Somewhere, Marnie's inner hack was weeping. And what the hell was she going to do to pay the mortgage?

"I've got a few plans afoot to keep us afloat but I can't share them with you yet," he said, with a smile playing on his lips.

Oh, thank God. If anyone could snatch victory from the jaws of defeat and save *The Sentinel*, it was Barker.

"For now, I've got to keep leading the band as the ship is sinking, which means we need to do something to restore your popularity among womankind."

He pulled a memo out of his drawer.

"I was saving this for a rainy day, when you had really upset me." He had a wicked glint in his eye.

"What do you need me to do?" Her throat had gone awfully dry.

He waved the memo at her: "It's a feature idea from Athena Maldon. She says you have agreed to it?"

"I haven't, exactly," said Marnie. She honestly thought Athena was just making idle threats with that silly feature about the popularity of large knickers.

"Well, I can't protect you from her any longer, your *Vision* article has seen to that," he said, slapping the sheet of paper down on the desk. "I'm afraid it's time for you to strip down to your underwear for the good of the newspaper."

Marnie wished, for once, she could make her excuses and leave.

⚜   ⚜   ⚜

If only Matt were here.

Marnie had so much she wanted to tell him – everything from how the boys were growing up day by day, to her latest debacle at work.

The house was deathly quiet with the kids soundly asleep and Dylan out drinking somewhere. She sauntered through to the kitchen and rummaged about in the freezer for some ice cream, to make herself feel better.

There, in the bottom drawer, were a series of little Tupperware boxes, each neatly labelled in Matt's handwriting – "Spag bol", "Lovely Lasagne!" and "Open in emergency only". She remembered how they'd laughed about that last one – she was such a crap cook, he had spent a Bank Holiday preparing little frozen meals for the kids, to help out. She remembered him, standing at the stove, sleeves rolled up, glass of wine in hand, stirring away so the mince wouldn't catch.

She had crept up and put her arms around his waist, giving him a squeeze and they had enjoyed that moment of just being together in the kitchen, as the kids hurled cushions at each other around the living room. It didn't matter that they were both knackered. They loved each other, they had something unbreakable.

Where did it all go so wrong? She sat down at the kitchen table, her appetite gone.

She and Matt had stopped really talking to each other in those last few weeks together.

She wasn't sure how that had happened.

Exhaustion with their lives had taken its toll, somehow. They hadn't listened to each other or really told each other what they were feeling – she'd probably been more guilty of that than he had. The little hugs around the kitchen had just petered out.

All her dreaming about Mr Make Believe can't have helped matters. It was easier to live in fantasy-land than to have to engage with her annoying, stubborn, grumpy, frayed-around-the-edges, preoccupied husband.

How could Matt measure up to the fantasy?

Shamefully, she found herself wondering whether he could live up to the reality of Maddox either.

She walked back into the living room, which suddenly felt cavernous without Matt schlomped on the sofa, as he used to do. Picking up *Vision* magazine and flicking through to the offending article, Marnie's heart sank.

What if Matt had read it?

The headline made her sound hateful.

She hadn't meant it like that! In fact, she hadn't meant to say any of it. She was just so angry with him, that's all.

A picture of them on their wedding day stood on the mantelpiece in front of her. She didn't want to take it down – for the sake of the boys, really. She was keeping things as normal as possible while Daddy was working away.

Marnie picked it up.

She looked so young and he was so handsome, kissing each other, while cutting their wedding cake. She was in Matt's arms, her hair falling in loose curls down her back, her wedding dress cascading into a little pool of silk at her feet.

The little figures on the top of the cake had been specially made for them – she was reading a newspaper and he was wearing a barrister's wig and they were holding hands.

Well, the icing on that cake had gone all crumbly now and the little figures had fallen off and slept with other people, from other cakes.

Marnie stifled a little sob.

She glanced up to the bookshelf by the fireplace, where the silk blouse that got ripped in her tussle with Zoe the stylist was sitting next to her grandmother's old sewing box, awaiting repair. The sleeve was quite badly torn but it should be possible to sew it back on.

Sewing hadn't been her strong point at school. In fact, she was banned from the sewing machines after accidentally stitching someone else's finger, and confined to embroidery instead.

But she was certain she could manage this.

She pulled the sewing box down, sending a cloud of dust flying, opened it and started to scrabble through, looking for some thread.

Of course, she didn't have the right colour when she needed it.

It was hopeless.

She put the torn blouse and the ripped sleeve back down on the arm of the sofa and returned the sewing box to the shelf.

Marnie sighed and turned the light off.

It was time for bed.

Outside, under a street lamp, Matt watched the lights go out.

He was still clutching the *Vision* magazine article.

Belinda was right. The headline said it all. Marnie didn't want him, she didn't need him. The boys were better off without him.

His shoulders drooping in defeat, he turned and walked away.

Chapter Thirty

The Sentinel Leg.

This was not, as Marnie had feared, some strange standby prop wheeled out of the fashion cupboard as a stunt double for subjects with really fat ankles.

No, it was a pose she was meant to perfect while standing in a studio wearing the most enormous pair of apple-catcher knickers known to man, or woman.

"Now, darling Marnie," said the photographer, Hugo Hansen, pushing his sunglasses further back on to his head and peering through his viewfinder, "this time try *The Sentinel* Leg a bit more."

She thrust her left leg forward, put her weight on her right leg and twisted her torso to the side as she had been shown. This was supposed to make her look thinner.

The look on Hugo's face told her it wasn't working.

The hair and make-up girl had done her very best to detract from the subject matter – Marnie's body – with an enormous backcombed hair-do adding at least three inches to her height, which, with her four inch heels, made her 5ft 9ins. She was practically as tall as a supermodel – under any other circumstances a cause for celebration.

If only she could put some clothes on. Athena Maldon's horrid "Big Pants" feature was an Editor's must so there was no way but the scantily-clad runway.

The Fashion Editor had provided an array of underwear that would make your granny proud. All of them made Marnie's short, curvy frame look even more rotund than usual. She'd had a stiff drink beforehand to give her the courage to go through with it, as well as a spray tan which had gone a bit streaky in places. No mother in her right mind would want to strip off for public scrutiny like this but she had to if she wanted to keep her job.

"Marnie, darling," sighed Hugo, "try putting your hand on your hip to make your waist look smaller and suck everything in."

She sucked everything in dutifully but nothing looked even one iota smaller.

"But you have to smile at the same time, sweetie," he said, trying not to sound too irritated. "Drop your chin and say Thursday."

"Thursday."

He fired off a couple of shots.

"Now, throw your head back and laugh."

Marnie gave a rictus grin, fighting the urge to cry.

"More Rihanna and less Red Rum," he shouted at her. "Yes, that's lovely, darling."

He muttered under his breath: "It'll have to do."

The feature made a double page spread in *Sentinel Woman*, with picture after picture of Marnie modelling everything from satin and silk forties-style drawers to French knickers (big mistake) and, worst of all, sensible cotton granny pants. "AT LAST! UNDERWEAR FOR REAL WOMEN!"

It was like a waking nightmare. She wanted to crawl into a hole and die of shame.

A massive bunch of yellow roses arrived at her desk at the same time as she did, almost eradicating the memory of the sniggers she'd had to endure from the newsroom this morning, especially Bryher, who had just returned from an investigative job, apparently, and was more full of herself than usual. Marnie could tell Bryher was dying to be asked about her secret mission but she didn't want to give her the satisfaction of gloating about it, not with the way she was feeling today.

She opened the little card attached to her flowers.

"Beautiful bottom, darling, but you know I prefer it without the big pants. Maddox x"

He was just being kind. But it was very chivalrous of him. She started to feel a warm glow inside thinking about Maddox, as she sniffed the blooms, sat down and took the phone off the hook.

Her email inbox was already full with a zillion emails from everyone she'd ever met and quite a few she wished she hadn't. People she went to school with – "Hello fatty!"; Zoe the stylist – "What the hell happened?"; and the headmistress – "Your brave article reminded me, I would welcome the opportunity to talk to you about the media and the obesity crisis."

And of course, Caveman had gone into overdrive, tweeting no less than six droll comments – in his opinion, at least.

She hadn't bothered replying to any of them.

"Mrs Make Believe gets her kit off and puts feminism back to the dark ages #doublestandards."

Although, the last one was a bit kinder: "Mrs Make Believe looks good in big knickers #liketoseemoreofyou."

Oh, God. He was trying to flatter her into responding now. Or was that just a bit creepy of him?

"Caveman can't help admiring Mrs Make Believe's form #notbadforherage."

She needed to take her mind off the whole thing.

Pulling out the scrunched up papers from her bag, she typed "Obduro drug" into the search engine, Cyberlook. She'd been meaning to do some research into Dr Tolko's drug and there was no time like the present. She scrolled through the search results and a couple of strange-looking Ibiza rave websites popped up. Clicking on them, she opened a chat thread.

Rave websites San Antonio next weekend? Obduro aka Stonk. Fort Stonk was sick at first cos I went all nite wiv the hos and byatches but it will screw u up big time. Took it for a month – horny as, even the dog started to look like it wanted to get jiggy wiv me. Know what I am saying? Avoid.

There were a few replies.

Stonk (Obduro) – Man, nevva touching it again. Stiffy for a whole day first time. Week after, the fugly chubsters started to look hot. WTF?

Marnie sighed. Her teen-speak was pretty poor but from what she could gather, Obduro seemed to have a role as a rave drug. And the side effect was a massively increased libido to the point that unattractive girls started to look quite appealing.

And Maddox had been on it when he bedded her.

She swallowed hard and felt her pride sticking in her throat.

She keyed Globotec, the firm behind Obduro, into the search engine and nearly fell off her chair. The main backer behind Globotec was Vladimir Shustrov, owner of *The Sentinel* and boyfriend of Athena Maldon.

Her mobile phone rang.

It was Maddox.

"Hello," he said. "Sorry I haven't been in touch. I didn't want you to think I was avoiding you."

"I didn't think that," she lied. She'd never been the type to want an actual affair, even with a gorgeous A-list film star but she couldn't stop her heart from skipping a beat, just to hear his voice.

Of course, now she realised Maddox had only bedded her because of some sex pill, it made her feel even more of a tragic failure than she did about an hour ago, when the whole of Twitter and the internet were having hysterics at her photoshoot.

"I wondered if you'd like to have dinner?"

Oh, that was unexpected.

"Maddox," she sighed. "The roses are lovely but I can't. I just can't. It's not you, it's me."

She heard laughter at the end of the line.

"Marnie, are you trying to finish a relationship I wasn't aware we were having?"

"Well, you asked me out to dinner!" she said indignantly. "And you sent me flowers!"

"I did ask you out to dinner, but it could be just dinner – although I'm always open to persuasion where you are concerned. And the flowers were because I knew you'd be mortified by that article, although, you really did look very lovely. Not sure about the French knickers though."

"Yes a few tent pegs and I could have been hired out for a fete in those," she giggled, finally seeing the funny side. "Look, Maddox, I don't know the rules of the games you play, but even dinner, to me, sounds very much like a date because we ... "

"Had great sex?"

"That, exactly," she mumbled. "And the thing is ... "

For some reason, she wanted to tell him all about her guilty dream about Matt the other night. It was all so effortless with him.

"I'm having fantasies about another man. It used to be you, you see, all the time, mostly in your film roles. But I think it was because I was bored with my life, actually."

"Well, that's nice to know," he laughed. "Don't spare my ego now, will you? Who are you dreaming about now?"

"Well, I did have quite a few rude thoughts about Seb Winter, the superspy."

"Oh, I bet you did," he teased. "Did he have time to take you in hand before he saved the world from the killer plague?"

She felt the beginnings of a blush: "Yes, I think he may have done but it's not him."

"So who is it?"

She paused. Even if she told him about how much she was missing Matt, that didn't mean she still loved Matt, did it? That would make her quite tragic. She was just getting it off her chest, that's all.

"It's my husband."

"Lucky bastard!" said Maddox. "Of course, you do realise this means that you probably still love him?"

Marnie didn't reply.

"I'm obviously disappointed if it means we won't be having any more little get-togethers," he added.

"I don't think we will be, you know," said Marnie, slowly, wanting to tell herself to shut up and keep that option open like any sane woman would, faced with Maddox Wolfe offering no-strings sex.

"I'm a simple woman, Maddox. Matt is not around but I still have a ring on my finger and for some reason, something in my stupid, broken heart appears to belong to him."

"Well," said Maddox, "I hope he realises what he is missing, leaving you on your own, while other men send you flowers, invite you out to dinner and chat to you on the phone about your secret fantasies."

"I'm quite certain that he doesn't give me a second thought, actually," said Marnie curtly. "He's too busy snogging his first love from university, remember?"

Maddox gave a hollow laugh: "Yes, sorry about that, sweetheart."

"Oh, and there's something else," she said, twiddling with her hair. "That night in Cannes, when I read your emails…"

"Don't remind me of that or I will be forced to come around and spank you again and we both know where that will lead," he said. "Especially now I know you'll enjoy it so much. I'll have to start calling you Katya."

She stifled a giggle.

"No, seriously, Maddox. You've been on a pill called Obduro, haven't you?"

"It's one of Cecily's health kick things," he muttered. "I took it for a bit but to be honest, I'm rubbish at remembering those sort of things."

"It is not a vitamin, Maddox. It's an impotence drug of some kind and from what I've read, it has some worrying side effects."

There was a silence at the end of the line and then Maddox whispered: "Like what?"

"It might give you – there's no easy way of saying this -problematic erections that go on for a while."

"Oh, God," said Maddox, "I had one of those during filming. But I hadn't started taking it. At least, I didn't know I'd started … " He wouldn't put anything past Cecily. What the hell had she been playing at, drugging him?

"And there's something else," said Marnie. "It might give you such a high sex drive that you fancy people who are not very attractive to you normally and, Maddox, I think that explains what happened between us."

He had been through quite a few call girls lately, but that was nothing new. Marnie was different.

"You think I only went to bed with you because of some sex pill?" he said, incredulously.

"Something like that," she murmured.

"Mar-nie, you are a very beautiful woman. You are all woman. I found you attractive because of who you are as well as what you look like. Obduro had nothing to do with it. I've a good mind to go and see that bloody Harley Street doctor of Cecily's and give him what for over this bloody sex pill, the fucker."

"No, please don't do that," said Marnie. "I think there's a big story behind it. It appears to be produced by a company owned by Vladimir Shustrov."

"What are you thinking of doing?"

"Well, the drug is being prescribed by Dr Tolko and it is not on prescription here but I have an email showing he knows it has worrying side-effects. It's produced by Shustrov's company, so it will be bad news for him if it gets out, which may be just what we need here at *The Sentinel*, because he is closing us down in a couple of months' time."

"No more *Sentinel*?"

"Just a celebrity news website and some kind of rubbishy internet TV channel, according to my boss."

"Oh dear, what will Middle England do?"

"You can joke, Maddox, but we are a newspaper and we do have an important role, plus it is my bloody livelihood and I have two young boys to support," she shouted.

"I'm sorry," he said.

There was a loud cough at the open door and Bryher walked in, flicking her lank hair over her shoulders.

She was in a very bad mood indeed, because her first column, *My Brilliant Life*, was basically just a paragraph at the top of the *News in Briefs* on page 48. That was not the deal that she had brokered with Barker, in return for going to Russia.

She'd already put salt in his triple shot latte but she was planning to have it out with him, especially as Marnie now appeared to be launching a television career, for parading around in her smalls. Bryher was miles better at stripping off than some mumsy type! It just wasn't fair.

"You've been invited on to *ChitChat* to talk about your knickers," she scowled, turning on her heel. "Car's downstairs waiting."

Marnie didn't budge.

"Oh, and Barker says you have to do it, or else," said Bryher, sticking her head back around the door, grinning: "See ya later, Big Pants."

CHAPTER THIRTY-ONE

The television studio lights were so bright, Marnie found herself squinting myopically at her hosts, Allie – with waist-length hair extensions – and Dee-Dee, whose eyebrows were so thickly defined that they appeared to be resting like two furry caterpillars above her eyes.

The trio perched on teeny stools behind a massive kitchen island, which doubled as a desk for the lunchtime chat show.

"Nah ven," said Allie, "all the tork is abaht wevver big pants is back, innit?"

There were a few whoops from the *ChitChat* audience. "Yeah!" said Allie, punching the air: "Who likes comfy knicks, girls?"

"Yes," said Dee-Dee, who had a pearl of a Home Counties accent to Allie's estuary dredge. "That is the question on everyone's lips today. It was just so refreshing to see a woman not afraid to bare all – well, almost all – as you did Marnie, given the state of your figure. We already know you as Mrs Make Believe, but is there any part of you that you *haven't* shared?"

There was hysterical laughter from the audience.

Marnie wanted to run away but she knew she couldn't. Barker had told her to go through with it. It was live so there could be no ducking out.

She cleared her throat.

"Well, I've talked about my marriage break up and shared my life experiences through *Mrs Make Believe*, which I think a lot of people can relate to," Marnie began.

"Aaah," said Allie, leaning forward and resting her hand on her chin. "Made me sad when yer fella dumped you."

"I'm glad you mentioned that, Marnie," said Dee-Dee, "because we've got some people we'd like to bring in to talk to you about your life."

Marnie worked hard to retain a relaxed expression but her heart was pounding ten to the dozen.

She was going to finally get to confront Caveman face to face, she could feel it!

Marnie started racking her brain for a witty put-down. What would he look like? The smart money was on ugly and thuggish or maybe he was a suave banker-type? That was banker, with a "w".

But Dee-Dee went on: "Please welcome childcare expert Alexa Joy and relationship counsellor Barbara Grudge!"

The camera swung around and closed in on Marnie's face as Barbara Grudge bounced on to the set followed by a strutting Alexa Joy. Her mouth fell open. Of all the experts to have to walk on to a television set, *ChitChat* had to go and pick those two ... Daytime TV producers should really use their superpowers for good rather than devastatingly awkward evil occasionally.

They perched themselves on leatherette chairs at the side of the kitchen island, with a little glass coffee table in front of them.

Dee-Dee got up and walked over with a mic, kneeling down by Barbara.

"So, Barbara, have you seen a lot of women facing similar issues to Marnie?"

Barbara fixed Marnie with the most steely glare: "Oh yes, Marnie's behaviour is sadly all too familiar to experts such as myself. It starts with dissatisfaction with their lot – their house, their work (or lack of it) – and that is projected, whole-heartedly, on to their poor, dear long-suffering husbands who are working their fingers to the bone just to provide.

"I like to call it Damsel in Distress Syndrome and Marnie is a prime example. Always blaming their partner, behaving like some spoiled little princess in a fairytale. And grasping at everything they can – a bigger house, a better car; some of the worst cases even start demanding a third child when they have two perfectly lovely ones at home!"

Marnie was dumbstruck.

Dee-Dee looked over to Marnie: "Anything you'd like to say about that, Marnie?"

"No, not really," she whispered. She was being eviscerated live on television. She hadn't expected this.

"I would like to add something, if I may," said baby guru Alexa, rapping her fingers on her bony knees. "Women such as Marnie usually fail to instil the loving discipline in their children that is needed to run a family efficiently and happily. They spend ages Twittering and Facebooking when they should simply be cooking a wholesome meal or caring for their offspring. Put simply, they are so lazy and self-centred that their young ones are allowed to run amok, with no proper manners and grubby little fingers. It is a clear beginning of criminal tendencies, in my opinion."

"Boo!" said Allie. "It ain't right not to be a proper muvver is it, girls?"

"No!" replied the crowd, with a few shouts of "Shame on you!" and "Wash their hands!"

"And the final issue here is total self-love," said Barbara, triumphantly. "Who but a selfish, self-obsessed Damsel in

Distress would stand up in a national newspaper in their underwear and practically show off their lady-parts? Only someone who loves themselves more than their children because, goodness knows, those children are going to look back in years to come and be ashamed, deeply ashamed, that their mother paraded herself like a common tart."

That was it. Something snapped in Marnie.

She ripped off her microphone, stood up and walked calmly over to Barbara.

Dee-Dee, sensing something was about to happen, got up and stepped back, a look of excitement sweeping across her plasticised features, thrusting her caterpillar eyebrows upwards into a funny little dance.

As Marnie approached, Barbara got out of her chair and opened her mouth to say something. But Marnie swung her arm back and delivered a resounding slap right across Barbara's face, before Barbara could even draw breath.

The camera panned in on a livid hand-print on Barbara's left cheek.

"You hit me!" she screamed. She clasped her hands to her face and stood there, looking almost triumphant, as Alexa Joy fussed around her.

The audience erupted.

Some people were on their feet cheering and clapping, while others cat-called and shouted at Marnie.

"You can call me a tart but nobody says I love myself more than my children," said Marnie, storming off the set.

⚜   ⚜   ⚜

Marnie hailed a cab, almost steaming with fury, and arrived home to find some of Fleet Street's finest already camping on her doorstep.

Flashbulbs went off all around her as she ran up the garden path.

"Nothing to say, sorry," she shouted as she fumbled with the key in the lock and ran inside, pulling the blinds down in the lounge to stop reporters peering in.

Her phone hadn't stopped ringing. She'd better answer. It was Barker.

"Consider yourself on gardening leave, you total fuckwit."

And he hung up.

She sat down at the kitchen table and cried, for God knows how long.

Dylan was ambling down the street on the school run when he came across the media scrum outside his sister's house.

"Are you her husband?" said one reporter, as Dylan tried to push past to open the garden gate and Rufus ran over one of the photographer's feet with his scooter.

"No, mate, brother. What's she done?"

"Has she ever slapped you?"

"Yeah, loads of times," he laughed. "I'm her kid brother, what do you think?"

"Does she hit the children?"

"Never," said Dylan, suddenly realising that Marnie was in some kind of big trouble. "Now, I think you lot better clear off before I call the police."

"Too late," yelled a photographer. "They're already here."

A panda car pulled up outside and a young PC stepped out.

Shielding the boys under his arms, Dylan walked up the garden path and shouted through the letter box for Marnie to open the door.

"Marnie Martin," said the officer as she stood on the threshold, teary-eyed. "I am arresting you on suspicion of common assault on Mrs Barbara Grudge earlier today on the *ChitChat* television programme. You do not have to say anything, but I have to warn you, anything you do say may be taken down in evidence and used against you in a court of law. And courts may also infer guilt from your silence, in certain circumstances, should you choose to remain silent. Now, will you please accompany me to the police station?"

⚜ ⚜ ⚜

"THE SLAP!" – screamed the headlines on every news website that evening and every national newspaper the following day.

"Mrs Make Believe lashes out and loses it as her life is laid bare" ran the strap line. "Brother admits: 'She hits me too!'"

She'd even had a slot on the television news, to her utter shame.

A clip of Marnie assaulting Barbara was trending on Twitter and all over YouTube.

"Blimey," said Dylan. "You really walloped her one. But she deserved it, Marnie. She's an utter cow."

Of course, Caveman was all over the story like a bad rash: "Mrs Make Believe has a mean left hook #shescaresme."

Trust him to put the boot in! She wouldn't even dignify his stupid comment with a response.

And Zoe the stylist had ditched her, which was a relief, actually: "I cannot allow my image to be tarnished by representing you a moment longer. Fashion rules. OK?"

Marnie sat down at the kitchen table and made herself a cup of tea. It was what she did best in a crisis. She was just a mother-of-two, trying to get by, not a celebrity. What on earth had she been thinking, getting caught up in the whole fame thing? Forgetting who she really was, thinking she was somebody special. She'd done something very, very stupid in the heat of the moment and it had put her role as a mother to her boys, which was the very kernel of her being, at risk. She'd been charged and was due to appear in court next week: the very words made her quake. What if the court sent her to jail? What if she couldn't be there for the boys? She'd be a jail-bird mother. What if Matt took the children off to Australia and moved in with Belinda? This thought left her gulping for air.

All of this had started with wanting another baby, Barbara was right about that, but it wasn't selfish was it? She had been driven by her maternal instinct.

She'd only started the Mrs Make Believe blog to vent and the column was supposed to make things better financially but look what she'd done. She'd ruined her marriage. She'd ruined her life.

After she'd read to the boys that night, she put a blanket on the floor beside their bunk beds and lay down in the dark, just to be near them, listening to their breathing as they slept.

CHAPTER THIRTY-TWO

M arnie had never noticed before but tea, when served in a polystyrene cup at the magistrates' court, tasted of desperation.

She made her way through a crowd of people to get into the courtroom. Some were waving placards emblazoned with "I SUPPORT THE SLAPPER".

Belle was waiting for her, like the good friend she was in her hour of need. She'd brought Gabriel, looking beautifully chunky in his baby papoose. The courtroom was already packed with press and the public gallery was full to bursting, although the ushers forced her supporters to leave their banners outside.

There, sitting beside her solicitor, whose flicky hairdo almost touched her bouncy ginger curls, was Barbara Grudge. She turned and gave the press bench an appreciative little wave and then stared hard at Marnie.

"Don't worry, M, we're right here for you," said Belle, shooting Barbara her dirtiest look, as Gabriel chewed his fingers. He was teething and she'd given him Calpol in the hope that it would keep him quiet enough for her to sit in during the court case. The usher had almost refused to let her in until she explained Marnie had no other friends or family with her.

Marnie looked around the courtroom, searching for someone. For some reason, she thought Caveman might show up. But of course, he could be here and she wouldn't even know what he looked like.

What would she even say to him?

Thanks for the sexist comments?

Marnie climbed the little steps into the dock, her backside wiggling a bit in her too-tight skirt and heels. She wanted to look smart but had a limited wardrobe after Zoe's edit. Plus, her nerves could only be calmed by bars of chocolate and bags of boiled sweets, which hadn't helped matters.

The magistrate, a kindly-faced man in his early fifties, dressed in a sombre suit and tie, walked in as the usher, an unkindly-faced man in his thirties, dressed in a black robe that looked as if it had been used as dishcloth, shouted: "All rise!"

The court clerk read out the charge of common assault.

He was a dour fellow with a round face, thin lips and button eyes.

It was like being told off by a grumpy Homepride Flour man.

Marnie stood up to answer her name and enter her plea.

"Guilty," she said, blood rushing to her face. "And I'm very sorry for what I did. It was terribly wrong."

Barbara smirked.

Reporters flipped open their notepads, jotting down every word.

The Crown Prosecutor stood up, picking up a file with his case notes in it, and began to read.

"It is the Crown's case that the accused, Mrs Marnie Martin, slapped the victim, Miss Barbara Grudge, on the *ChitChat* television show, in an attack which was unprovoked ... "

Belle started to smell something bad. Gabriel had gone red in the face and was straining. People were leaning away from her.

"I'm sorry," she whispered to the woman next to her, "he's teething."

There was a horrible squelching sound and Belle felt his nappy growing warmer on her lap.

"Silence in court!" said the usher.

"Sorry," Belle mouthed at him.

"As I was saying," the prosecutor continued. "The victim suffered shock, anger and humiliation at the hands of the accused, who is also known by the *nom de plume* Mrs Make Believe. The effects of this disgraceful incident are still being felt today. In fact, she is still undergoing counselling."

Some of Marnie's supporters sniggered openly, and one said: "She'll be able to talk to herself then," leading Mr Homepride Flour, the court clerk, to look up and stare menacingly.

"May I remind the court," he said, "that it is possible to jail people for contempt?"

Gabriel then broke wind rather loudly, setting off another round of giggling in the public gallery.

"I'm sorry," said the usher, leaning towards Belle and then recoiling as he got a whiff of Gabriel, "you'll have to go outside with that baby."

"But I can't, she's my friend! She needs me!"

The doors at the back of the room swung open.

A tall man swept in, his face a picture of determination, black robes flapping, wig slightly askew and beads of sweat trickling down his neck from the effort of running from the tube station.

"If I may address the court?" said Matt, to gasps from the press bench and the gallery. Marnie's solicitor blanched visibly but Matt leaned over and whispered a few words in his ear and he sat down, shuffling a few papers around. There was no way he was going to argue with a barrister.

The magistrate sighed: "And who are you exactly?"

"I am the defendant's barrister, and husband."

Marnie gulped a great mouthful of air and gripped the dock so tightly that her knuckles turned white. What on earth was he doing here?

She was torn between the need to run away and the desire to run over and slap him, but given that she was already in enough trouble for that, she concentrated on trying to breathe normally through her windpipe, which appeared to have contracted to the size of a drinking straw.

The magistrate raised an eyebrow: "Go on, then. But be quick." It was nearly noon and he had a full list of motoring offences to get through later, so he wanted to leave time for a decent lunch break.

"I would just like to say, in mitigation, that my wife has suffered the extreme provocation of being married to me for more than ten years, which may have driven her to a kind of temporary insanity on this occasion," he said, as if he were reasoning with a small child, totally calm and in control.

Marnie was transfixed.

He had lost so much weight, it was like looking back 20 years. The bastard was so happy that he had lost his appetite! His back was as broad as ever but his suit seemed to hang off his waist now.

As Marnie studied him more closely, she realised that his weight-loss had, perhaps, not been due to happiness. There was a hollowness under his eyes.

She felt her pudgy middle, straining against the waistband of her skirt. Her emotions needed feeding, which made her feel even more guilty – and quite cross.

The magistrate raised an eyebrow: "Indeed, Mr Martin. But your good wife must realise she cannot go around slapping people, even if she disagrees with what they are saying, or feels aggravated. The pen is mightier than the sword, as they say. Is it not, Mrs Martin?"

Marnie nodded and then looked back at the floor as Matt turned to face her.

She didn't want to look directly at him or she would go to pieces. Barbara folded both her arms across her chest and whispered into her lawyer's ear as Matt spoke. Barbara still had the winning hair but Matt was speaking for Marnie and that counted for something.

Matt continued: "I would urge the court to be lenient, because the defendant is the best mother in the world and has two young sons who love her and need her. Her husband has let her down and failed to provide the support she needs. She has a host of friends who will swear to her good nature. None of this would have happened if I had appreciated her and told her that I loved her, in fact that I love her and the boys more than anything in the world. I should have come back, Marnie. Please forgive me."

This was all too much. Honest communication had been drowned out by the deafening din of everyday living and now the words she'd longed to hear were gushing out of Matt's mouth…she couldn't take it all in.

He loved her, not Belinda the temptress from Down Under.

But she bloody well hated him for what he had done. And what about what she had done with Maddox?

The court room appeared to be spinning.

The magistrate coughed loudly and said: "Mr Martin, now is neither the time nor the place to start declaring your affections for your wife."

"I meant to say, she was thrust into the limelight at a time when she was weakest emotionally due to strain on her marriage and not robust enough to withstand the onslaught of criticism foisted on her during the *ChitChat* television programme. This was a moment of madness from a woman who has the kindest heart."

She wanted to yell: "No, I don't have a kind heart. I cheated on you with an A-list film star!"

Instead, she stood there watching him defend her honour, with guilty written all over her face. He was oblivious to the fact that she had broken her marriage vows just as badly as him – worse in fact, because she'd slept with the object of lust for every right-thinking woman over the age of 35 and thoroughly enjoyed it.

The reporters couldn't get enough of Matt's outpouring of emotion and were scratching away frantically in their notepads but the magistrate had had enough of his court turning into a session with Relate. Although, he did quite enjoy Judge Rinder.

"Very well, stand up Mrs Martin." Marnie stood, her fingers clasping the edge of the dock. Her legs had turned to jelly. "You have apologised to your victim. Having heard the rather *lengthy* mitigation from your husband, I accept there were extenuating circumstances. This was a crime of passion, if you will." That would be bound to get his name in the papers, what a great quote. His clerk turned and gave an appreciative little nod.

"I will give you a conditional discharge and bind you over to keep the peace for 12 months. If we see any repeat of this behaviour, you will find yourself being dealt with very severely indeed, do you understand?"

"I do," she said meekly.

"Very well. The court will retire."

"All rise," yelled the clerk.

Matt stood up, fiddling with his lucky cufflinks – which almost made Marnie sob. She remembered him coming home, exhausted, taking off those cufflinks and putting them beside his dinner plate, night after night, or leaving them on the kitchen island, or losing them down the back of the sofa. Oh, Matt.

She twisted her wedding ring around her finger. After everything they'd been through, she still hadn't taken it off. And he was still wearing his.

Matt smiled at her but she looked away. Marnie's insides were churning. He still loved her. He said so, but it was all too late.

What had they done to their marriage? Did he think it could just be repaired by saying sorry? And, anyway, she'd ruined everything by cheating on him. Their whole life had changed, it couldn't be glued back together that easily. This was not some stupid fantasy relationship.

A flood of tears threatened to spill down her cheeks. Her supporters were cheering her now but she could barely manage a smile for them.

Belle helped her down from the dock and they pushed their way through the scrum as she walked out through the court room. Matt looked crestfallen as she brushed past him. If only someone could mitigate on his behalf to save his marriage.

❧　❧　❧

Marnie would have loved to go out for a walk down by the river at Kew to clear her head but she didn't dare leave the house, in case any Press were lurking.

Rufus appeared at her side, clasping a letter with her name on it.

"I found this," he said. "Postman Pat has been."

She recognised the hand-writing straight away.

With the envelope in her hand, she rushed upstairs to her little office and sat down at her desk. She opened it and felt tears welling in her eyes as she read:

Darling Marnie,

I have tried so many times to write to you and beg your forgiveness. Today, at last, I was able to show you how much I care, but I am not expecting you to want me back.

If you can bear to read on, I just want to explain things.

Marnie, I lost sight of myself and I lost sight of what matters most: you and the boys.

I behaved so foolishly, I was flattered by my pupil into booking that hotel suite. I got seduced by the idea of having fun, not by her. I swear nothing happened. She had other plans, with the head of Zenith Chambers, who will soon have to explain the patter of tiny feet to his long-suffering wife.

When you said you didn't trust me, Belinda seemed to have all the answers. I felt so low, something in me snapped. By the time I realised my mistake, it was too late – I had betrayed you, Marnie. I betrayed you long before that, by letting you struggle on your own and failing to see what you were going through.

I am deeply ashamed. When all is said and done, I cannot forget the happiness we had and everything we have created together. I failed to appreciate the joy of just living with you and the boys. Every day was so special, but I took it for granted.

Can you forgive me? I can be a better person but I need you by my side.

Matt xxx

CHAPTER THIRTY-THREE

"Please mind the gap, between your expectations of what life will be and how it actually turns out."

Did the tube announcer really just say that?

Marnie stepped off the train, clasping a copy of *The Sentinel*, with its screaming headline: "MRS MAKE BELIEVE SAVED BY LAWYER HUBBY!" This infuriated her more than ever.

Matt's letter was burning a hole in her handbag. She was still working out what to do about that but, meanwhile, she had bigger fish to fry: getting her job back.

Her swipe card at *The Sentinel* still worked. Crossing the atrium, she ignored the stares of everyone from hacks to the cleaners, and stepped into the glass lift. It was empty but with Marnie's feelings spilling over, it was starting to feel quite confined in there. What was she supposed to make of everything Matt had said to her? He had just dropped out of her life and then suddenly he expected to slot back into it, like some bloody fairytale? Well, it wasn't going to work like that! She was getting along just fine with things as they were – if you ignored the bit where she went off the rails and ended up in court.

Matt had to ruin everything by coming back and behaving so perfectly, didn't he? Sweeping in, like some handsome hero, and pouring out his heart to her and saving the day; even expressing his feelings in a letter, for God's sake! When had he ever done *that* before?

Now, he was going all touchy-feely on her and expecting her to just give in!

It all looked good on paper – let's face it, he was good at his job, which involved being very persuasive – but in the cold light of day, with a sink full of washing up and two screaming kids at his feet, would he live up to his declaration of love, or would that turn out to be just another fantasy?

And what about Maddox?

She'd loved every minute of being with him but had felt terrible about it ever since. Now she was going to have to confess it to Matt and feel guilty, all over again.

Why should she, after all he had put her through?

She would like to take hold of her stupid conscience and give it a really hard shake or a stern talking to – or both.

She was Mrs Make Believe and Mrs Make Believe was above saying sorry to her wayward husband, no matter that he had apologised to her in public and saved her from going to prison. Had she forgotten everything he had done to her: walking out of her life, dumping his kids and taking up with Belinda?

And what about the months, no, years of being taken for granted and treated as little more than the chief cook and bottle washer?

That wasn't who she was, was it? She had thoughts and feelings and ideas and, thank God, *Mrs Make Believe* allowed her to express them and get paid for it at the same time.

Mrs Make Believe was a dream come true.

She had taken control of her own fantasy and that turned out, strangely, to be her saviour. She wasn't going to allow Matt to just waltz back in with a few well chosen words of apology. Her readers would expect more of her than that.

Yes, she really deserved to be given another chance at *The Sentinel*. She'd been under so much pressure as Mrs Make Believe, that she had snapped, that's all.

And, in any case, she had a brilliant story to whet Barker's appetite.

The door to the lifts opened and Marnie stomped into the newsroom with a look of such anger on her face that Bryher did a bodyswerve.

Bryher had always suspected it, but the court case had proved it – Marnie was hardcore. That drippy motherhood stuff was all an act.

Marnie marched into The Bunker, Barker's office lair.

"Oh, Mrs Slap Happy," said Barker, barely glancing up from his newslist. "I saw you got off. But you are still on gardening leave. Why are you here?"

"You need to see this," said Marnie, taking a seat without waiting to be asked.

She pulled out her Obduro research. This story proved she could still cut it as a journalist, in case Barker needed to be reminded of that. Yes. Mrs Make Believe was in no mood to take any crap from anyone today.

Barker's face lit up as he scanned the page.

"That is bloody brilliant!" he said. "I have almost forgiven you for being the worst behaved member of staff since Harry Hedgeson was so hung-over he puked on the carpet at Number Ten."

"I know we are owned by Shustrov but I really think this is a story. It shows what kind of a man we are dealing with," she said, leaning forward over the desk to make her point. "The drug is produced by Shustrov's firm and is being peddled by a leading Harley Street doctor, who has a massively A-list clientele. I have also got this stuff from the Ibiza rave scene, but it is rather anecdotal."

Barker read the chat threads.

"It's largely Swahili. But it doesn't matter. It will sit nicely alongside Bryher's exclusive from Russia. All of it might make the Monopolies and Mergers Commission think twice about having someone like Shustrov controlling such a large slice of the media."

Marnie looked puzzled: "But he is shutting *The Sentinel* down, isn't he?"

Barker sighed: "Yes, but Peppa Pig is not Prime Minister, Marnie. You need to keep up with current affairs a bit more. Shustrov has a takeover bid in for *Future News* to get into satellite telly, big time, which will make him quite a player, as well as controlling what is left of this news operation."

Bryher sashayed in and parked her ample bottom on the edge of Barker's desk.

"I found out the truth about Shustrov," she said, her pillowy lips parting slightly in a smile of pure pleasure, as her kohl-rimmed eyes grew wider. "He was a very naughty boy indeed."

"Right," said Barker, tearing up his newslist, "let's get on. Bryher, you can start writing the splash. Marnie, you can oversee and feed in your copy. We are all screwed anyway, let's go down fighting."

Barker was giving her a second chance! Marnie felt like skipping around his office and planting a big kiss on his reptilian lips, but this was *The Sentinel*, so she merely gave a little, self-satisfied smile. She was back in.

Bryher almost hissed at Marnie in anger.

"It's OK, Bryher, you will get the first byline," she soothed, experiencing a feeling of such joy at getting her job back, that she could almost hug the hateful Newsdesk secretary: "It is your exclusive."

Bryher was struck dumb in the face of Marnie's kindness.

"Shall I get us some coffees, before we get going?" said Bryher, eventually. Now that she had arrived as a journalist and had to write the front page, she hadn't a clue how to start the story. It was quite terrifying.

Barker stood up, tucked his shirt into his trousers and rubbed his hands together. The old adrenaline was flowing again and it felt great. He marched into the newsroom to address his troops.

"If Stalin gets wind of this he will stop the presses. My career is fucked either way. I'll get a dummy front page sent around to Shustrov for first edition, to buy us more time. It may only be a newspaper but it is the best in Fleet Street. I am proud to say I work for *The Sentinel*. Write for your lives."

⚜ ⚜ ⚜

OLIGARCH'S SHAME: MURDER AND DODGY SEX PILLS

Vladimir Shustrov, one of the wealthiest Russian media owners in Britain, was convicted of killing a prostitute in communist Russia in a sex game that went wrong, it can be revealed today.

Shustrov, owner of The Sentinel *newspaper, who is also bidding to takeover the Future News satellite network, spent five years in a grim work camp east of Moscow for his crime, committed in the early 1980s.*

Sources at Zhukovsky Camp 17 said the sex-worker, from the neighbouring town of Skotoprigonyevsk, was strangled at an orgy for communist party bosses. Shustrov was named eventually as the killer after locals fought a cover-up by apparatchiks, but despite his past, Shustrov was able to use his connections to make millions exporting platinum after the fall of the communist regime.

One former colleague, who did not wish to be named for fear of reprisals, told The Sentinel: *"He made his fortune in precious metals doing business with everyone who was anyone. Anyone who wouldn't deal with him got their legs broken."*

As well as backing the spy thriller, Harsh Winter, his interests now include the Globotec drug firm, which has pioneered a new treatment for erectile dysfunction, called Obduro. The drug, being prescribed privately to celebrity clients by Harley Street cosmetic specialist Dr Igor Tolko, has shown alarming side-effects in tests carried out overseas, including problematic erections and dramatic increases in libido.

Emails obtained by this newspaper show that Dr Tolko and Mr Shustrov were both aware of these problems at the time that it was prescribed to clients, including an A-list actor.

Clubbers in Ibiza, who have obtained supplies of the drug illegally, have reported suffering priapism and sex mania.

⚜ ⚜ ⚜

Barker ran his fingers through his hair.

He was the first News Editor to openly attack an owner on the front page. His career was sunk. Not that he cared that much about his career – although, he did have a wife and three kids to support – it was the worry about his staff which had kept him awake all night.

The paper's first edition made it into print before Shustrov, as predicted, pulled the whole story.

It didn't matter – the Shustrov sex and drugs story had grown legs and was scampering about all over the internet, other newspapers and television networks worldwide.

Some bloke called Ivan in Russia was even waxing lyrical about Bryher's charms.

The hacks at *The Sentinel* were all still staring redundancy in the face but politicians from all parties were now questioning Shustrov's suitability as a media owner, at least.

Barker was glued to *Future News*, which had been doing rolling coverage – including, unfortunately, replaying the clip of Marnie lamping Barbara Grudge on *ChitChat*.

The TV anchorman, who oozed charm and used too much Brylcreem, said: "One of the journalists behind the story was recently bound over to keep the peace after this unprovoked attack on a counselling expert during a day-time television chat show. The other journalist is, according to our sources at least, well known in public houses and nightclubs around West London but has so far failed to distinguish herself as a writer."

"That was uncalled for!" said Bryher, putting her feet up on Barker's desk in The Bunker. She was on such a high, she was acting as if she owned the place. If the rumours from the business correspondent were true, Bryher could easily afford to buy the place. Shustrov was apparently so furious he was planning to sell *The Sentinel* and everything in it, for a nominal pound.

Marnie checked Caveman's Twitter feed, just to pass the time.

Yes, he'd read her story and surprise, surprise – he had another acerbic comment for her.

"A real news story and not just gossip or knickers from Mrs Make Believe #makesachange."

Barker's phone rang. He cupped his hand over the handset and motioned for Bryher to get her trotters off his blotting pad and leave him in peace.

Then, he darted out of the office and disappeared into a lift in the back corridor of power.

The minutes ticked by.

A hush fell over the newsroom as a tall, striking man strode in with Barker.

Barker spoke: "This is a proud moment in the history of *The Sentinel*. After the extraordinary events of the last 24 hours, I would like to introduce, if introduction were needed, Maddox Wolfe, one of Britain's leading actors."

Hacks were murmuring to each other as confusion swept the newsroom.

"But the BAFTAs are months away," mumbled sozzled reporter Harry Hedgeson, rudely awoken from his afternoon snooze, under his desk.

Barker continued: "And the new owner of *The Sentinel*."

There were gasps and people tore themselves away from their computer screens, hung up their mobile phones and started to make their way towards the Newsdesk.

Maddox addressed the crowd: "These are difficult times for the industry but I believe, with the right direction, we can turn that to our advantage. I'm hoping to get to know more about the way the newspaper runs over the days and weeks that follow, but what I will promise you now, is that I will take my lead from your boss and I will not meddle where I am not wanted. I intend to invest in quality journalism. *The Sentinel* has a bright future indeed.

"Now, you'd better get back to it. There's a paper to produce, isn't there?"

A ripple of applause washed across the newsroom.

Maddox watched Marnie intently and then wandered over to her.

All eyes in the office turned to look at Marnie and the movie star, as she struggled not to blush beetroot.

"And if you would like a little exclusive, I'm no longer in the frame for role of Seb Winter in *Harsh Winter*," he said.

"No!" she said, rather loudly, before she could contain her disappointment. "I mean, why not?"

"The bosses thought I was too old for the role," he said, softly. "And the fact is, they are probably right. They are giving it to Byron Hunt instead. Young blood and all that."

"I'm so sorry," said Marnie, touching his arm briefly and then taking her hand away before Bryher or any of the others noticed. "I can't think of anyone better to play Seb Winter than you. You make him so … masterful." She couldn't say that last word to his face, so she looked at the floor instead.

"That's very sweet of you, Marnie, and I'm delighted you feel that way but it's fine," he said. "There comes a time when actors have to face facts and move on. And in any case, I have a feeling I will have my hands quite full here, don't you?"

CHAPTER THIRTY-FOUR

The azure sea was so calm and still, the yacht barely rocked in the water, as Athena Maldon lay down on the sumptuous, king-sized day bed on the deck and cried her eyes out.

Hollywood had called and it was not good news.

The offer for her to play the leading role of sexy spy Katya in the long-awaited *Harsh Winter* film had been withdrawn, in the light of *The Sentinel*'s outrageous allegations about her boyfriend Vladimir Shustrov. Once again, Marnie Martin's name was on the story which put an end to her dreams.

It just wasn't fair.

She pounded the linen pillows with her fists, her bronzed legs flailing as she howled her distress.

A large shadow loomed over her.

It was Shustrov.

She turned over and stretched out like a cat, squinting up at him with red-rimmed eyes, as the sun's rays beat down.

Athena was naked but for a gun-metal grey pair of side-tie bikini bottoms.

"What ever is the matter, little dove?"

"It's that bloody newspaper. My next film role has been cancelled, thanks to their article about you. You should have closed the rag down when you had the chance, like I told you to!"

He rested his hands on his hips as he spoke: "Are you giving me orders?"

Athena lowered her eyes and crossed her arms to cover her breasts: "No."

"Don't cover yourself. I want to look at you."

She hesitated.

"You are very disobedient today. I think you want me to punish you, little dove."

He half-smiled at her, his full lips curling slightly at the edges and his eyes, a clearer blue than the sparkling sea, seemed to glow, as if a light were shining behind them.

Her heart was beating faster and she felt her nipples growing hard.

He moved towards her.

"You like me to do this, don't you, Athena?"

She stared at him and pouted, but said nothing.

"Don't be insolent. Answer me!"

She uncrossed her arms, arched her back – so that her breasts jutted – giving him a salacious little smile as she nodded. A huge five carat diamond glinted on a platinum chain around her neck.

The water lapped against the glossy sides of her boat, which he had named after her, just as he had promised he would.

He leaned over and started to kiss her throat as he murmured: "You are such a bad girl."

Athena put both her arms around his neck and kissed him, hard, her tongue mingling with his, as she inhaled his musky scent and felt his broad, muscled shoulders. He sat down beside her.

"Who needs Hollywood? I will make you a star, dorogaya. I promise. Let me talk to some of my friends in television, hmmm?"

Next to him, she was just a helpless little bird. His hands travelled down to her waist, holding her, firmly.

Then he flipped her over his lap, lazily stroking the silky fabric, which barely covered her bottom. He took his time, slowly pulling the side ties of her bikini pants, so they fell away, showing off her tan lines.

Last time, he had shaved her bare. Her skin was soft and smooth as he traced his fingers between her thighs, which she parted for him. She was already getting wet.

Athena wriggled with pleasure and gave a little moan as he gently placed one hand underneath her, cupping his fingers, so that she would push against them with every slap. He whispered in her ear: "How many this time? Twenty? Thirty? Until you come?"

Then he lifted his other hand and brought it down so hard that she yelped loudly, jolting forward into his thighs, squirming as she awaited the next blow.

The crew turned up the sound on the deck stereo to mask her cries. Shustrov liked to put out to sea first but sometimes Athena couldn't wait and the boss didn't want any trouble from the harbour authorities in Cannes.

Athena was a bad girl every day.

CHAPTER THIRTY-FIVE

Training for Astral Prep Sports Day had begun, in earnest, just after the Easter holidays, which did seem rather excessive.

Year One had been thoroughly drilled in the sack race, hopscotch and the egg and spoon, working on their speed and agility with more dedication than your average Olympic athlete.

Marnie had tried to explain to Rufus that it was best not to attempt practice runs around the house with a raw egg from the fridge – but several nasty splodges on the living room carpet were evidence of him, and her brother Dylan, ignoring this decree.

Teachers, flustered in the heat of a June afternoon, were handing out coloured bibs to the assembled children, while the shoutiest parents were gee-ing up their offspring from the sidelines.

The mothers were the worst.

Particularly the Amazonian blonde Felicity Harper-Bilge, who had been a bit funny about Marnie's success with her *Mrs Make Believe* column, to be honest.

"You've stopped writing that dross then," she said, looking Marnie up and down, through her Kors sunglasses. "Did they fire you after your court case?"

Marnie had been in rather a hurry to get here and

had to resort to her trusty denim cut-offs and a pair of Birkenstocks. Felicity was wearing a very pretty tea-dress.

"No, still writing happily," she said. "I've just been rather busy of late."

But her reply was drowned out by Felicity bellowing across the field: "Come on, Ptolemy! Stuff the opposition!"

She turned back to Marnie: "Sorry, what were you saying?"

"Just admiring Ptolemy's running form," said Marnie, melting Felicity's glacial exterior by a millimetre at least.

Rufus looked a bit miserable standing in the crush of other kids, his blue bib over his games kit, which was not as pristine as it could be, really. Marnie waved to him but he didn't see her.

The games master fired the starting pistol and a stampede of little legs began.

"See how Ptolemy has a much superior grip on his spoon when he is running!" crowed Felicity.

"See how the little bugger is cheating by holding on to the egg," muttered Marnie, under her breath.

Rufus was neck and neck – or spoon and spoon – with Ptolemy now. Ptolemy stuck his foot out and Rufus, who was not the most co-ordinated of children, dropped the spoon and fell over.

"Another win for Ptolemy! Hurrah!" yelled Felicity. "I expect he will get the most medals at the end."

"I expect so, yes," said Marnie. Rufus limped to the finish line in last place and burst into tears on seeing his mother. Marnie ran to him and gave him the biggest hug: "You did very well darling, don't worry."

Rufus looked at her with little round brown eyes, which were a miniature version of hers: "I am rubbish and he cheated. He is the s-word."

"We don't swear Rufus."

"The S-word is stupid, Mummy. That is what he called me in class the other day because I can't read as fast as him."

Marnie looked around her. She had spent so long thinking about her own problems that she had neglected what mattered most – her children's happiness.

"Just have fun in the sack race," she said, patting him on the head as he went off to rejoin the class.

"Fun?" said Felicity, incredulously. "Fun? Is that what we are paying for here? I don't think so! I want my boy to be the best at everything, so that he reaches his full potential. What is the point of being an also-ran in this life? But, then again, I'm not the kind of mother who goes around slapping total strangers. Perhaps we have different standards." She turned her back on Marnie.

"Yes," said Marnie, looking around her, at the crowd of pushy parents, whose ambition for their children to be the best and to trample over everyone and anyone to get there seemed to seep from their very pores; and at the teachers, lining the children up like nine pins. "I think we do."

She marched over to the sack race, where Rufus was struggling to clamber into his bag, and whispered in his ear: "C'mon, let's get out of here."

And they skipped together, to the lasting astonishment of Astral Prep School, up the race track and out of the sports ground.

Chapter Thirty-Six

Mrs Make Believe

DOES SORRY EVER WORK?

I am pondering whether just saying the word is enough. When you think about all the water that has flowed under the bridge in a relationship, does there come a point at which you cannot go back? Like a little pooh stick that has been thrown in and is just bobbing away on its own down the river, to be carried along to pastures new.

No, no, no. That was rubbish. She'd have to tear it up and start again. Her column was supposed to be witty and amusing at the very least.

She re-read the letter from Matt, explaining how his old flame Belinda had promised to help him find himself, fuelling his fantasy of being a younger man with no responsibilities. Well, it was a good excuse, but rather late, in her opinion.

She tried again:

Well, girls, The Husband has said the words I never thought I'd hear – not "Here's my credit card, go shopping" (which would be quite nice, actually) – just: "Sorry."

How many times have you heard that one? Has it ever stopped him staying out late with his mates at the pub, failing

to remember your anniversary or even just do the washing up?
Didn't think so! So, does it cover going off with another woman?

Yes, that was a bit better. She'd omitted, of course, to mention that she had gone off with another man. What purpose would it serve to admit to it in print, anyway?

Mrs Make Believe was not supposed to be a love cheat. It wouldn't be good for her image. She needed to bear in mind what the readers thought of her, especially as she'd only just got her job back after her court debacle.

There was a knock at the door.

It was the postman delivering a parcel for Dylan. She laid it down in the hallway and then Marnie climbed the stairs back to her little box room, which doubled as an office.

She sighed and took another sip of coffee as she stared out of the window at the trees, which were now clothed in their summer finery, to the church spire beyond and the aeroplanes coming in to land at Heathrow. And glancing back into the street, to the black Mercedes pulling up outside. And to Maddox Wolfe stepping out and trying to work out which house was hers. Oh my God!

She scarpered into the bedroom and ripped off her jogging bottoms and yanked on a pair of jeans, which were torn at the knee but she could at least do up.

The door bell rang.

She released her hair from its scruffy ponytail, then, catching sight of herself in the mirror, pulled it back up again, before scampering down the stairs. She opened the door, reminding herself to pretend that she didn't know he was standing behind it.

"Maddox! What a total and utter surprise!" Yep, he would definitely know she'd seen him from the window from that performance.

He produced a bunch of red roses from behind his back, beaming as he looked her up and down.

"I thought you might like these," he said extending the flowers towards her.

"Gosh, how lovely of you, thanks," she said, remembering that she hadn't done the washing up yet and there was a massive pile of laundry waiting to be folded on the kitchen table, plus the nail varnish on her toes was quite chipped.

Did she really have to invite him in?

"How did you find out where I live?"

She hovered on the doorstep in her bare feet, cradling the flowers.

"Well, I own the newspaper now, so that was easy," he said, as the Newsdesk's driver peered through the window of the Mercedes and waved at her.

"Yes, of course, amazing."

That was it. Next time she was in the office, she was going to put cyanide in the driver's tea, instead of sugar.

"I expect you're far too busy to bother coming in?" she said, unable to disguise the note of desperation in her voice. Surely he would take the hint and leave? She hadn't even had time to brush her hair this morning!

"No, all the time in the world. I'd love to, thanks," he replied, stepping over the threshold and into the hallway, with scuff marks from the kids' scooters and jammy handprints on the woodwork.

"Things are a bit chaotic," mumbled Marnie, hurriedly sweeping a pile of unopened post into the kitchen drawer. "Can I get you a coffee or something?"

"That would be nice."

What was he even doing here?

"Do sit down." She said a silent prayer, that he should not inspect the cleanliness of her coffee cups too closely.

Maddox pulled out a chair to sit – it was covered in stuck-on bits of cereal.

"Maybe not that one," said Marnie, cringing and pulling out another chair for him, which was covered in ketchup.

"Why don't we sit outside in the garden?" she said, brightly.

The white wisteria was in full bloom on her little pergola, with pink clematis winding through it and into a cherry tree. It was quite a pleasant garden, if you ignored the patchy grass and the kids' toys scattered about. The iron garden chairs scraped on the flagstones as they sat down opposite each other, parking their coffee cups on the table in front of them.

Some of the wisteria flowers were shedding their petals. It looked like confetti.

"Cecily's pregnant," said Maddox, watching her face closely.

"Oh," said Marnie. She added quickly: "Oh, congratulations, I mean."

"It has come as a bit of a shock," said Maddox, slowly.

"Is it yours?" said Marnie. Her hand flew up to her face. "I'm sorry, I shouldn't have said that."

Maddox gave a little laugh, his blue eyes twinkling: "It's OK, Marnie. The same thought crossed my mind, but she assures me it is mine. She only started screwing Byron Hunt once she had conceived with me."

"Ugh," said Marnie. "That is disgusting. I mean, I shouldn't make value judgements on other people."

"It's OK," said Maddox, with a wave of his hand. "She wants to come back to me and of course, I want her back, she's my wife. Although, there is someone else who's been on my mind a lot lately."

"Really?" said Marnie, trying to sound nonchalant.

"Yes, I'm thinking about her more often than I should. In fact, I even had a dream about her the other night. Would you like me to tell you about it?"

Marnie looked into his eyes. He had such a level gaze, there was no hiding from him and he didn't seem to want to hide from her. It was terribly unnerving and rather sexy at the same time. He could have her, so easily. He knew it and she knew it but that didn't make it right.

And, anyway, he could have any woman he wanted. He was a movie star, for goodness' sake. She was just a chubby house-wife/ journalist/ scandal-starting blogger from Chiswick.

"Why are you telling me this?" she whispered.

"Well, she's hung up on her husband. So, she's become a sort of fantasy for me."

"But if you did have her, if she was available, you'd soon get bored, wouldn't you?"

"I don't think I would, she's quite a handful, you see. I'd take her to bed and love her very thoroughly. I think that is what she needs most of all, don't you?"

He was propositioning her and it sounded delicious.

Maddox went on: "I'd take her out to the finest restaurants, whisk her off on lovely holidays, buy her things she deserves. I'd give her everything her foolish husband doesn't."

Marnie gave him a wry smile.

"I'd ask her to tell me what she was really feeling and then I'd listen," he said.

Oh, bloody hell. Maddox had got her number alright.

"But what you are offering isn't real is it?" said Marnie, crossing her arms.

"It's as real as you want it to be, Marnie."

They sat in silence for a moment, just looking at the garden.

"Well, you're going to be a father again, which is lovely," said Marnie, eventually.

He laid his hand on her arm.

"If you don't want to take things further with me, why don't you at least let your husband come home?"

"I can't," she said, moving her arm away, as if he had scalded her. "I'm Mrs Make Believe and Mrs Make Believe doesn't need a pathetic, unfaithful husband, no matter how much he grovels and says sorry and wants to come home. I have to think about my readers, you know."

Maddox pretended to take a sip of coffee to disguise the massive grin that was spreading from ear to ear.

She spotted it.

"You don't really believe that, do you?" he said.

"I might do," she mumbled.

He was being downright nosy with her, so she would be just as nosy back: "So, how do you and Cecily manage to keep it all together? You know she's been cheating on you. Does she know you have cheated on her?"

"Well, we do this every couple of years," he sighed. "We have to both come clean with each other."

"You can't tell her about me!" said Marnie, horror-struck.

"Don't worry," said Maddox, "I don't go into that kind of detail. I just say there have been a few flings, nothing serious. Then, we usually go away somewhere quiet and luxurious together and spend time just enjoying each other. That sort of rebalances things for me and Cecily."

"That sounds easy enough for you, Maddox, but I've betrayed Matt!" Marnie cried. "Can you imagine how he will feel if I just come clean with him? We are not used to shagging around, particularly not with film stars!"

She caught the wounded look on his face, and murmured: "I mean, having an open marriage or playing games or whatever it is you do. I thought I was a one-man woman, with occasional fantasies." She felt herself colouring up: "And the trouble is, I have had another man – from one of my fantasies – which makes me, God knows what, never mind what my husband got up to with his old flame from university."

"Don't be so hard on yourself," said Maddox. "He cheated on you, which is not an excuse, but he did and you were on your own, and something happened between us. So, just tell him there was a fling on a job in Cannes and that was that. You might even have been a bit drunk."

"Yes, but I wasn't, was I?"

"We are all failed human beings, Marnie. You have to forgive yourself before you can forgive him, I think."

Then, Maddox said: "The great thing about marriage and kids is that everyone can tell you what it's like, but there's no point because until you have experienced it, you don't know how you are going to react to those pressures or even what the pressures will be."

"It's hardly the same for film stars!" she scoffed.

"Yes, I accept that we don't always have the same money worries, maybe, but there are long absences, trust issues, egos. We all have problems."

Marnie stared into the bottom of her coffee cup. She really would have to get some new dishwasher tablets because there was a definite murky ring around it.

"What about *The Sentinel*? Are you going to close it down or use it to just promote Cecily's latest film?" said Marnie, unable to keep the sarcasm out of her voice.

"No, not at all," said Maddox. "I'm going to be a very hands-off owner."

"How can you even afford to run it? I know it was going cheap, but the salaries alone … "

"Well, I'll let you into a little secret," he said, squinting as the sun reached its midday peak. "Years ago, and I mean years ago, when I was a struggling actor in LA, I meet a geeky guy in a coffee shop, who had a notion that the computer he was using at university would one day be as common as cars, and everyone would have one, and would need a way to get information. Bonkers, right?"

Marnie laughed.

"So, I piled my meagre savings into his research project for something he called a search engine, which I thought was a stupid name at the time."

"But, that means you are worth millions and millions," she gasped.

"Cecily's never known about it till now. I'm not kidding myself, it might have had something to do with her desire to return home, but anyway. I've been a sleeping partner in the business from the start. I always planned to use the cash for my retirement, then I heard this national treasure was under threat and I have quite a soft spot for one of its more bolshie reporters."

Marnie could feel the beginnings of blush. Why did he do that to her so easily?

"You didn't have to buy the newspaper to help me, Maddox."

"I didn't just do it for that reason," said Maddox. "*The Sentinel* – love it or hate it – is as British as cricket or tea and toast. I think the world would be much greyer, scarier place without it. But on a serious work note, Marnie, I have been going through the sales figures with Barker and, in spite of the all drama surrounding your court appearance, circulation peaks on the days when your column comes out. We'd like you to turn *Mrs Make Believe* into a book. It's a natural step for *Mrs Make Believe* and we can do a launch party as soon as next week. We're doing a reader competition and the winners will get to meet you. What do you think about that?"

Marnie felt something approaching panic. This was beyond her wildest dreams for *Mrs Make Believe* – but being on show, putting herself out there and actually meeting the readers, was terrifying. What on earth would she wear for a start?

"I have a feeling," said Maddox, with a sly little half-smile, "that Mrs Make Believe is going to turn out to be something of a star. Perhaps she will even be as well-known as Seb Winter. She could become a fantasy figure for mothers everywhere."

A half-strangled sound came from the back of Marnie's throat.

"You might have to spice up her love life a bit, I'm sure we could work on a few ideas together," said Maddox, his smile turning into a wicked grin and lighting up his eyes.

Marnie's heart flip-flopped.

"No," she said, recovering herself, "I think Mrs Make Believe is just a mother, like everyone else, and ordinary mothers might dream about famous actors but they definitely, absolutely, do not go around having sex with movie stars. It wouldn't be good for her image."

And she plonked her coffee cup down on the table, quite hard, as if she were putting a big full stop at the end of that sentence.

"Suit yourself," said Maddox, standing up to leave and pulling her to him to steal a kiss, before she even had time to protest. "But, as one of Mrs Make Believe's most avid readers, I would love to see her living out her fantasies a bit more. Think about it, Marnie."

He swept up both empty coffee cups in his manly hands and headed back to the house, taking her vain hope that the matter was closed along with him.

CHAPTER THIRTY-SEVEN

*M*rs *Make Believe* was going to be a book.

Marnie could barely contain her excitement and called Belle to tell her the latest.

Then, she did a victory lap of the kitchen island, squeaking with delight, before emptying the washing machine and hanging out the laundry.

Belle arrived with Gabriel in his pram to help her celebrate her big news.

Marnie noticed her friend looked so much happier these days: Belle's shapeless t-shirt was covered in the remnants of Gabriel's lunch and her hair was a total mess but she was smiling and had a glow about her. Gabriel had splodges all over his Babygro and smelled like he needed a change. In short, they were a perfectly normal mother and baby combo.

Belle bent down and pulled a bottle of chilled prosecco from the shopping carrier underneath the buggy. "I never thought of putting it to such good use before," she laughed. "But we really do have something to celebrate!"

As the cork popped, Belle put her hand momentarily on Marnie's shoulder.

"Why don't you call and tell Matt the good news?"

Marnie winced.

"Why on earth would I do that?"

"Because you still care about him. He'd be so happy for you, you ought to at least give him a chance to talk things through…"

"Look, Belle, I know you want us to get back together but it's not that easy. I'm Mrs Make Believe now, remember?"

"What's that got to do with it?"

"Mrs Make Believe doesn't need her rubbish husband back, does she? Imagine what the readers would make of that!" said Marnie, over-filling the champagne flute so that bubbles spilled all over the work top.

Belle raised an eyebrow.

"*Mrs Make Believe* doesn't have to rule your life, Marnie," said Belle. "I know it is a column about your experiences, but you could just make a bit up now and then. You could let Matt come home and not write about it? You still have the right to a private life."

"But I don't, not any more!" said Marnie. "I am supposed to be telling it like it is. I owe it to the readers, who believe in me. I can't let them down."

"Oh, come on," said Belle. "Half of what goes in those columns is made up."

"My column isn't!" cried Marnie. "It's the truth, the whole truth and nothing but the truth and that is why it is so good."

"OK," said Belle, realising her friend was on her soapbox and there was no chance of getting her off it, other than by changing the subject entirely. "What are you going to wear for the big book launch?"

"I suppose I'll have to wear my hideous circus frock again," sighed Marnie.

"No!" said Belle, before she could stop herself.

Marnie looked rather hurt: "It's not that bad, is it?"

"It's not really you, Marnie," said Belle, tactfully. "Let me babysit for you and you can go and get yourself something lovely to wear. In fact, I can bring Gabriel and we will have a sleep over. That way you can really relax and enjoy your big night out, without leaving it all to Dylan."

"Oh, Belle, thanks," she said, brightening. "You are a true friend. I will find an alternative to my frocky horror show." As she sipped the champagne she felt a tidal wave of sadness at the thought of achieving so much with *Mrs Make Believe* and not having Matt beside her.

"I won't ever be happy again," she said, putting the glass down on the kitchen island, with a sob. "I've had my chance."

"That's not true," said Belle, giving her a hug. "There is still hope. Maybe you just need to talk to someone? You could think about getting some counselling, perhaps?"

She caught the look in Marnie's eye and said quickly: "Or, perhaps not. Maybe you and Matt just need time to chat to each other, and get to know each other again."

Marnie pulled a tear-stained letter out of the kitchen drawer and showed it to her friend.

"He's been writing at least one letter to me a day," she said.

"What's he been saying?" said Belle.

Marnie was so secretive about her feelings. Why hadn't she told her about it?

"He's just finding different ways of saying he loves me and the boys and is so sorry. He wants a second chance."

"Well?"

"I'm scared to let him back because I don't want to go back to the way we were before and I don't know if I can ever forgive him. Or if he can forgive me."

"What's he got to forgive you for?"

Marnie swallowed hard.

"I cheated on him."

"When?" said Belle. She'd been so wrapped up in her own little new babyworld with Gabriel and Jonah that she hadn't realised half of what was going on with Marnie.

"It was while I was in Cannes. It was just a one night stand, Belle. I'm not going to do it ever again." Marnie picked at a few crumbs on the table and then wiped her eyes on her sleeve.

"I'm not judging you, Marnie," said Belle. "I think it's good that you enjoyed yourself, to be honest."

"I can't bear to think about it," she said, with a look of despair. "What if I did enjoy it? What kind of a person does that make me?"

"It makes you a woman," said Belle, "A woman who is too hard on herself."

Marnie put her head in her hands.

"I don't want to keep it a secret from Matt but I don't want to have to tell him about it either."

"I can understand that, but he hasn't got a leg to stand on, Marnie, when it comes to cheating," said Belle, adding hurriedly: "Not that I am judging or saying anything bad about him. The main thing is, you need to talk to him. Why don't you just ring him up and have a chat?"

Marnie wanted to run a mile from that question.

"I'm just too busy with stuff right now," she said.

Belle raised an eyebrow but said nothing.

"The truth is, Belle, I'm scared to face it all," said Marnie, as the last of the prosecco bubbles fizzled themselves out.

❧ ❧ ❧

Once she'd waved Belle and Gabriel off, Marnie's thoughts turned to tea for the boys – fish fingers and oven chips, to be precise. And ketchup – which almost counted as a vegetable, didn't it?

With Dylan slumped in front of the telly, Marnie had just enough time to have a quick read through the penultimate chapter of *Harsh Winter*, to see if she could work out the ending, before going to her book club.

She turned the page and began to read.

The dying embers of the fire are still glowing in the half-light.

 She is already awake.

 Without speaking, she clambers on top of me.

 "Again?" I ask, with a smile.

 She nods and eases herself downwards. I love taking her in this position, with every inch of her beautiful body on display.

 But this time her eyes are cold and unfathomable.

 She starts to squeeze me.

 "Katya, that is very impressive," I moan, but she doesn't stop. She keeps squeezing, trapping me with her pelvic floor muscles, creating such a wave of pleasure that I start to feel light-headed.

 Before I can flip her onto her back and take control of the situation, she puts her hand beneath the pillow, pulls out a syringe and stabs it into my arm.

 The room starts to spin away from me.

 "You'll regret this," I mumble, aware that she is still bringing me to the most earth-shattering orgasm I have ever experienced.

 "It seems winter is coming to an end," she murmurs, riding me harder.

 The last thing I see, before the room turns black, is her head thrown back in ecstasy, her eyes half-closing and the most evil smile playing on her rosebud lips.

When I wake, it is morning. The fire is dead and the room is cold. Katya has gone and taken the antidote with her.

I check my equipment.

It is still working, thank God, despite her strangle-hold, perfected, no doubt, in some strip joint in Singapore.

The memory of her haunts me but I have no time to dwell on that, because the fate of the world still rests in my capable hands.

Crikey. Who would have thought it? So, Katya had out-witted Seb with her scary pelvic floor muscles and broken his heart at the same time, but not, thankfully, his equipment. What a woman!

She pulled on her coat and grabbed her bag, sighing to herself as she stepped outside.

Scrabbling in her handbag to check she hadn't for-gotten her door-key, Matt's latest letter worked its way between her reluctant fingers. She'd stuffed it in there earlier, to give her time to think. She pulled it out and glanced at it.

No, she still really needed more time. She couldn't face reading it properly, anyway, because it made her feel quite tearful. She was too busy with *Mrs Make Believe* and every-thing else to have to deal with all Matt's emotional outpour-ings, in any case.

Her phone bleeped.

It was another stupid tweet from Caveman, this time about her latest column, which was up on *Sentinel Online*, as a teaser for tomorrow's paper.

Caveman, unfortunately, appeared to be her biggest fan.

Now he was taking objection to her pondering whether she should accept her husband's apology! As if saying sorry was enough to make up for colossal disinterest and infidelity. Pah!

Caveman was always siding with her husband. It was like some stupid, blokish bro-mance.

She fired off a quick tweet: "You don't know all the facts #mindyourbusiness." Yes, put a sock in it, Cave-twit.

As she cut a solitary figure, walking up the road lined with lime trees, their leaves sticky with summer sap, she couldn't stop Caveman's tweet running through her mind: "What hope is there for anyone if you can't accept sorry? #onlyasking."

CHAPTER THIRTY-EIGHT

Marnie was amazed to discover that, without the demands of running the house and looking after two little boys, she did have a half-decent dress sense.

It wasn't a showy dress or on-trend or whatever the awful stylist would have called it. But it made her look good and more importantly, she felt good in it. The black silk crepe draped beautifully over her bust and cinched in her waist, without clinging too much. The length was just right too. It seemed to enhance her curves without making her feel like she was trying to fit into something for a skinnier model. She might even look quite stylish.

And it cost a small fortune. But, hey, this was supposed to be her big night for *Mrs Make Believe*, and working it out on a cost-per-wear basis, if she wore it to every event she was invited to for the next five years, it could turn out to be a bargain!

It was slightly off the shoulder, which meant she would have to go shopping for some new underwear. The woman in the lingerie department brought armloads of knicker and bra sets for her to try. Marnie glanced at the price tag and nearly fainted. Seventy-five quid for one pair of pants? She pulled on a pair which had looked a bit complicated on the hanger. Once she'd got them on, she turned around to have a look at her rear view in the mirror. Her heart fluttered as she gazed at her reflection. They had a criss-cross of stretchy black lace that seemed to wrap around her curves, while giving a tantalising flash of her naked bottom beneath. They were very, very sexy and there is no way she would ever normally consider wearing something like this.

Marnie thought back to Matt buying her tarty knickers as an apology before she kicked him out. They were not sexy in a classy way like these ones, but she understood now. He had been trying to say he found her attractive. He really had. In his cack-handed, blokish way with his silly furry handcuffs for a bit of fun. She could have just told him thanks and then gone shopping for something she liked. But, no, instead she'd flown off the handle, forced him into counselling and into the arms of Belinda, the witch. She sat down on the little padded stool in the changing room, still clutching the matching bra.

"Is everything alright?"

The assistant was hovering outside the curtain.

"Fine," said Marnie. "I'm just thinking."

That was an understatement.

She was having a relationship epiphany in the under-wear department of Selfridges.

"It's all gone rather wrong," said Marnie.

An overly-made up face appeared around the curtain: "I've got lots of sizes, just ask."

"Sorry, I didn't mean the knickers," said Marnie. "They are lovely."

"Bra?" said the assistant, who sounded rather impatient.

How could Marnie even begin to explain?

"Sorry," she said "I will just try it on and tell you."

The curtain was yanked shut again.

Marnie stood up and sighed. She needed to talk to Matt. She could barely face it. The thought of discussing everything flooded her with so many feelings: guilt, anger, shame, despair, more anger – at herself, at him.

Besides, she had to get the *Mrs Make Believe* launch out of the way first. *Mrs Make Believe* was her priority now. She clung to it, like a life-raft, after leaving the shipwreck of her marriage. *Mrs Make Believe* had finished that off, really, and she was determined now, more than ever, to make some good come of it. She had to, for the sake of the boys.

She pulled on the matching bra, which was strapless in the same black lace. It seemed to work miracles, holding her in whilst lifting things up and pushing them out, in the right way, with no risk of slippage. She checked the price tag. That must be worth the hundred quid she was going to have to pay for it.

She stared at the curvaceous woman staring back at her, looking not only comfortable in her own skin for once but actually working a set of expensive lingerie.

What had happened to her?

Marnie fleetingly imagined Maddox seeing her dressed up like this. Would he like them?

What on earth was she even thinking about him for!

She was going to have to see him at the *Mrs Make Believe* event later and it was strictly business between them from now on. She'd decided on that for sure.

Hadn't she?

❧ ❧ ❧

Maddox had spared no expense in the launch of her *Mrs Make Believe* book for *The Sentinel*, which of course was planning to serialise it and make as much capital out of her success as possible.

Marnie gasped as she walked in to the grand Edwardian town house overlooking Park Lane.

She'd been expecting a few drinks and sandwiches in a little hotel somewhere but everything about this building, with its bow windows and Baroque, gilt staircase, was breathtaking.

She could hear the chatter of people upstairs.

A waiter showed her to the drinks reception, out on the terrace overlooking Hyde Park.

Huge containers of box and olive trees lined the terrace, which was already full to bursting with guests taking cocktails from silver trays or sitting down on the wooden benches, scattered with cushions, and talking animatedly.

There were a few clouds on the horizon but the sun was still shining through, bathing the sandstone terrace in such a warm light.

It was all too lovely for words.

Barker spotted her and raised a glass in her direction. Smiling back at him, she took a glass of champagne from the tray of a passing waitress and raised it back.

It was quite odd, the boss being so nice to her, for once.

A string quartet started to play, something classical, she couldn't tell what.

She moved through the crowd, chatting to people from the office and the first of the readers who had won the competition to meet her.

"You inspired me to leave my husband," said one rather rotund woman, clasping her hand and glowing with delight.

"Oh, no!" said Marnie, before she could stop herself. "I hope it is the right decision for you?"

"It is," she said, "because I've traded him in for a much younger model."

Marnie managed a little laugh but felt quite awful. Was she really having that much effect on people? She didn't want to be a marriage-wrecker or someone that people turned to as a role model.

Bryher breezed up, waving a sheet of paper under her nose.

"Duty calls, Marnie," she simpered. "One down, only nine more to go!"

Marnie glanced at the list of readers she was going to meet tonight. What would she find to chat to them all about? Her eyes travelled down to the last name on the list and she almost had heart failure.

It said Caveman.

What on earth was going on?

Marnie seized Bryher by the elbow: "Who let this guy Caveman win the competition?"

"Oh, that was down to me," she said. "He kept ringing me up and pestering me. In the end I was persuaded by £250-worth of Selfridges vouchers and a massive box of chocolates. I do hope that doesn't cause you too much trouble?"

And she walked away, towards a handsome publisher, cackling her head off.

Marnie glanced around the terrace, trying to spot Caveman.

Bryher was such a bitch but part of her was intrigued to find out what he looked like.

"You look beautiful," a voice whispered in her ear.

She span around, her heart in her mouth.

It was Maddox.

"So, are you enjoying yourself?"

"It's a wonderful party," she said, staring at the floor. "It's more than I deserve, thank you."

"Of course you deserve it, more than anyone I know," he said. "And it's business too, Marnie. *Mrs Make Believe* is a major selling point for *The Sentinel*. We want more women readers and you know how to hook them in, so this book deal about your life is crucial to take things to the next level."

"Yes, of course," said Marnie, desperate to shift the focus off herself and on to something, anything else because he was giving her that funny, floaty feeling just by standing beside her.

"How's Cecily? Is it all going well with the pregnancy?"

"She's more insufferable than ever, fussing about putting on weight and what this pregnancy is going to do to her body," he said, fiddling with his cufflinks. "I think she's having another affair – with her personal trainer. In fact, it's boring to talk about her."

He tried and failed to disguise a look of deep hurt. Who would believe that the gorgeous Maddox Wolfe was being cuckolded once more by his wife, even when she was pregnant?

Marnie wanted to give him a little hug to make it better but she suppressed that urge. This was a work do and she needed to keep things professional. Although, he did look very handsome in his immaculately tailored suit, the dark violet of his silk tie making his eyes seem bluer than ever.

"I'd rather talk about you," he said, flicking her one of his little smiles. "Have you let your husband come home yet?"

"No," she said. Did he have to keep interviewing her like this?

"In that case, I've booked a suite at Claridges," he murmured in her ear. "You're welcome to come and misbehave with me later. No strings, just fun, or a drink – whatever you prefer."

His eyes were twinkling and she felt herself melting at the very thought of him. She was so lonely. But she couldn't go to bed with him. It wasn't fair on Cecily for a start. Although, Cecily wasn't exactly being fair to Maddox. Maddox brushed his hand against her cheek and tucked a stray strand of hair behind her ear. His aftershave smelled of limes, so fresh and crisp.

She felt a tingle of desire spread down her neck, as he let his fingers linger longer than was necessary.

Why did he have to be so good at this?

She didn't stand a chance.

Marnie felt someone watching her. Glancing up to the doorway leading on to the terrace, she saw Matt. What on earth was he doing here?

She froze.

He had seen it. He had seen Maddox touch her and, in that split second, he realised what had happened between them.

The horror of it swept across his features and he turned and walked away, his broad shoulders almost clipping the doorframe.

Maddox was still smiling at her, oblivious to what had just happened.

He bent his head forward to say something else but there was a crack of thunder and the heavens opened, splashing a volley of giant raindrops on to the party, which responded with shrieks and laughter.

"I think it may be raining," he whispered in her ear. "Or don't you mind getting wet?"

There was no mistaking the look of pure lust in his eyes as he spoke.

Marnie couldn't respond. Her head was swimming as the rain soaked through floaty party dresses all around her.

Guests, who had arrived early to make the most of the free cocktails, turned their faces skywards, giggling at the silliness of it all.

A crowd of people started to surge off the terrace, laughing at the typically British weather.

She was swept along with them.

Who would have thought it? What a pity it's raining!

She felt Maddox's hand in the small of her back, guiding her gently up the steps and into the grand drawing room.

Now, Marnie was being called to the little stage to give a speech about the book, with bloody Bryher smirking at her.

People's lips were moving but she couldn't hear what they were saying any more.

There was a roaring in her ears and the walls of the oak-panelled room seemed to be closing in.

Bryher handed her the microphone.

The faces in front of her started to blur.

She couldn't do it, any of it.

Dropping the microphone, she turned and fled, running blindly, down the stairs, out into Park Lane, with the traffic rushing past and the rain hammering down on the pavement.

Where had he gone?

She looked frantically around her for Matt, almost stepping out into the path of an oncoming cab, which blared its horn.

Shocked, she threw herself backwards and someone caught her as she fell.

She found herself gazing into the depths of Maddox Wolfe's blue eyes, as he pulled her gently to her feet.

"Marnie, whatever is the matter?"

"I can't," she said, her bottom lip trembling. "I can't."

She started to cry, so many tears, cascading down her face, her whole body shaking.

He held her close as she wept in his arms.

"It's OK, we don't have to do anything you don't want to, Marnie."

He threw his jacket around her shoulders and led her to his limo, which was waiting with the engine running.

✤ ✤ ✤

Maddox pushed open the grand rosewood doors to his suite at Claridges and ushered Marnie inside. He led her through the drawing room, sauntered over the bar and started to fix them some drinks.

"I'm sorry," she said, standing there, not knowing what to do with herself, his suit jacket still slung around her shoulders.

She glanced around at the beautiful barrel vaulted ceiling, the sunflower yellow walls, the views on to a little terrace with flagstones glossy in the evening rain and back to Maddox, who was heartbreakingly handsome, and felt thoroughly miserable.

"There's nothing to apologise for," he said, shooting her a look of concern. "I left the launch party in Barker's capable hands. I told him you were taken ill and he knows better than to question me. Now, are you going to tell me what made you run off like that?"

His voice was soft and she felt his words touch her like a caress. It was intoxicating and unbearable at the same time because she knew she was powerless to resist him.

She inched over to the sofa and sat down, the wet silk of her dress sticking to her thighs, and began wringing her hands in her lap.

"Marnie, you'll catch your death if you stay like that," he said, shaking his head. "Let me find you something dry to wear."

He returned a moment later with a clean shirt and a towel.

"Stand up," he said.

She did as he asked and was surprised to find she was trembling, as he removed his jacket from her bare shoulders and tossed it over the arm of the sofa.

"Turn around," he murmured.

He slowly unzipped her dress, exposing her back.

She didn't stop him, her arms and legs were leaden.

Maddox leaned in closer, his breath warm on her neck. It seemed to be melting her.

As the dress fell at her feet, she hesitated for an agonising second before stepping out of it, suddenly very self conscious of her black lace underwear. Who was that supposed to be for? She knew who she had been thinking about when she bought it and it wasn't Matt.

That thought only made her feel worse.

Studying the floor, as she stood there in her outrageously sexy knickers and push-up bra, she felt him drinking in her voluptuous curves.

She glanced up at him, heart pounding. A great wave of longing swept over her.

Maddox gave her a brief smile and said nothing but bundled her up in the towel and hugged her. Then, he carefully unwrapped her and slipped the shirt on.

She fumbled with the buttons.

"Here, let me do that," he said, his fingers working their way deftly down the midline of her body, her underwear disappearing from view as he buttoned her up. The shirt hung to her knees.

He rolled the cuffs back for her and stroked her arm, his touch sending pulses of electricity down her spine.

"Are you still cold?"

"Yes," she said, teeth chattering slightly.

He went to the bedroom and returned with a quilt, wrapping it around her, before sitting her back down on the sofa and topping up her whisky glass.

"Drink this, slowly, but drink it all," he said.

She did as he asked and felt the liquid warming her from the inside as it slipped down her throat.

She found her voice.

"It was Matt," she said, struggling to meet Maddox's gaze. "He turned up at the party and he saw you standing with me. He realised we'd... " She couldn't even finish the sentence.

"How could he know that? We were only standing together," said Maddox, with a shake of his head.

"I've been married to him for ten years, Maddox, trust me, I know he knows. And the thing is, it's the worst feeling ever. It's like I've cut myself in two, hurting him like that."

"But he hurt you first!"

"Yes, he did, but first loves can be very powerful. He got caught up in his own fantasy about being carefree again, without family ties, and having the time to just 'find' himself, whatever that means. She promised all of that, without the arguments over the washing up and putting the kids to bed."

Maddox raised an eyebrow.

"You can smirk, Maddox, but that is how it is, in the real world, without celebrities and hot and cold running nannies."

"Fair point," he said.

She went on: "The problem with you is, Maddox, you were the fantasy and you became the reality and I liked it – I still like it, too much. I think that is what he saw when we were standing together."

He sat down next to her for a moment, running his fingers over her forehead: "Stop over-thinking and come to bed with me."

He took her by the hand.

"Please," she said, her distress etched on her features, "I can't do that now."

"I meant to sleep, Marnie," he said, tugging her gently to her feet. "It's late and you are tired. I just want to hold you, to make sure you don't get pneumonia for a start, you silly girl."

⚜ ⚜ ⚜

His fingers were curling around hers and Maddox's arm was a dead weight across her as he slept, cuddled into her back.

Very gently, so as not to wake him, she unclasped their hands and crept out of the bed.

The birds were singing in the trees and it was light outside.

She glanced at the clock – it was barely 6am. She dressed in silence.

He slept on. He was so perfect, his even features, his broad shoulders, the sheet pooling around his lean hips.

Oh, part of her wanted to stay, to get back in that bed, and wake up with him.

But that was just a fantasy.

It would be wonderful, she knew that from their time in Cannes, but the guilt that gnawed away at her told her she didn't want the fantasy, she needed the reality.

That reality was not a movie star, but a man who was rather frayed around the edges by the demands of life, a wife and two little boys. He was moody and mean at times; stubborn and argumentative. He didn't know how to work the washing machine and could barely load a dishwasher.

The kids bored him when he was really tired or his mind was on his job but he loved them as much as life itself, she never doubted that.

They had been together for ten years – longer than that, really, if you counted all the time they'd had at university and during their twenties, before they got married.

Long enough to second guess each other, to know all about those annoying little habits, to have heard each other's stories time and time again, to take each other for granted, to stop appreciating the things that made each other special in the first place; to take off the rose-tinted spectacles that made him her hero and her, his muse.

Everything that was fresh and wonderful and sexy and fun had got buried beneath the piles of washing up and laundry, lost in the rows and the hurt.

Staring at the movie star, the man she had spent so many hours dreaming about in her fantasies, the truth dawned.

She loved Matt.

She'd been so busy thinking about *Mrs Make Believe*, she had lost sight of the most important thing: living her life with Matt, as a family.

She'd been waiting for the right moment to try to talk to Matt about things and, of course, there would never be a perfect moment to confess to her adultery and face her feelings about what he had done too. To try to resolve it all, they would have to live it together. She could see that now.

Pulling some paper from the writing desk by the window, she began to write:

Maddox,

I think you may have stolen a piece of my heart. However, the greater part belongs to someone else, who got there first.

You are every woman's fantasy and more. I just need to try and work things out with the reality. I know you have so much to look forward to with Cecily and being a father again. I think we both need to give what we have in the real world a chance.

Love,

M x

CHAPTER THIRTY-NINE

Strolling in the early morning sunshine through Hyde Park, past joggers and cyclists, Marnie struggled to work out the best way to explain to Matt why she had betrayed him.

What on earth was she going to say?

"He really wasn't *that* great in bed."

Or, how about: "His body wasn't as stunning in real life."

"His six-pack got in the way, rather."

"Once you got right up close and personal, you couldn't really tell how extraordinarily good looking he was."

"I didn't notice his rock hard abs and firm bum, honest."

"With the lights off, I couldn't tell you apart."

Maybe this was better: "I closed my eyes and thought of you."

A bus sped by, with Maddox Wolfe's image plastered on the side, advertising his latest film.

Oh, God.

There was no escaping him.

Would she have to throw out all of her favourite box sets as well? That could make quite a dent in her movie collection.

Why couldn't she have had an affair with someone else's husband from school, or a man she met through work, or in the gym, like other women?

In the end, somewhere between Notting Hill and Shepherd's Bush, she decided a simple text would have to do for a start.

It said: "It only happened once. I love you, not him."

Abandoning her idea of walking home to Chiswick to clear her head, because her feet were killing her in these shoes, Marnie hopped on a bus, glancing at her phone every now and then. By the time she reached Chiswick, she was desperate to get her Ugg boots back on, just to feel their softness around her poor little feet.

She turned the key in the front door lock and was greeted by Belle, peering down at her from the top of the stairs.

"Are you OK, Marnie?" she whispered.

Marnie didn't reply.

Belle came down the stairs: "Well, do you have any exciting news?"

"You think I slept with someone because I stayed out," said Marnie, flatly.

Belle nodded and then looked rather embarrassed: "It's just, I thought you and Matt might have ... "

"He turned up at the book launch and saw me with someone, someone I had the fling with in Cannes," said Marnie, watching a look of horror creep across Belle's face, in much the same way as it had done Matt's. "It's just too awful to talk about. Shall we have some tea?"

As the morning wore on, she kept checking and rechecking her phone and her emails – just in case he had decided to forgive her. She even listened to the messages on the landline answer-phone – and she never did that, judging by the angry tone from the dentist who was threatening to remove her children from his practice because they hadn't had a check-up in over a year. What a bad mother she was.

Belle whisked the kids off to a soft play area to give her some space – which really was beyond the call of duty. She was still inexperienced enough not to know it was best to avoid such places, which were designed not only for the delight of little people, but the torture of grown-ups.

By lunchtime, it became abundantly clear to Marnie that Matt was not going to respond to her in a hurry, if at all.

Who could blame him? She had virtually let Maddox Wolfe seduce her, right in front of his very eyes.

And all the while she'd been too stubborn to forgive him, too scared to face the mess they'd got themselves into.

What kind of a wife was she?

And what kind of a columnist? *Mrs Make Believe* was supposed to be a warts-and-all look at her life, yet she'd missed out the bit that cast her in a bad light – the fact that she had cheated on her husband.

Was she any different to the likes of Athena Maldon and her stupid *Living the Dream* columns, peddling nonsense about being a perfect housewife, while actually being a total diva?

There was only one thing for it: Mrs Make Believe was going to tell the truth.

She ran upstairs to her little office and, still wearing her party dress, took a deep breath as she started to write her own headline.

Mrs Make Believe

MR AND MRS MAKE BELIEVE

When I started this column, I was caught up in a fantasy about a movie star I fancied.

He was my Mr Make Believe.

I preferred to spend hours watching his films or daydreaming about him, rather than facing the problems in my own marriage.

When my husband ran off with his first love from university, The Wicked Witch, I shared my stories of The Husband's deceit and the daily trials of being a mother.

I was only too happy to peddle you all the fantasy of me as the wronged woman, bravely coping with everything life could throw my way.

It wasn't a total fantasy but it certainly was one large, adulterous step removed from the reality.

I cheated on my husband too.

And, to make matters worse, it was with Mr Make Believe – but this time, for real.

He was kind enough to find me attractive when I was at my lowest ebb. The guilt I feel for what I did won't go away because I still love my husband.

I have betrayed you all too.

I promised to tell the truth – to tell it like it is – but I ended up lying.

I'm tired of living the fantasy of being Mrs Make Believe.

You deserve better.

And I need time to work on the reality.

The odds seem to be stacked against us, Matt.

I can't promise we can ever work this out, but I think we owe it to each other and the kids to at least give it a try.

Mr Make Believe is not a patch on what we have shared together as a family.

You are not perfect and neither am I – but I think we might just be perfect for each other.

I love you, Matt, and that is not make believe.

Can you forgive me?

Marnie glanced at the clock. It was just after 1pm, which meant Barker would be at his desk recovering from the monstering he had received from the Editor in lunchtime conference.

She rang him.

"Are you over your stage fright?" He growled those words, which was not a good sign.

"I'm so sorry," she said. "I suddenly felt really sick and had to leave the party."

"Not as sick as I do, I've got to give the competition winners a tour of the sodding office later to make it up to them," he said. "Now, where is your copy for this week?"

"I've filed it."

There was a pause as he checked his emails.

She heard a sharp intake of breath. "Christ, Marnie, are you sure about this?"

"Certain," she said. "It's the truth and the readers deserve to know the truth."

"OK, but I'm not protecting you from the fall-out. You're on your own this time, Mrs Make Believe."

⚜   ⚜   ⚜

Marnie's confessional column caused a media storm. *ChitChat* called three times asking for Marnie to come on and talk about her infidelity – she refused, on the grounds that she now didn't trust telly people as far as she could throw them, particularly now that Athena Maldon was making her debut as their new panellist. Marnie had been busy all morning with radio interviews anyway.

"Doesn't it make you feel like a hypocrite?" asked the presenter.

"I am a hypocrite. I'm also human. I want the readers to know the truth and let them decide what they think of me.

But, mainly, I want to let my husband know the truth and see if he wants to come home or not."

"Have you heard from him?"

Marnie swallowed hard: "No."

Mercifully, just as she could feel her emotions about to get the better of her, the presenter started talking to callers.

A woman, sounding suspiciously like Bryher, was on first.

"I think she should be sacked," said the caller. "She's a big, fat liar. She's painted herself as the victim and all along she was bed-hopping! Besides, there are some brilliant, younger columnists out there. There is one at *The Sentinel* who is only allowed a few paragraphs a week to talk about her single life. She is totally under-rated and underpaid too. Let's hear more from ..."

The presenter cut her off before she could hog the airwaves any longer. It was time for the traffic news.

Supportive tweets started to flood Twitter.

"I admire Mrs Make Believe's honesty #sheisonlyhuman."

"Why so guilty? #wishicouldgetabloke."

"Don't beat yourself up #loveisalongroad."

Barker called: "Have you got any more skeletons in the cupboard that I need to know about?"

"No," she said, flatly.

"It's just, sales are up by fifty per cent on last week and we are pretty sure it's due to your confession of adultery, which is still trending on Twitter.

"Can't you make something else up? Didn't you do it with the milkman or the window cleaner as well?"

"No, I bloody didn't," she said, with a hollow laugh. "You obviously haven't read between the lines, David. I am giving up all this fantasy stuff. I don't want to be Mrs Make Believe any more."

"Oh, I don't think I heard you say that," he said, airily. "I think there were some hormones on the line and your resignation wasn't very clear. Did you just say you wanted a pay rise? I think I can get you one. But first you will have to talk to some annoying bird from *Vision* magazine who seems to think you are best pals."

Marnie sighed.

"Just think about it," said Barker. "You're such a success it would be criminal to kill you off, although sometimes, you do make me feel that the prison sentence would be worth it."

She'd add Portia from *Vision* to the long list of people she didn't want to hear from. There was no word, of course, from Matt.

Just when she didn't need it, Caveman popped up on Twitter.

"Why don't we put this silly war of words behind us?"

He must have been so cross not to meet her last night – especially given the amount he had lavished on Bryher to secure an invite.

"Trying to get your money's worth?" she tweeted back. There, that would shut him up.

"Let's meet for a drink to bury the hatchet."

What?

He tweeted again: "Preferably not in my back."

"Why would I want a drink with you, sexist pig?"

"You're afraid you might fancy me. Chicken."

"I certainly am not a chicken."

"Are too. The Ship in Hammersmith. 8pm. Tonight."

She wasn't going to commit to it.

He sent another tweet.

"Be there, Mrs Make Believe, or I will know your cluck is worse than your peck."

✤ ✤ ✤

She knew she was reaching the end of the book, but part of her didn't want it to stop.

When she was younger, Marnie couldn't wait to find out what was going to happen and would flick to the end, just to be sure she knew what was coming. Or sometimes she'd speed read those final few chapters, racing to the best bit, then wish she'd taken it more slowly.

Harsh Winter was different. She'd relished every page – and been interrupted so often – she simply didn't want it to finish.

But it was time.

It is summer when I finally catch up with Katya, on a sun-soaked beach in the Caribbean.

I know it is her, the moment I see her perfect figure undulating out of the waves, her miniscule bikini the same colour as the amethyst pendant at her throat.

She strides across the golden sand, towards me.

"Mr Winter, I've been expecting you."

I enfold her in my arms. We kiss, for what feels like an eternity.

"Why did you do it Katya?" I murmur in her ear.

"I met someone who made me realise that I could save the world if I wanted to and change my destiny."

When she abandoned me in Russia, rather than taking the antidote to her spymasters, she handed it over to my bosses, who made sure it got to those in need, sparing millions of lives from the plague and scotching the terrorists' plans.

She looks up at me and I notice that her grey eyes are flecked with green. It is as if I am seeing her for the first time, in the sunlight, as she really is.

My eyes are drawn to her tanned belly, which is already showing the faintest curve.

"I did it for us, Seb. All three of us."

I feel the world start to spin away from me.

Are my hands capable enough to cope with this?

No!

It wasn't supposed to end like that!

How would sexy superspy Seb save the world if he was knee deep in nappies?

Katya had gone and got pregnant using her amazing pelvic floor muscles, in an act of sperm banditry. Did she know she was ovulating at the time or was it a happy accident?

Hopefully the author would do the decent thing and just kill him off, rather than trying to make Seb Winter some new-man type who was good at the laundry, as well as safeguarding national security and looking hot. It wouldn't be right. It would ruin the fantasy, for a start.

She put the book down and trudged upstairs, feeling rather cross about Seb and Katya and their happy ending.

Rufus and Charlie, freshly scrubbed and in their pyjamas, looked just adorable, huddling together in bed, waiting for Marnie to read to them.

Gabriel was spark out in the travel cot beside them, his arms aloft like a little parachutist. Marnie stroked his cheek. He was such a perfect little thing but the longing was not there anymore. She really did have her hands full with her two.

They had worn themselves out, running around the garden and playing countless games of hide and seek with Belle, who was babysitting again.

The boys would be asleep in no time.

She started to read them their favourite fairytale.

Well, she altered it a bit as she went along, to be fair.

"And so Sleeping Beauty, who was beautiful but not so very beautiful – she was more liked for her kindness and interesting conversation, actually – decided she would marry the handsome prince, who was also a very nice person."

Their eyes were closing a bit as they listened to her voice.

"Sleeping Beauty told him that she would expect him to do half of all the household chores and he readily agreed, because he was a very good prince. He liked washing up, cooking and cleaning and didn't think that was just for the girls.

"They then had a long discussion about who would go out to work and who would look after the children. After a great deal of thought, they decided to take it in turns, in the interests of fairness. They agreed to review the situation at regular intervals, chatting nicely to each other, with no raised voices.

"And they all lived happily ever after."

Belle poked her head around the open bedroom door, suppressing laughter.

"That was a very right-on ending, Marnie," she whispered, leaning into have a peek at Gabriel, who was still fast asleep.

"Yes, well, I just thought I'd try to manage their expectations, for the future, you know," she mumbled.

They walked down stairs and into the hallway, just as a taxi honked its horn in the street outside.

She still hadn't heard from Matt. If nothing else, tonight would take her mind off her total and utter misery. Her marriage was shredded in bits after what she had done and there was no repairing it. That much was clear from his silence. She was going to be on her own for the foreseeable future.

Barker had offered to increase her salary by 50 per cent, given the huge spike in sales.

She was thinking it over, but the harsh reality was that if she was going to be a single parent she would need to make *Mrs Make Believe* work now, more than ever.

So, getting rid of the irritant that was Caveman was a smart career move.

"Go and have fun on your date!" said Belle.

"It's not a date, Belle," said Marnie, "it is just work. I am sick to death of Caveman and his constant goading. It's time to draw a line under it all."

Belle smiled to herself: "What if you find out you quite like him?"

"I will not like him!" cried Marnie. "I hate him! Caveman has been a constant thorn in my side these past few weeks. He's always cropping up with some smart-arse comment, right when I don't need it. Well, I am planning a charm offensive to put a stop to it."

"You are going to use your feminine wiles on him?" said Belle, raising an eyebrow.

"No, I am not," said Marnie, who had gone rather red. "I don't know what I am going to do. I will play it by ear once I get there."

"How will you know what he looks like?"

"He sent me a tweet saying he will be the tall, dark, handsome one. Can you believe that?"

"I bet he is sixty, fat and balding, with a squint and one leg shorter than the other," said Belle, with a guffaw of laughter.

"Thanks for nothing, Belle," said Marnie, as she stepped, heart sinking, through the front door and into the warm evening air.

❧ ❧ ❧

Why was she even bothering to go through with this?

Couples were basking outside under the last rays of the sun, holding hands, lying on the lawn beside the river as they watched little boats sail by. A pair of swans glided past on the water, as Marnie pushed open the door to the pub and looked around. A few men drinking at the bar turned to glance at her and then went back to their pints.

In a darkened corner of the room, a karaoke machine started to play.

Oh, bloody brilliant, karaoke night. This was hardly a classy place to come for a drink, was it?

She marched up to the bar, plonking her massive bag down in front of her, and ordered a lemonade. Caveman had better hurry up and get here. What if he stood her up? What if those blokes at the bar were his mates, sent to laugh at her and see how long she would wait for him to arrive? Oh, the whole thing was so stupid!

She took a sip and glanced up at the flat-screen on the wall behind the bar, which was scrolling the name of the song and the karaoke singer who had chosen it.

Marnie jumped.

It said "CAVEMAN", followed by "Islands in the Stream".

She span around, her heart in her mouth.

She instantly recognised the curls framing his face, the curve of his cheek, his full mouth and his expressive, brown eyes, gazing at her.

Matt was standing there, with the microphone in his hand.

He was Caveman! Of all the lowdown tricks to play on her.

Suddenly all those beastly Caveman tweets made sense.

It was Matt, doing his best to pique her interest, knowing full well that she would roll her sleeves up, get on her soapbox and engage with him in a slanging match on social media.

He knew her so well.

She didn't know whether to laugh or cry.

Part of her wanted to storm out of the pub and out of his life forever.

Her mouth opened to say something – or shout it – but he gave her such a smouldering look, it silenced her completely.

She felt a pull towards him. It was almost magnetic, the attraction. It was undeniable. It was maddening.

They were 19 again in the student union and he was signalling for her to come up and join him for the cheesiest song on the playlist.

When most sane people would have walked – or run – away, she found herself striding across that floor and picking up the other microphone.

She was Dolly Parton – well, a few cup sizes smaller – and he was Kenny Rogers.

It was a living, breathing thing her marriage. It was the two of them. They were islands in the stream like the song said. And life had this way of clogging up the stream with old bits of junk and used shopping trolleys but so what? She didn't want to escape it any more.

He looked deep into her eyes, and sang: "You do something to me that I can't explain. Hold me closer and I feel no pain. Every beat of my heart, we got something going on."

With tears in her eyes, and not just because she had a terrible singing voice, she replied: "Tender love is blind, it requires a dedication, all this love we feel, needs no conversation."

They both sang: "We can ride it together a-ha", making several people at the bar cringe, as they were both a bit out of tune on that part.

He whispered tenderly: "Would you like to come and visit my cave sometime soon? It's got Neanderthal wall art and a bear skin rug."

She smiled: "Oh, I'm so sorry, Caveman, I think I'm busy later, washing my hair, in my well."

"I'm prepared to wait as long as it takes for you to be available, Mrs Make Believe. A lifetime, if necessary."

He moved closer to her and reached out his hand.

She hesitated for a second.

There was no fairytale ending and no guarantee of happiness. The reality was flawed, darker in parts and, perhaps, more beautiful for it.

She stepped towards him and fell into his arms.

They hugged each other for a while, the karaoke words scrolling past them on the screen as their embrace lasted a verse and a chorus and another verse.

"Matt, I've done some terrible things to our marriage," she said, eventually, tears rolling down her face, "I'm not even sure I will ever want to tell you."

He gazed into her eyes and brushed them gently away.

They both knew what she was talking about.

"Marnie, so have I. I don't want to know and I don't need to know. I don't want to go through life without you."

Just admitting her infidelity to his face felt like a huge weight off her shoulders.

"You and the boys are my life; the reason I get up in the morning and the last thing I think about before I go to sleep at night," he said. "I know I've taken you for granted and I cheated on you, which I will regret until the day I die. I didn't listen to you, I barely spoke to you some days.

You just slipped out of view and by the time I realised you'd gone, it was too late. I wish I could turn the clock back on all of this."

Tears were welling in his eyes now.

"I thought I'd lost you forever," he said, his features falling in anguish.

She put her arms up around his neck – she could just about reach – and hugged him: "We can't go back, Matt. But I do want to go forward," she said, "with you."

His whole face lit up and he smiled, showing his dimples, which melted her heart.

"I've thought about this a lot. We can try for a third baby if you want. I just want you to be happy," he was swaying her gently from side to side in time to the music.

"Matt, I don't know that another baby is really the answer but just knowing we can talk about it makes all the difference to me."

"Will you write about this in your *Mrs Make Believe* column?" he said, with a worried look.

Marnie smiled up at him: "I'm not sure about that. I think Mrs Make Believe has met her match in Caveman, don't you? But there's one thing I'm dying to know," she said, pulling him gently across the pub, past the drinkers who failed to register that two people had just made the monumental decision to get back together, over a karaoke song. "How did you know I would even bother to show up?"

"Easy," he said. "I knew if I wound you up enough, you'd be hooked and you wouldn't be able to resist me. I know you love a good argument almost as much as you love me."

He really was insufferable.

"Shall we go home now?" she said, as he grinned at her.

There was so much they needed to sort out, but the bedroom was a good place to start.

They walked out of the pub, arm in arm, along the river, looking just like any other couple out for an evening stroll.

By the A4, with lorries thundering past, Matt gallantly hailed a cab.

They huddled in the back like a pair of teenagers, murmuring to each other, while the driver tried to engage them in conversation about the state of the road-works up in town and the menace of men in lycra on bicycles.

A huge, full summer moon was suspended in the night sky, glowing low above the houses, as the cab turned into their little road in Chiswick. The chatter from next door's telly could still be heard through an open living room window.

Hand in hand, Marnie and Matt walked up the garden path to the house, where the boys were sleeping soundly.

They would probably be awake by six.

But the night was still young.

"There's a book I read that I want to tell you about," said Marnie.

EPILOGUE

Mrs Make Believe

FAQs

My effort has not lived up to my expectations. I followed the recipe, I thought I had all the right ingredients but my bottom sank, the middle spread and the icing ran off. Where have I gone wrong?

Did you enjoy making it? Did it taste good? If so, who cares if it is not perfect? I often find a troublesome bake can still be saved with a bit of TLC.

My usual fare is wholesome and tasty but I'm worried it might be getting a bit boring. Do I need to be more adventurous?

How can it be wrong if you love it? Always remember to mix thoroughly and don't be afraid of adding some spice now and again. However, as a general rule, I find you can't beat your favourite dish.

⚜ ⚜ ⚜

The latest edition of *Vision* magazine lay open beside her keyboard. There was Cecily Haywood, smiling for the camera, looking older but happier, with her new baby and husband Maddox Wolfe by her side.

An email flashed up on her screen from Barker: "Where is your sodding *Mrs Make Believe* copy?"

She shifted a bit in her seat and smiled to herself. She was planning a column on fantasy and reality in marriage but her mind kept wandering to what she and Matt had got up to last night.

Another message popped up from Barker: "Caveman has already filed his column. What a total pro! Then again, he is a bloke, so I would expect no less."

Her phone rang.

It was Barker again: "Are you sure he won't be identified? The Editor wants you to do a full chat with him."

"Oh no," said Marnie, doing her level best to sound bored: "I had to promise total anonymity for his column or he wouldn't do it. And, anyway, he really isn't that interesting in real life. And his wife! The less said about her, the better..."

ACKNOWLEDGEMENTS

Writing a book is a bit like going through labour: a long and – at times – difficult process in which you want to leave the room and cry but you can't. The end result is worth it, though.

I would like to thank my agent, Tim Bates, of PFD, for believing in me and my writing, reading the drafts and listening to me drone on about the tribulations of being a mum. A huge vote of thanks to Kate Evans and Faye Johnson of Ipso Books for getting my sense of humour, taking me on and guiding me through the editing process and so much more. What a brilliant team you are. I am very proud to be a part of the Ipso gang.

Thanks are also due to the wonderful Maddy Pickard for dragging me into the 21st Century and teaching me to love Twitter.

Thank you to my family, my husband Reuben and my boys, Idris and Bryn for everything you are. And to my friends, Mark and Jo, Sally and Marcus, Sarah H, Sallyanne and Steve, Tania, Siusai, Nicky S-H and Nicky B and anyone who got half as excited as I did about this book. To the girls at Wendlebury Gate, Newt and Murray, thank you for many happy hours not thinking about words and the same goes to Sensei Sue and the team at Kilburn Shotokan Karate Club, who made me believe anything is possible.

Lastly, thanks to my Mum, for telling me that I should write.

WANT MORE FROM THE WORLD OF MARNIE MARTIN?

B e the first to know about new books from Beezy, peek behind the pile of laundry at the real lives that inspire her work and access exclusive stories featuring Marnie and Belle as they continue to muddle through life, love and inevitable mishaps...

Just visit www.beezy-marsh.com for more information.

Made in the USA
San Bernardino, CA
27 March 2017